THE PROMISED ONE

L.W. Coscia

Dedication

This book is dedicated to Bill and Barbara Coscia, and to all of the poor and needy of the world.

<u>Jesus Christ loves you!</u>

Foreword

Here is an interesting and impressive story about the early years of Jesus Christ and his earthly parents. It is a fictionalized account which details the trials of Joseph and Mary as they prepare for the Savior's coming and their journeys through the Holy Land and Egypt to escape Herod's wrath after Jesus' birth. The author has created a lively and personalized story; the main characters are quite "lifelike" and consequently the story is realistic and believable. The Promised One is a book for today. In these troubled times when people are becoming more and more confused about the true meaning of life, this a story that can be of much help.

Table of Contents

CHAPTER ONE 1

CHAPTER TWO 12

CHAPTER THREE 24

CHAPTER FOUR 29

CHAPTER FIVE 39

CHAPTER SIX 51

CHAPTER SEVEN 59

CHAPTER EIGHT 69

CHAPTER NINE 79

CHAPTER TEN 89

CHAPTER ELEVEN 99

CHAPTER TWELVE 110

CHAPTER THIRTEEN 116

CHAPTER FOURTEEN 122

CHAPTER ONE
The Journey to Bethlehem

Joseph walked briskly through the fields of Chimki; he knew that Nazareth was some six hours further and he was anxious to be with Mary again. His trip to Jerusalem and Bethlehem in search of lumber and a place to build a home had taken longer than he anticipated.

"There is more work to be had near Jerusalem," he thought. "Many caravans pass that way and may be in need of a carpenter to repair their carts or baggage. And I can build a small house and shop near Bethlehem close to the inn of my friend Abila. The people of Nazareth are poor and there are not enough trees for lumber. It is difficult to support Mary and the child will be delivered soon. Perhaps we can leave before the Feast of the Pasch."

The fields were beautifully illuminated by the almost full moon behind him. His shadow elongated and shortened on the changing terrain of rolling hills. Joseph, now in his forty-sixth year, was tall and thin, he had prominent cheekbones, a fair complexion, a high open forehead, brown hair and beard with a trace of gray.

He was thirsty. The water in his leather bottle which was almost gone was warm from the heat of his body. He knew of a spring nearby and went to it, praising God for the water He provided. He bent low over a small pool, scooped up a handful of the crystal clear water and threw his head back to drink. As he did so a beautiful young man with golden hair surrounded by a brilliant light suddenly appeared before him. Joseph stared at the youth; he noticed that his feet were bare and he hovered about six inches above the ground. Joseph was afraid to speak and unable to move for he knew that an angel of God was before him.

"Fear not, Joseph," the angel said. "I bring you instructions concerning Mary and the child. Upon your return to Nazareth, prepare to leave at once for Bethlehem. It is there that the Child will be born. Take with you only those things that are necessary for the journey."

Joseph remained motionless and very much surprised. The angel continued, "Mary is to ride upon an ass and you are to obtain a she-ass of one year which has not yet foaled. The she-ass you shall let run at large and follow the road it will take. Peace be with you, Joseph."

The angel vanished. Joseph resumed his journey, thinking often of the angel's commands and wondering if it was all a dream.

The house in Nazareth was given to Mary and Joseph by Anne, Mary's mother, as a wedding gift. It was small and had a stucco-type exterior. The courtyard was small and nearby was a well dug by Joachim, Anne's first husband, many years before his death. The rear of the house was triangular in shape, slightly higher than the front and faced away from the sun. There were no houses nearby except Anne's which was connected by a stony path. The foundation was placed on rock and the roof was flat with drains through the parapet at each corner. Mary's bed chamber was in the rear and was divided by movable partitions made of coarse wicker. It was here that the angel appeared to Mary and announced the conception of Jesus by the Holy Spirit. A fireplace made of smooth stones was in the middle of the house and also separated Mary's chamber from the rest of the house. In the chimney wall were several shelves that Mary used for small cups and other vessels for cooking and eating. There were two windows in Mary's chamber, one facing the hill at the rear and the other toward the east. Striped curtains made of wool hung loosely over the window sill. That morning Mary was awakened by the rays of the rising sun that reflected off the vessels stored in the chimney nook. She rose quickly and as she was accustomed to do, knelt in prayer of praise and thanksgiving. She wore a white woolen garment with a narrow blue girdle around her waist. Her hair was auburn and long. She had dark eyes and brows, fine and curved, a high forehead, long dark lashes, a straight nose, delicate and a little long, small lovely lips and a pointed chin. She was of medium height and she moved very gently and humbly. Her head was covered by a yellowish veil, and she crossed her hands upon her breast as she prayed. During her prayers she reflected on the angel's announcement and her visit with her cousin Elizabeth until the birth of John, her first born, She repeated the canticle of thanksgiving that she and Elizabeth said frequently during her visit.

"My soul does magnify the Lord, and my spirit has rejoiced in God, my Savior. Because He that is mighty, has done great things to me; and holy is His name. And His mercy is from generation unto generations, to them that fear Him. He has shown might in His arm: He has scattered the proud in the conceit of their heart. He has put- down the might from their throne, and has exalted the humble. He has filled the hungry with good things, and the rich He has sent away empty. He has received Israel His servant, being mindful of His mercy: As He spoke to our fathers, to Abraham and to His descendants forever."

At the moment she finished her prayer she heard Joseph calling her name. He was a short distance away from the house.

"Mary, Mary! I have returned," he called out. Mary's mother, Anne, who remained with her while Joseph was away, was awakened by Joseph's call. She and Mary met him at the entrance and embraced each other warmly with tears in their eyes. There was much joy in Mary and Anne for his safe return.

Mary asked Joseph, "What did you find in Bethlehem? Tell us about your trip."

Joseph smiled and said, "Sit with me before the fireplace and I will tell you of a most wonderful happening in the field of Chimki."

Mary and Anne did as he asked and patiently waited for him to begin his account.

" An angel of God appeared to me and spoke as I stopped for water during the night. His instructions are for Mary and I to journey to Bethlehem and remain there until the child is born. We are to take only that which is necessary for the journey. And we are to obtain a small she-ass not yet foaled which will be our guide."

Joseph took Mary's hand in his, squeezed it gently and looked into her eyes. Mary looked into his for a moment, lowered her head and said, "The Lord's will be done. The prophecies are to be fulfilled."

She knew that the Savior was to be born in Bethlehem and lovingly submitted to the Divine Will.

Anne assisted Mary with the preparations but in her heart she was worried. The journey she knew would be difficult for Mary in her condition and the weather was getting worse. It was cold among the hills they must cross and the valleys were covered with snow and frost.

Joseph placed a comfortable crosseat upon the back of their ass, then hung their baggage and provisions on each side. Anne said, "I will accompany you as far as the fields of Chimki. I have pasture land there and a small she-ass I will give to you."

Two of Anne's servants joined them and the journey began. When they arrived at the pasture the servants found the she-ass drinking from the spring near to the place where the angel spoke to Joseph the night before. Anne embraced Mary and Joseph sadly, bid them farewell and blessed them saying, "The Lord bless you and keep you! The Lord let his face shine upon you, and be gracious unto you! The Lord look kindly upon you and give you peace! "

With tears in her eyes she turned away and returned to Nazareth.

Joseph and Mary continued southward into a very low valley, on the road between Jezrael and Samaria that was covered with frost. Mary was very cold and she was hungry.

She asked Joseph, "May we stop for a while? I can go no farther."

Joseph directed the animals to a large pine tree and arranged a place for Mary to rest under it. He helped Mary to dismount then built a fire for her warmth and to prepare a little food. Their supplies consisted of pigeon meat, small coarse loaves of bread and water. Joseph looked about and he saw several small fires in the surrounding hills.

He thought aloud, "There are many shepherds tending their flocks here. I wonder if any of their houses are nearby."

Mary ate a little meat and bread to gain her strength then she prayed, "Lord, I thank you for all that we have to endure but I implore you, do not let us freeze."

At once a feeling of warmth passed through her entire body. She stretched out her hand to Joseph and as he grasped hers the warmth entered his body as well. At that moment the little she-ass approached them and remained motionless, as if asleep.

While they rested Joseph spoke to Mary about the accommodations they would find in Bethlehem.

"I know you will find our lodgings at Abila's inn to your liking Mary the rooms are pleasant and clean, and he will charge us little," he said confidently.

Mary was comforted and encouraged by the things he told her. After a long rest, they continued their journey south. Joseph concerned about Mary's discomfort hoped to find an inn where they could retire for the night. Two hours passed when Joseph noticed lights coming from a large farmhouse. He asked the man, who answered his knock, if they might stay the night.

"This is not an inn!" he replied gruffly. "Try further down the road."

Joseph was hurt by his response but said nothing. He and Mary continued on until they came to a small shepherd's shed. Standing near the shed was the she-ass, so they entered. However, it was occupied by four shepherds who also sought protection from the cold.

"Welcome," said one of the shepherds.

"Peace be with you," Joseph replied.

Mary entered behind Joseph. She smiled, pulled her veil over her face, but said nothing. The shepherds were immediately aware of Mary's condition and her fatigue. They were good men and they sensed the goodness of Joseph and Mary.

"Come, sit by our fire and warm yourself." said the oldest. "We will fix you a place to rest with fresh straw near the wall." said the youngest.

He and another proceeded to pile clean bundles of straw near the wall until there was a comfortable place to recline.

"You are very kind," said Joseph, "my wife is close to her time and she is very cold."

Mary sat on the new straw with her back against the wall; her veil remained over her face but she nodded her head as a sign of thanks.

"We can not stay here tonight, "whispered the oldest shepherd, "they should have some privacy. Let us go to the farmer's house. He will take us in for the night. We have some of his sheep in our herd."

Joseph overheard them but said nothing to Mary. "We must be going now," said the oldest, "we are to stay with a farmer just down the road. We hope you will be comfortable here. We will leave you these bundles of reeds for the fire. Peace be with you."

"Peace be with you," the others said in unison. They then left the shed and walked slowly down the road.

Joseph turned to Mary who now lowered her veil. They smiled at each other then Joseph picked up a bundle of straw and took it out to the little she-ass and the ass Mary had ridden.

The four shepherds arrived at the farmhouse a few minutes later. They mentioned to the farmer about meeting Mary and Joseph and how they were affected.

"What a beautiful, what an extraordinary woman! What an amiable, pious and humble man! What wonderful people those travelers are!" they exclaimed.

The farmer told them that they had come to his house but sent them away. His wife heard him and promptly scolded him for his unkind behavior.

" Are you not ashamed of yourself? How could you send them away on such a cold night? We have many rooms and they must stay in a drafty shed," she said very sternly. " I will go to them and beg their Pardon," she exclaimed. "I will go with you," said her husband, "I must seek their pardon. It was me that sent them away."

The farmer and his wife hurried to the shed but hesitated going in at first. The farmer's wife nervously knocked on the door and then held the arm of her husband. Joseph opened the door slowly and asked them to enter. He recognized the farmer and was very glad to see him. Mary had risen from her couch of straw and stood behind and to the side of Joseph.

"We have come to apologize and beg your pardon," said the farmer, "'I should not have sent you away; please forgive me. I am a stupid and selfish man."

The farmer's wife looked at Joseph and then at Mary. There eyes met and a feeling of awe and joy filled her entire body. She knew not why, but it was a wonderful feeling.

Joseph placed his hand on the farmer's shoulder and said, "Peace be with you, brother. I bear you no ill feelings. This shed is comfortable enough for us to rest and eat awhile. I am looking for an inn but have not seen one along this road."

"There is a small inn a short distance further on," said the farmer. "I will take you there. This shed is no place for a woman in her condition," he continued as he turned his head toward Mary. "Come, follow us. It is not far," said the farmer's wife. Let us help you with your things," she added.

Mary and Joseph walked beside them on the road, which was steadily rising to the top of a mountain. They spoke of the land, farming and family life. Mary tired a little, so Joseph helped her to the seat on the ass. The little she-ass frolicked in the fields alongside the road just a little ahead of the travelers. One half-hour passed when they arrived at the inn. The farmer and his wife wished them well, then returned to their home. Joseph inquired of the innkeeper if there was a room available.

He replied, "There are no rooms available tonight. Many are traveling to Jerusalem and tomorrow is the Sabbath. I am sorry but you will have to try somewhere else."

As he was speaking Mary entered the inn and begged, "Sir, we have traveled far. We are cold and very tired. Will you give us some shelter, please?"

Suddenly the man's attitude changed. His wife also was affected when Mary spoke. They apologized and quickly arranged a shelter for them in a shed nearby. It was in much better condition and warmer than the shepherd's shed. The innkeeper stabled and fed the ass. The little she-ass remained in the fields and was seen only when needed. Mary and Joseph rested well that night. In the morning Joseph suggested that they remain there another day because it was the Sabbath. The morning frost melted rapidly as the sun's rays warmed this side of the mountain. The inn was located on the east slope and was surrounded by gardens, orchards, and balsam and pine trees. A small brook ran between the shed and the inn which had several houses, a few sheds and a large stable for the guest's animals.

Following their morning prayers of thanksgiving, Mary and Joseph saw to their ablutions and partook of a light meal. The inn-keeper and his wife visited them very early in the day and implored them to remain with them a while longer. They promised to prepare a nice room for them in the main house. Joseph and the innkeeper discussed this while walking in the fields, and the innkeeper's wife showed Mary the room they would have.

Mary replied to her entreaties, "You are most kind, dear lady," but I am afraid we must be on our way. My husband and I are anxious to reach our lodgings in
Bethlehem and to prepare for the birth of the child. I am most grateful for your consideration, but we must be on our way following the Sabbath."

Both the host and hostess were disappointed at their leaving. They had felt a great warmth toward Mary and Joseph and were concerned about Mary's condition. .

The road they took, as they resumed their journey, led eastward away from Samaria and down into the plains of Sichem. The little she-ass trotted slowly ahead of them; occasionally running into the fields to drink from a brook or eat a little of the dry grass. It was much warmer here and the vegetation was thicker and greener than at any place they had been. Mary walked beside Joseph at times and they ate of the berries and fruits that had not fallen from the trees. Shortly after dark they arrived at an isolated house on the road to Lebona. Joseph knocked on the door several times before he received an answer.

"What do you want? Why are you bothering me? Your knocking interrupted my rest. Go away!" the owner said quite rudely from behind the door.

"My wife and I are seeking shelter for the night. She is with child and we are very tired. I will pay whatever you ask for a room," Joseph answered.

"This is not an inn. I will not have that knocking. Be off with you!"

The door remained closed all the time and suddenly the lights from within were extinguished. Joseph turned away very sadly and they continued down the road. The little she-ass was no where to be seen.

"Do not be discouraged, Joseph. I am sure we will find shelter a little further on," Mary said softly.

The road was narrower here, walking was difficult and only the moon lit their way. The ass was having little difficulty and Mary felt very secure on its back. After traveling a short distance, Joseph spied the she-ass standing near a large shed. Joseph entered it; it was vacant. He lit a few lamps and prepared a couch for Mary and himself. Mary assisted him as best she could. Before they retired he brought the ass into the shed and gave it whatever straw or fodder he could find. The little she-ass left them and frolicked in the fields through the night. Joseph decided to leave before first light because Jerusalem was ten hours distant.

Before dawn the movements and sounds of the animal awakened Mary. She immediately began to contemplate the birth of the child Jesus and was suddenly filled with a pleasant anxiety and great joy. Kneeling in prayer she lifted her heart and mind to God giving thanks as David did in the Psalms:

"I will praise you, O Lord, with my whole heart: for you have heard the words of my mouth. I will sing praise to you in the sight of the angel. I will worship towards your holy temple, and I will give glory to your name. For your mercy, and for your truth: for you have magnified your holy name above all. You answered when I called to you: you shall multiply the strength in my soul."

Joseph awoke and joined her for the remainder of the psalm: "May all the kings of the earth give glory to you: for they have heard all the words of your mouth. And let them sing in the ways of the Lord for great is the glory of the Lord. For the Lord is high, and looks upon the lowly, and the proud cannot hide from him."

"If I shall walk in the midst of tribulation, you will keep me safe: and you have stretched forth your hand against the anger of my enemies: and your right hand has saved me."

"Lord your love endures forever. Complete the work that you have begun."

As Joseph rose from his knees he looked thru a small opening and saw the she-ass approaching the rear of the shed. He then spoke to Mary about the remainder of the journey.

"At this time of the year the road through the mountains is very difficult. I think it best to leave this route and travel through the country between here and the Jordan. If we approach Bethlehem from the east the terrain will be much better, although the distance will be greater."

He added, "If you have had enough rest, Mary, let us eat a little bread and fruit, then begin again."

Mary replied, "I am fine, Joseph. Do not be worried about me. We can leave whenever you wish."

Joseph placed the baggage on the ass and they continued their journey. He saw the she-ass running through the fields in the direction that led to the Jordan; he smiled and began to walk confidently in the same direction.

Late in the day they arrived at a large public house near the Jordan, which was frequented by many travelers and was staffed with many servants. Mary and Joseph were warmly greeted by the innkeeper who promptly directed the servants to wash Joseph's feet at a spring running between the main house and a stable. Joseph was supplied with fresh garments while those he wore were cleaned. Mary was provided the same services by a maid servant. As they were entering the main house the innkeeper's young wife approached them but greeted them warmly. She was very beautiful but very vain and jealous of anyone with equal or greater beauty.

"What is your destination?" she asked. "And why are you traveling in your condition?" she directed to Mary but not really concerned. Joseph continued on to inspect the lodgings with the innkeeper and did not reply.

Mary spoke kindly to her. "Your concern for my condition is very kind. We are traveling to Bethlehem. My husband has relatives there and he hopes to find more work than was available in Nazareth, the village we came from." The innkeeper's wife was surprised at Mary's gentleness and very much agitated by Mary's beauty. She rudely turned away and hurried to her room where she remained all the while Mary and Joseph were there.

Joseph followed the owner to a rather large room that was used by many of the travelers. A great many beds were rolled against the wall and each sleeping place was separated by straw mats rolled down from the ceiling and covered with heavy curtains for privacy.

"Is this all you have?" asked Joseph.

"Yes" the owner replied, "we have no separate rooms here. This is the best you can expect. Do you wish to stay?"

"My wife needs much rest," Joseph answered, "this will have to do. Will you have your servants assist me with our baggage and our animals."

"Certainly." replied the innkeeper and he hurried off to give the commands.

Mary joined Joseph in their sleeping space. They prepared themselves for sleep, thanked and praised the Lord for what they received and retired. The servants stabled and fed the ass and the she-ass, then reported to the innkeeper. They discussed the beauty and gentleness of Mary and the humility of Joseph when they helped him with the change of clothing and the washing of his feet. The innkeeper declared that a feeling of warmth towards them flowed through him when he first greeted them. He had not felt anything quite like it before.

"Who are these good people? Where are they going? And how can we help them?" he asked quickly.

One of the servants replied, "We shall rise very early in the morning and attend to all their needs. Perhaps they will remain with us until the child is born. The woman appears to be close to delivery."

"Perhaps," said the innkeeper, "I will ask them to stay in the morning."

All retired, pondering over this very special couple.

Early the next morning, Mary and Joseph prepared to leave. The servants were most considerate of their needs. They prepared a light meal for them and packaged some food for them to take with them. Their cleaned clothes were returned to them and their sleeping space was put in order. The servants did not speak to Mary or Joseph except to greet them when they opened the curtains.

The innkeeper greeted them most cordially when they appeared in the eating room and asked, "How are you this morning? Did you sleep well? And how does your wife feel today?" Not waiting for a reply to each question he continued, "I do not know your destination nor do I know how long you have been traveling, but I am certain that your wife has endured a great deal of discomfort traveling in her condition. And she is very close to her time of delivery .Will you consider staying with us a while longer; at least until the child is born. One of my maid servants is an experienced midwife and we can provide the privacy you desire."

Joseph listened and thought, "How considerate this man is and he has only just met us." He then replied, "Sir, you are very kind and your servants are most considerate. Our stay here has been pleasant but we must be on our way. I am anxious to arrive in Bethlehem as soon as possible. Only a few more hours of traveling are before us. Thank you, but we must leave."

The innkeeper addressed Mary, "You cannot be certain you will arrive in Bethlehem before the child is born, daughter. You may be alone and on the road when it is time."

Mary answered with certainty in her voice, "Kind sir, I have yet eight and thirty hours until the child is born."

The owner wondered how she was so certain of the time, but he felt that she knew as women do know about such things, even though she was younger than his own wife who bore him two sons and a daughter.

Joseph was informed by the other travelers that lodgings were difficult to obtain in Bethlehem because of the census. But Joseph replied with much confidence, "A friend has lodgings for us in his inn. I'm sure that Mary and I will be well received."

Joseph repeated this to Mary as they continued their journey.

As they proceeded westward toward Bethlehem, about three hours from the public house, Mary spoke to Joseph about her need for rest and refreshment. Joseph recalled a resting place for travelers nearby and he moved in that direction. The she-ass trotted just ahead of them. They came to a fig tree that was laden with fruit when Joseph visited it last. The tree had seats built around it and a small brook was near to it. But when they arrived at the tree, they were disappointed to find the tree barren of fruit. Mary rested beneath the tree for an hour before they returned to the road entering Bethlehem. The road broadened as they approached the city. It was lined with trees of many types and behind the trees were people encamped in tents. Joseph was surprised at their number. When he last visited the city he saw no tents anywhere along the roads. The number of Roman soldiers present concerned him as well.

A short distance from the east wall they arrived at a large building surrounded by several smaller ones. Joseph knew this place well, it once belonged to his father's family and it was originally the family mansion of David the King. The Romans used it as a custom-house for collecting taxes from those that arrived for the census decreed by Caesar Augustus. Only those who owned no establishment or real estate were required to register in their own town. All those who owned property or their own business had been paying taxes for years and were not required to move about the country.

Mary and Joseph enjoyed this part of the journey. The weather was much better, warm, dry, very little wind and the sun shone brightly on the mountains to the north, between Jerusalem and Bethania, which they could see from where they were. Joseph noticed that the she-ass had run off toward the south wall of the city.

"The she-ass has run off." he said to Mary, "I wonder where we will find her next."

Mary smiled but gave no answer.

As they walked toward the custom-house, they were instructed by a Roman soldier. "Tie your animal at the rear of the building, leave your baggage and report to the officer on the second floor. Be quick about it!" he ordered.

Joseph did as he instructed. He helped Mary down from the ass and they entered the building together.

"Wait here, Mary." he said. "I will go up to report to the officer."

There were several women on the lower floor waiting for their husbands who were being interrogated as Joseph was. They were very considerate toward Mary offering her something to eat and drink, and arranged a comfortable seat for her away from the traffic. Many Romans, Pharisees and Sadducees, priests and elders were in the upper rooms questioning the travelers, examining any papers they presented and referring to large rolls of writing that contained the genealogies of the families of David.

"You are late, sir, do you have any identification papers?" a clerk asked.

"No", replied Joseph. "I am Joseph, son of Jacob, whose family once lived in this house. I have traveled with my wife from Nazareth in search of lodgings and work."

When the elders heard Joseph say this, they immediately welcomed him as they would a distinguished visitor.

"Peace be with you, Joseph, son of Jacob," said one of the elders. "I am Joatham, son of Azor. Your father and I were friends for many years but I have not seen you since his death. I am happy to see you. Tell me where have you been and what have you been doing all these years?"

"Peace be with you, Joatham. I do remember you. It is good to see you again," Joseph responded. "After my father died I lived near Taanach where I was a carpenter for a well-to-do family. I was happy there, but following the death of the head of the family, I moved to Tiberias, lived alone near the sea and continued working at my trade. Several years ago I moved to Giah near Jerusalem and married this past year in Nazareth. My wife is waiting below. She is pregnant and very close to giving birth to our first born."

Joatham took hold of Joseph's arm and introduced him to the priests, elders and clerks that were present, ignoring the Roman officer and his men watching from the rear of the room. The officer listened as Joseph spoke to those he was introduced to. Suddenly he directed the clerk to continue questioning Joseph and the man called Joseph to his table.

"Where is your wife?" he asked.

Joseph told him and he directed one of his subordinates to go below to question Mary. Joseph followed down the steps and stood by as Mary was questioned, and he was surprised to learn that Mary was also of the house of David through her father Joachim. The Roman officer decided that since Joseph owned no establishment or real estate and because he was in need of work, he did not have to pay the taxes immediately. He directed Joseph to return in three months from that day to make the first payment. He then gave Mary and Joseph permission to leave. As Mary and Joseph walked through the large courtyard many memories flashed through his mind. He saw what was once their garden with a small, stone wall around it and a stone springhouse in the center. Only weeds and grass were in the garden now because it received no care for many years. The lower story of the house had no windows, just a door at the front and one in the rear. The upper story had several circular openings and a broad gallery which ran around the entire house. Joseph and his brothers had sleeping quarters in the upper story. The memories were painful to Joseph. He was badly treated by his brothers; three were of his mother and two were step brothers. Joseph was different from them. He was talented and learned quickly, but his tastes were simple, he was gentle, pious and humble. They harbored a jealousy toward him; taking every opportunity to abuse him or destroy anything he had grown or made. Gardening pleased Joseph but his brothers either stepped on his plants or pulled them out of the ground. While in prayer in the courtyard, they would ridicule him and kick him until he fell to the ground in pain. But Joseph never complained or sought revenge nor did he report the abuses to his parents. He just moved to another spot, more secluded, and continued his prayers. Joseph endured these abuses until he left home at the age of eighteen, returning only when his father was ill and died. His step-mother died while he lived in Tiberias and had no knowledge of it until he returned to Jerusalem many years later. But before he left home he learned his trade from a master-carpenter who took a liking to him. Joseph never told Mary about his poor treatment at the hands of his brothers; he spoke little about his family because it pained him to do so.

Mary and Joseph entered Bethlehem through a portion of the wall that once held a large gate but had since crumbled and was never repaired. The activity within the city was surprising to Joseph. People and animals were moving quickly through the streets and in and out of the city. Animals were purchased and slaughtered by many who paid their taxes with cattle. Roman soldiers could be seen everywhere.

Joseph brought Mary through the crowd riding on the ass. He headed directly for the inn of his friend Abila which was not far from the wall. Mary remained on the ass as Joseph entered the inn to speak to his friend and inquire about their lodgings. Abila was standing near a large wine jar filling a pitcher.

He walked to him and said, "Peace be with you, Abila". Abila turned and stared at Joseph for a few moments but with a worried look.

"Joseph, my friend, peace be with you," he said in return. "Wait here for a moment while I bring this pitcher of wine to those Roman soldiers."

He hurried to their table, poured wine into their cups, placed the pitcher in an opening provided for it in the center of the table, wiped it a little, said something to the soldiers and returned to Joseph .The worried look remained on his face .

"Joseph, where have you been? I expected you to be here two days ago."

Our journey from Nazareth was longer than usual because of the weather and the condition of the roads. It was necessary for us to travel east to the Jordan from the plains of Sichem, south along the Jericho road and then west to Bethlehem. Mary's condition caused her much difficulty and discomfort. We arrived here as soon as we could."   "I am sorry to tell you this, Joseph, but I was forced to give your room, just this morning, to a Roman official who learned that the room was vacant from one of my servants. She did not know that it was reserved. I have no other room or space available. You can see for yourself how busy we are."

"What am I to do, Abila?" Joseph asked. "Mary is about to deliver the child. We need a place to stay. Do you have a shed that we may use?"

"Everything is filled," replied Abila. "There are four men sleeping in each of the sheds and in tents on the roof. I have nothing for you."

"Listen," he continued, "there is a small out-of-the-way inn not far from here. I know the owner well. Try there, he may have a room that is vacant. Hurry, the city is swelling with travelers."

Abila gave Joseph the directions, wished him well and turned to attend to his customers.

Joseph came out to Mary; he was visibly concerned. Mary saw this and asked, "Joseph, what is wrong?"

He answered, "Abila was forced to give our room to a Roman official this morning and he has no other room or space available. He suggested we try another inn not far from here and to hurry."

Mary replied, "Do not worry, Joseph. We will find a place to stay this night."

Joseph prodded the ass in the direction he was given and walked as fast as the crowds would allow. They came to the street within a few minutes. Joseph left Mary near a large tree and hurried up the street to the inn. He was gone for sometime but when he returned Mary knew as she looked at him that he had no success.

"Perhaps we should try the center of the city." Joseph said. "The inns there are not as available as these near to the gates."

They moved slowly through the streets and Joseph inquired at all the inns along the way. The responses to his inquiries were always the same, "We have no vacant rooms. Try somewhere else."

As they approached the south wall of the city, Joseph recalled a cave used for storage by the shepherds. He remembered the many times he used the cave as a refuge from his brothers who taunted and abused him.

"Most likely the cave will be deserted this time of the year," he thought as he pointed the animal in that direction.

"If any shepherds are using it, we can make friends with them. And we can remain there until the crowds leave the city; lodgings will be plentiful then."

He walked very confidently and felt much relieved. Meanwhile it had grown dark.

CHAPTER TWO
The Nativity

As they passed through the south wall gate Joseph wondered if they would ever see the she-ass again. She had disappeared so suddenly. Perhaps, he thought, she was no longer their guide. The wind was stronger beyond the protection of the walls; the night was beautifully clear but growing colder. Joseph and Mary marveled at the brightness of one star just above the crest of a hill to the east. They traveled along a narrow trail, through rows of pine, fir, and cedar trees that ended at the base of a hill upon which was the cave they sought. Mary was extremely uncomfortable and anxious to reach shelter.

Joseph, is it much further?" she asked.

Joseph pointed and replied, "There it is about halfway up. Can you see the small wooden roof at the entrance?"

"Yes. Oh! Thank you Lord for this welcome gift" she exclaimed.

Climbing was not difficult the grade was slight on this face of the hill, but there were many rocks and fallen trees to avoid. Several small cedar trees were directly in front of the cave's entrance, which was covered by a heavy coarse wicker mat.

"The mat will shelter us from the wind," Joseph declared. " And I will build a fire."

Joseph pushed the mat aside and to their surprise stood the little she-ass.

"Joseph it is surely the will of God that we should be here," Mary exclaimed. As they walked to the rear of the cave Joseph was very much bothered by the debris and old straw covering the floor. He felt ashamed for having to bring Mary and the child to such a place. But Mary welcomed the privacy and the shelter. No one was using the cave and there were no animals stabled in it. Joseph lit a small lamp and began to clear a path for Mary. The cave was narrow at the entrance but widened toward the rear.

"Several air holes are through the roof, "Joseph said. "I will close them off and build a fire at the entrance. I am sure we will be comfortable here. And I will stable the ass nearby to help warm us."

He gathered the cleanest straw he could find and prepared a resting place for Mary. After which he continued to put the cave in order; he prepared a sleeping place for himself in a small recess about halfway into the cave. He filled it with straw and reeds that he had gathered at the base of the hill. Mary rested awhile on the straw using the baggage as a headrest and ate and drank a light meal of bread and fruit. She felt her strength return then prepared a place for herself and the child.

"Mary," Joseph called from the entrance, "I am returning to the city for more food and dishes. I will return as soon as possible. Please rest while I am gone."

Mary smiled, nodded her head, went to her sleeping place and lay down. Soon she was asleep.

At the first inn that he found Joseph purchased bread, meat, fruit and dishes, obtained a pan full of glowing coals and hurried back to the cave. While Mary slept he prepared a warm meal.

Mary awoke to the pleasant odor and said, "Let us give thanks to our Lord for all that he provides, for his goodness and his love."

They knelt facing each other and recited one of the Psalms. Joseph started and Mary joined him: "Sing a new song to the Lord; Sing to the Lord all the earth.

Sing to the Lord and bless his name: show forth his salvation from day to day. Declare his glory among the Gentiles: his wonders among all people.

For the Lord is great, and exceedingly to be praised: he is to be feared above all gods.

Let them all be confounded that adore graven things, and that glory in their idols. Adore him all you his angels: Sion heard and was glad.

And the daughters of Juda rejoiced, because of the judgments, O Lord.

For you are the most high Lord over all the earth: you are exalted exceedingly above all gods."

Mary returned to her straw couch. Joseph brought her a small bowl of the stew he prepared, filled a bowl for himself then sat beside her. They ate in silence. Joseph suddenly felt fatigue take hold of him that he had been fighting off. Mary, too, felt a strong drowsiness, finished her stew then lay down on her bed. Joseph covered her with a light blanket they brought with them. He extinguished the lamp, placed a few pieces of wood on the fire and retired to his sleeping place. Within a few moments he was in a deep and restful sleep.

At first light Joseph awoke feeling much stronger and anxious to make the cave more habitable for them. He knew of a small stream nearby in which he filled their leather bottles with water they would need for washing and cooking. When he returned to the cave the small she-ass ran up to him. He welcomed her with soft pats upon the neck and asked, "Are you hungry little friend? Come I have some straw for you and a place for you to rest."

He prepared a place for her under the small wooden roof over the cave's entrance. Mary slept while he quietly removed the remaining debris and straw and prepared several lamps to be used that night. As he carried fresh straw to the ass at the rear of the cave Mary awoke. She, too, felt much rested. Enough to assist Joseph in his chores and prepare a light meal for them. Following the meal, Joseph returned to the city for additional supplies. He obtained several vessels and dried fruit. Upon his return to the cave, Mary asked if he would place a small trough near her sleeping place. The trough was used to feed the animals. She filled it with fresh straw and covered it with a small woolen coverlet. They spent the remainder of the day doing small chores to make the cave more presentable. Joseph was concerned about Mary's activity and begged her to rest.

As evening approached Joseph suggested, "I will return to the city to find some very good women I once knew to assist you when the child is delivered."

Mary replied, "Dear husband we have several hours yet before the child is born. You will see that no assistance will be needed. But I beg you dear husband to join with me in prayer so that his coming will be most favorably received and for all those whose hearts were hardened toward us when we sought shelter. The Lord Our God gives this child to the world so that all may be saved; He is to be thanked and praised exceedingly for this."

Joseph marveled at her words. He could make no reply. They both knelt and prayed for a long time.

Later that evening Mary said to Joseph, "Dear husband, the time is at hand please return to your resting place and continue praying."

"Are you certain you will need no one to assist you?" he asked.

"Yes. I am certain." she answered. "Do not fear. The Lord Our God is with us. He will see to all."

Joseph's worry was evident in his face but he returned to his place as she asked and fell to his knees. He turned his head toward Mary for a moment and saw her kneeling also and facing the rear of the cave. Mary's white robe was spread out before her and her hands were crossed upon her breast. The light from the lamps shown through the pale yellow veil covering her head. Suddenly he saw the cave filled with a brilliant light that emanated from Mary. She was entirely enveloped. The light grew brighter and brighter. Joseph was frightened and unable to speak. The light continued to grow brighter until he could no longer see the lamps he lit nor the walls and roof of the cave. Mary's head was lowered and her eyes closed; she was completely ecstatic. Joseph turned away and fell to the floor of the cave; he could no longer look at Mary. She remained in this state of ecstasy for some time and the light from her became even more resplendent.

Shortly after midnight, Mary, still in the kneeling position slowly lifted off the floor. Her robe spread out around her just barely touching the rug she had been kneeling on. Suddenly the Child appeared below her emanating a light more brilliant than that coming from Mary. He lay on the small rug but made no sound. A few seconds passed before He let out a cry. Mary heard the cry and slowly descended to the floor and covered Him with the red woolen cover she had placed over the trough. But she did not touch Him. He kicked his legs against the cover while making a stronger cry. At that Mary reached down and with the cover around Him drew the Babe to her breast. The Child was fair, had dark hair and dark eyes. Joseph heard the cry but was unable to move. The entire cave was sparkling with light now. The stones on the walls and floor glowed like diamonds. Several angels appeared around Mary and the Child, first bowing then laid prostrate before them. At the same time beautiful sounds filled the cave. The angels wore dazzling white robes without a girdle, had golden hair which rested upon their shoulders and their faces were like those of children yet strong in character. They began to sing most beautifully with sounds but not words.

Mary held the Child gently against her breast. She was so filled with love and joy that she could not move or speak. Slowly the light enveloping them faded. Several minutes passed when Mary called to Joseph.

"Dear husband the Child is born."

Joseph sprang to his feet and looked about the cave; he was still dazzled by the light that filled it. Most reverently he approached Mary and the Child. At the manger he fell to his knees bowed his head then put his face to the ground as a sign of his love, joy and humility.

Mary placed her hand on Joseph's hands and asked, "Do you wish to look upon our Lord's sacred gift from Heaven?"

Joseph rose slowly and asked Mary if he might hold the Child. Mary quickly removed the cover, wrapped the Child in a red cloth up to the arms, covered him with a white cotton veil then placed Him in Joseph's arms. Joseph nervously but tenderly caressed Him. He was almost overcome by his joy. Gently he placed his lips upon the Child's forehead, eyes and hands then gazed upon the Infant's face. While Joseph held the Child, Mary prepared His crib. She covered the fresh straw with a fine moss that Joseph had gathered on his last trip to the city then placed the Child in the crib and covered Him. Joseph came and stood by her side; both had tears in their eyes. Mary began to pray as they fell to their knees in adoration.

"Come let us praise the Lord with joy: let us joyfully sing to God our Savior. Let us come before his presence with thanksgiving; and make a joyful noise to him with psalms. For the Lord is a great God, and a great king above all gods. For in his hand are all the ends of the earth: and the heights of the mountain are his. For the sea is his, and he made it: and his hands formed the dry land. Come let us adore and fall down: and weep before the Lord that made us. For he is the Lord our God: and we are the people of his pasture and the sheep of his hand."

The Holy Child lay quietly on his bed of straw and moss. Mary and Joseph remained beside the manger for sometime praying, singing softly or just quietly adoring.

Joseph was suddenly aware that he did not inquire about Mary's condition. He turned to her and asked in an apologetic manner, "Mary, are you alright?"

"Yes Joseph," she replied, "I am fine. I feel no weakness or sickness at all."

"Is He not beautiful?" she asked in return.

Joseph smiled and nodded his head. The Child began to cry softly, then a little stronger. Mary realized that he needed to be fed and informed Joseph. He promptly walked to the entrance of the cave placed some wood on the fire and walked thru the small pines shielding the entrance. Mary picked up the Child and held Him to her breast. He drank of her milk then slept contentedly.

The sky was clear and filled with stars, the moon had set an hour earlier and all the shepherds had settled down for the night except those on watch. Amos walked quickly through the herd of sheep in his care when he saw a strange light in the sky. A light so bright that he could clearly see the herds and the tower manned by the other shepherds on the nearby hill. His pace quickened as he cleared the herd; he was anxious to reach the top of the hill to determine the source of this light. At the hill crest, he could not believe what his eyes beheld. On a distant hill he saw a light brighter than the moon that just set emanating from the cave the shepherds used for storage. He ran back to his companions sleeping under a small wooden shed.

"Jorim, Joda!" he called, "Awake! Awake!"

"What is it?" answered Jorim. "What is wrong?" Are the herds alright?" asked Joda.

"Yes! Yes! Everything is fine but come with me to the top of the hill. Our storage cave has a strange light coming from it. Look there! You can see the brightness above the hill from here."

"Something is burning." said Joda. "We had better see what it is."

"It is too bright for just a fire," added Jorim. "And I have a strange feeling about this night. Do you not sense it?"

"Yes. I do," replied Amos. "What is happening? Everything is so still!"

The three men picked up their cloaks and staffs and ran to the hilltop. There before them was the light still emanating from the cave, a brilliant light. While they gazed upon this strange sight a cloud descended upon them. Within the cloud were many figures in robes moving about. They were very frightened.

One of the figures approached them. It was a young man dressed in a bluish robe that reached to his ankles. The shepherds could see that his feet were bare and appeared not to be touching the ground.

"Do not be afraid," said the young man. "For behold, I bring you good tidings of great joy, that shall be to all people; for this day, is born to you a Savior, who is Christ the Lord, in the city of David. And this shall be a sign unto you; you will find the infant wrapped in swaddling clothes, and laid in a manger."

Suddenly many more figures appeared around the shepherds. They began praising God and said, "Glory to God in the highest; and on earth peace to men of good will."

Slowly the figures and the cloud lifted. Amos, Jorim, and Joda stared in amazement. Then in an instant all disappeared. The three shepherds remained at the top of the hill pondering all that had just taken place.

After quite some time Joda asked, "Was all this a dream? Is it true? Has the Christ come?"

"We all saw and heard the same things," replied Amos, who was the oldest and wisest of the three. "How can we all have the same dream? No, it really happened. Come! Let us prepare to visit the Child."

"But where shall we find the Child?" asked Jorim. "Bethlehem is a large city and there are many travelers living in tents on the hills all about it."

Amos reflected for a few moments then turned toward the cave and pointed to it.

"There we will find the Christ Child. In the cave filled with light. That is heavenly light we see."

"Yes," agreed Joda. "But what shall we bring as gifts? What do we have that is worthy of the new-born Savior?"

Amos responded, "We have our herds do we not. We shall select the finest that we have and there are the pheasant and quail we caught yesterday. We have no gold or silver or precious ointments; the animals and birds are all we can give."

"You are right, Amos." declared Jorim. "We must choose them quickly. Let us not delay a moment more than necessary."

The three ran excitedly toward the shed, then began the selection of the sheep. Each one was carefully selected, as the lambs chosen for the Pasch, then placed in a small corral until they numbered thirty. The selection was not completed until the first rays of the sun shown above the eastern hills. Now it was light enough for them to move the herd toward the cave.

Joseph had risen as usual at first light. He went to a nearby spring and returned with two bottles of fresh water. A light mist rolled down from the hilltop and the ground was covered with a heavy dew. Joseph returned quickly for he was anxious to prepare some food for Mary and himself before Mary awoke. As he neared the cave he was met by the three shepherds with their small herd.

"Peace be with you," said Amos.

"Peace be with you," answered Joseph.

"We have come to visit the Child and to present our gifts. May we enter the cave?" Amos inquired.

"How is it that you know of the Child?" Joseph asked. "He was born during the night and I have told no one."

"We were visited by Angels!" Jorim said excitedly.

Joda interjected, "The Angels told us of the Child's birth and that He is the Promised One, the Savior. And we were to find him lying in a manger wrapped in swaddling clothes. We saw a wonderful light coming from this cave just before the Angels spoke to us and my friend Amos felt certain that the Child was here."

"We have brought thirty of our best sheep and these birds as gifts," Amos added. "Please accept them on behalf of the Child."

"You are most kind," said Joseph. "I do accept them on behalf of the Child and his mother. But will you stable them in the cave to the right, there is not enough room in this one."

They did as Joseph asked then returned to introduce themselves since in their excitement they failed to do so. Joseph invited them to enter but to wait at the entrance until he was certain Mary was awake and the Child was fed. Joseph walked quietly to the rear of the cave where Mary and the Babe slept. He found Mary sitting on a rug near the manger with the Infant on her lap.

"Mary, we have visitors. Three shepherds who have come with gifts for the Child. May they come in?" Joseph asked.

He was concerned for Mary's privacy.

Mary pulled her veil across her face and answered softly, "Bid them enter, Joseph. The Child is awake."

"Come in my friends," Joseph called. "The Child and His mother are awake."

Amos led, Jorim followed, then Joda behind him. When they rounded the turn in the cave they hesitated for a few moments taking in the picture of mother and Child, then fell to their knees with tears flowing. Silently they adored the Child. They were filled with an indescribable joy. After a long while the three visitors simultaneously repeated that which the Angels said on the hill.

"Glory to God in the highest; and on earth peace to men of good will."

Mary smiled but kept her head lowered. Joseph watched somewhat amazed by the shepherd's adoration. His eyes filled with tears as well. Joda raised his arms toward the roof of the cave, looked upward and slowly recited a Psalm. Jorim and Amos accompanied him.

"Sing to the Lord a new song: because he has done wonderful things.

His right hand has wrought for him salvation, and his arm is holy.

The Lord has made known his salvation: he has revealed his justice in the sight of the Gentiles.

He has remembered his mercy and his truth toward the house of Israel.

All the ends of the earth have seen the salvation of our God.

Sing joyfully to God, all the earth; make melody, rejoice and sing. Sing praise to the Lord on the harp, and with the voice a psalm: with long trumpets, and sound of cornet.

Make a joyful noise before the Lord our king: let the sea be moved and the creatures therein: the world and all that dwells within.

The rivers shall clap their hands, the mountains shall rejoice together at the presence of the Lord: because He comes to judge the earth.

He shall judge the world with justice, and the people with equity."

As they rose to leave, Mary beckoned to them to draw nearer. She then rose to her feet and presented the Child to them. Each held Him most tenderly and tearfully in his arms. Then after returning the Infant to Mary, they turned to Joseph and each embraced him.

Joda spoke first, "This cave needs to be cleaned and made more comfortable for you and your family."

"Yes," Jorim agreed. "And we will have our wives and some of the town's widows help with the cooking and washing."

Mary and Joseph did not refuse their offers; they knew how happy they were to serve them. That afternoon the women arrived at the cave. And to Joseph's surprise some were the women he knew when he hid in the cave from his brothers.

"Peace be with you, Joseph," one of the women called out.

"Peace be with you," he answered as they neared the entrance.

Although many years had passed since Joseph last saw them, he recognized each one and called them by name.

"Dina, Johana, Veronica, Sarah! I am happy to see you again."

They embraced him, kissed his cheek then stepped back and stared at him. Joseph stared back. Each one had many memories passing through their minds.

Finally Johana asked, "And where is your wife and child? We are anxious to see them."

"Mary and the Child are at the rear of the cave. Please, go in. She will be pleased to meet all of you."

Joseph also invited the other women to visit. All had brought gifts of silk garments and linens for Mary and the Infant and small bundles of fruits, nuts and wood. They spent some time adoring the Child and speaking with Mary then began to serve the Holy Family according to their skills.

Sarah started singing the words, "O Child, blooming as a rose are you! You came forth as a herald!"

The other women repeated the words and sang it joyfully several times.

In the early evening when all the visitors had departed the cave, Mary sat near the manger with the Child in it, making garments from the linens and silk brought as gifts. Joseph busied himself making shelves and mounting them on the wall of the cave. Later that evening two women approached accompanied by their daughters; two were eight year old twins and a third was nine years of age. They were dressed well and had an air of distinction about them. Joseph greeted them as they came near the entrance.

"Peace be with you, ladies."

"Peace be with you," the women replied. "We have been traveling for three days now so that we may greet the new born Savior. Is the Child here?"

Joseph was amazed at this statement and asked, "How is it that you knew of His birth before it occurred? The Child was born only this past night." With her veil covering her face, the elder of the two women began their story as she introduced all in the party to Joseph.

"I am Agatha of Suphan, this is my dear friend Barbara of Socoth, her daughters Sebia and Orpha, and this is my daughter Mary. Barbara and I received instructions in a dream to leave our homes and seek the Christ who was to be born in the city of David. That we would find the Child in a cave wrapped in swaddling clothes and lying in a manger."

Barbara added, "I quickly traveled to Suphan to tell Agatha about the dream when behold I met her traveling to inform me of the same dream. We left with our daughters without delay."

"May we visit the Child?" asked Sebia, Barbara's daughter. "We have many gifts to present to Him."

Joseph was very touched by their account; tears filled his eyes as he escorted them into the cave. They brought with them baskets of grain, small fruits, and a cluster of thick, triangular, gold leaves that were stamped with a seal. They approached Mary, now holding the Child in her arms, slowly and reverently. The three young girls remained close to their mother's side, clinging to their dresses with one hand and holding some of the gifts in the other. Mary lowered her eyes as they approached, then raised them for a moment during her greeting.

"Welcome, and the blessing of the Almighty God be upon you."

Mary held the Child out to Agatha. Agatha received the Child and pressed Him tenderly to her breast. Silently she gave thanks to God then passed the Child to Barbara who did the same but held Him much longer. Their daughters watched silently and were deeply impressed. Mary took the Child and placed Him carefully in the arms of each of the children, they kissed Him and then smiled at Mary. Mary then returned him to the manger. The visitors gazed down upon the Child and adored him silently and most reverently.

Joseph waited for some time before he asked, "Will you rest awhile and eat with us? You have traveled a great distance."

Mary added, "Yes, please do. You are most welcome to share what we have."

Barbara replied, "We will stay but let us prepare the meal while you tend to the Child. This would give us much joy."

Mary and Joseph smiled and allowed them to do as they suggested. A stew was prepared by Agatha and the food was distributed by the children. They spoke of little things with Mary and Joseph as they sat and ate, still filled with an overwhelming joy. The Child slept.

Late that night, the visitors declared that they would be returning to their homes in the morning but would sleep that night in the home of a relative located a short distance west of the city. Their departure was mixed with joy and sadness. This night was colder than it had been when they first arrived; before retiring Joseph saw to the fire at the entrance, placing several pieces of wood on it. He stepped outside to see to the she-ass but the animal, their little guide was gone. As Joseph turned to enter the cave he was greeted by Joda the shepherd.

"Joseph, I have some thing to tell you," he said anxiously.

"What is it?" Joseph asked.

"News of the Child's birth has spread throughout Bethlehem. Several of Herod's spies are in the city making inquiries. If they come here to speak with you, do not trust them and keep Mary and the Child out of sight until they leave. Do not trust them I beg you."

"Thank you, friend, " Joseph answered. "I will do as you say. But do not worry we will be safe."

Joda left after promising to return when the spies had left the city. Joseph said nothing to Mary about the spies. He joined her in prayer at the manger then retired. During the night, Mary was awakened by the cries of the Infant. She nursed him, and she sang to Him a song Anne had taught her. Joseph heard her singing and came to her; he sat next to Mary, held her hand for a moment and then gazed adoringly at the Babe.

The ass that was stabled near them walked forward and stood facing the Child. Suddenly the good beast fell to the knees of its forelegs and lowered its head to the ground. Mary and Joseph were greatly surprised and moved to tears. Joseph got to his feet, stroked the neck of the animal and led it back to the stable. Once the Babe was asleep, Mary and Joseph retired again.

Early the next day two servants of Mary's mother came to the cave; they had traveled from Nazareth and brought with them many things that the Holy Family needed. One of the servants, called Athalia, was a widow who lived in Anne's house. The other, an elderly manservant, called Joses had served Anne's family for many years but resided in the servant's quarters. The couple were moved to tears of joy when they presented themselves to the Child. Athalia was instructed to remain with the Holy Family; Joses returned to Nazareth with news of the Child for Anne.

While Joseph busied himself making shelves, Mary asked the servant Athalia to accompany her to an adjacent cave where with the Child concealed themselves behind the sheep brought by the shepherds. Mary gave no reason for her actions but they were gone only a short time when four men, dressed in attire that identified them as belonging to Herod's household, approached the cave.

Joseph greeted them in a friendly and respectful manner.

One of them said, "Bethlehem is excited about a reported miraculous birth here in these hills. We have come to see for ourselves if the report is true."

Another said, "Tell us who you are and what you are doing here."

Joseph answered, "I am Joseph, son of Jacob. I am a carpenter and I have come from Nazareth with my wife and child with the hope of finding work here and to build a home. We are living in this cave because there were no lodgings available in the city."

"A Nazarene," one of them said with contempt. "Why are we bothering with this fool? The one we seek is of the house of David. Let us look elsewhere."

Joseph smiled and bowed to them in the customary manner. All four were filled with scorn because of Joseph's humility and simplicity. They laughed disdainfully as they walked away. Joseph felt more secure now that the spies were sure he was not the one they sought.

Shortly after the spies left, Mary, the Child and Athalia returned to the Nativity cave and prepared the midday meal. Joseph continued putting the cave in order; he placed many of the gifts near the entrance of the cave and some on the shelves. Realizing that they had more food than they needed he carried some of it to the city and distributed it among the poor and the widows he knew. He returned with several small carpets which he spread on the cave floor. His desire was to make the cave as comfortable as he could for Mary and the Child. Living in the cave did not suit Joseph, but he realized that obtaining permanent lodgings was not possible until the crowds left the city. Mary was content with their temporary home; it afforded them the privacy and isolation she desired. Her daily routines of preparing meals, making garments and caring for the infant Jesus pleased her. Occasionally Joseph heard her praying or singing Psalms as she moved about.

On the seventh day after the birth of Jesus, Joseph and Mary while eating their midday meal discussed the preparations for the Child's circumcision.

"Tomorrow is the eighth day," Joseph declared. "The Child must be circumcised and receive his name. I will enter the city early in the day and seek the priests to perform the rite."

Mary was troubled about the pain she knew the infant must endure. She pondered Joseph's plan for a few moments then said, "Yes, Joseph. The law must be fulfilled."

She continued, "Athalia and I will prepare the food and a place to eat it while you are gone."

Joseph had been constructing an arbor just outside the entrance with lumber brought as gifts and wooden strips he purchased in the city. Joseph was a good carpenter and he liked his trade. He learned quickly when taught by the master carpenter and he was as skillful at building cabinets and furniture as he was at building homes or making repairs on carts. He hoped to finish the arbor in time for the occasion, but saw that not enough time remained before dark.

While he worked he recalled the angel's words to him in a dream concerning Mary and the Child. 'Do not be afraid, Joseph, son of David, to take unto thee Mary thy wife, for that which is conceived in her is of the Holy Spirit. And she shall bring forth a son: and thou shall call his name Jesus. For he shall save his people from their sins.'

Although many months had passed the angel's words and appearance were very vivid in his mind. Evening came, and the darkness prevented any more work on the arbor. Joseph spent the rest of the night working within the cave which was well lit by the many lamps he placed on the walls. Mary and Athalia tended to the Babe then gave Him to Joseph to hold before he retired. He caressed the infant Jesus and spoke to Him with endearing words. The Child was wrapped in cloths up to His arms and covered with a small red blanket. As Joseph bent his head to kiss the Babe, the Infant placed his left hand on Joseph's cheek. Joseph was very touched and moved to tears. Mary and Athalia saw this and were filled with great joy.

Early the next morning Joseph completed the arbor, and after his morning meal, which was prepared by Athalia, he left for the city. He found the streets just as crowded with people and animals moving in every direction as the day they arrived. It was nearly noon when he arrived at the Synagogue. The priests could give him no audience until late afternoon because they were preparing for the holy feast of the Maccabees that would begin in two days. Many vendors lined the walls of the synagogue and the adjacent streets. Joseph went among them and purchased plates and vessels to be used at the meal prior to the circumcision. He also purchased small gifts to be given to the poor who always followed the priests when they are about to conduct a ritual or take part in a ceremony. The sun had just set when Joseph and five priests, who agreed to attend the ritual, started for the cave followed closely by a score of men, women and children. Others joined them as they walked single file through the streets and along the trail into the hills. Some carried oil lamps; others held burning torches high above their heads. Joseph and the eldest priest led the way. Athalia was placing rugs and cushions at the place where the meal was to be served when she saw the lights winding through the groves of trees.

"They are coming, " she shouted to Mary. "There appears to be many people following Joseph."

Mary came to the entrance with the infant Jesus in her arms, stood next to Athalia for a few moments, then returned to the rear of the cave. After placing the infant Jesus in the manger she knelt to pray.

"Happy are they whose lives are faultless, who live according to the law of the Lord. Happy are they who follow his commands, who obey him with all their heart. Surely they do no wrong; they walk in the Lord's ways. You have given us your laws, and told us to obey them faithfully. How I hope that I shall be faithful in keeping your rules! If I pay attention to all your commandments, then I will not be disappointed. As I learn your righteous rulings, I will praise you with a pure heart."

Joseph and the priests entered the cave, but those that followed waited a short distance from the cedar trees. The priests went directly to Mary and the Child. Joseph introduced them then left to assist Athalia with the preparations. Mary gave the infant Jesus to the eldest priest; he held Him for a few moments then gave Him to the others.

"Your husband is of the House of David, is he not?" asked one of the priests.

"Yes," Mary replied. "His father was Jacob, son of Matthan, who lived all his life in Bethlehem."

"Ah, yes! Jacob was a dear friend of my father," declared the youngest priest. "His family lived in the house now used by the Romans."

The other priests, not natives of Bethlehem, came there after Jacob's death. They were pleased to learn that Joseph's father was known to one of them. At that moment, Joseph joined them.

The eldest priest asked, "What name will you give to the Child?" Without hesitation Joseph replied, "His name will be called Jesus."

The priest turned to Mary; she nodded her head in agreement.

"Jesus!" one of the priests repeated. "Do you have an ancestor with that name?"

"No," Joseph answered. "None of my ancestors were called by that name; nor were the ancestors of my wife called Jesus. But that is the name we want for Him."

"We will seek the Lord's guidance in this," said the eldest. "We will pray for confirmation."

Athalia came forward and announced, "The meal is ready. Please come to the entrance where we will eat."

Joseph led them to their places; Mary and Athalia saw to the distribution of the food. After the priests were served Joseph brought some food and the gifts he purchased for the occasion to those waiting outside. All were very grateful and blessed Joseph several times. Mary and Athalia sat apart from the men. The infant Jesus was awake but lay quietly in the manger, which Joseph had moved to the place where Mary reclined. Following the meal the priests retired to the rear of the cave and began praying and singing. Each of them in turn held the Infant. Their praying and singing continued for hours; they stopped only to canvas each other for approval of the name. As dawn approached only one priest had a doubt. Mary, Joseph and Athalia waited patiently and occasionally joined in the praying. The infant Jesus made no cry or sound all the while.

At sunrise Mary and Joseph saw a radiant angel suddenly appear before the doubtful priest holding a tablet about twenty inches in length. Upon it was inscribed the name JESUS. The priest did not see the angel but he felt deeply moved by some inner force. Taking a piece of parchment from his tunic he wrote down the name "JESUS" in bold letters and handed it to the eldest priest. "Praise the Lord!" he exclaimed. "We are unanimous; the Child's name will be Jesus."

All rejoiced.

After the Priest returned the Child to Joseph, who in turn gave the Child to Mary, she comforted Him for a while then returned Him to the manger. The priests brought with them a small wooden stool which was hollow and contained a chest full of small clothes, and an octagonal shaped stone slab about two feet in diameter. A small metal box containing medicinal fluids and the circumcision knife was located in the center of it. One of the priests covered the stool with a red cloth then placed the stone upon it. When all was ready, Joseph took the Child from the manger and placed Him on the stone. Several prayers were recited as the circumcision was performed. The Infant's first cry stung Mary deeply; she was much troubled and anxious to hold Him. After the fluids were applied Joseph lifted the infant Jesus from the stone and handed Him to His Mother. He quickly quieted as Mary pressed Him against her breast and walked back and forth near her sleeping place. The priests and Joseph continued praying; then ended the ritual singing a psalm of thanksgiving.

"I thank you Lord, with all my heart; I sing praise to you before the gods.

I bow down in front of your holy temple and praise your name, because of your constant love and faithfulness, because you have shown that you and your commands are supreme,

You answered me when I called to you; with your strength you strengthened me.

All the kings of the earth will praise you, Lord, because they have heard your promises.

They will sing about what the Lord has done, and about his great glory.

Even though the Lord is so high above, he cares for the lowly, and the proud cannot hide from Him.

Even when I am surrounded by troubles, you keep me safe; you oppose my angry enemies, and save me by your power.

You will do everything you have promised me; Lord your love is constant forever. Complete the work that you have begun."

After a morning meal, which was served by Athalia, the priests returned to Bethlehem. Behind them were the people who waited through the night, but before they left Joseph distributed more gifts of food and coins. Several times during the day and through the night the infant Jesus cried because of the pain. Mary and Joseph held Him, caressed Him and walked up and down the length of the cave trying to comfort Him.

That night while in meditation Mary received the knowledge that the Incarnate Word offered these first drops of blood and pain as a promise that He would shed it again for mankind's redemption and to satisfy the debt of the sons of Adam.

CHAPTER THREE
Elizabeth and Anne

Zachary's home was situated upon a hill remote from the village of Juta, a suburb of Hebron which was once as large as Jerusalem. Zachary, now in his seventy-fifth year was a highly respected priest because of his piety and he was a direct descendant of Aaron. He was tall, lean and presented a majestic appearance in his priestly robes. His wife Elizabeth, now entering her sixty-first year, was also tall, not as thin as her husband and had a very delicate face. The miraculous birth of their first child, John, now six months old, caused a stir throughout many of the villages and towns in that area. They were extremely happy to finally have a child after so many years of prayers and supplications. At last the derision and ridicule inflicted on Elizabeth by some of her neighbors was now ended.

By divine revelation Elizabeth knew that from her line the Messiah would be born, and she knew that Mary, her cousin, was the mother of the promised Savior. Mary had visited them nine months earlier and remained with them until their son was born. Again through divine revelation she knew Mary had given birth to the Savior and where to find the Holy Family.

After obtaining Zachary's permission to leave John in the care of a very capable servant in order to travel to Bethlehem, Elizabeth and a servant departed early on the morning of the day following Jesus' circumcision. She rode upon a female ass outfitted with a cross-seat covered by a wicker canopy. The servant walked just ahead of the beast which was loaded with several packages of gifts and necessities. They traveled for several hours over many hills and through very fertile valleys; stopping only to rest and eat fruit still on the trees. Elizabeth wore a dark woolen underdress covered by a grayish one with a blue girdle. Her head was covered by a brownish veil and her mantle, which was also brown, had a cowl and bands of white designs on the front. It was not an easy journey for her but the joy she felt more than compensated for the difficulties. By evening they were climbing the hill upon which the cave was situated. Joseph, who was again working at the entrance, saw them coming.

Excitedly he called to Mary, "Mary, your cousin Elizabeth is here."

He ran to greet her.

Mary was nursing the infant Jesus at that moment; her heart beat rapidly because of the joy she had. And so too the Babe when he sensed the excitement. Athalia, never having met Elizabeth, hurried out to meet her. Joseph reached them quickly and helped Elizabeth to dismount. They embraced, then Elizabeth kissed Joseph on both cheeks.

"What a wonderful surprise," Joseph exclaimed. "I am so pleased to see you again. How are you?"

"A little tired from the journey," she replied, "but otherwise I am fine."

"Mary will be so pleased to see you!" Joseph declared. "The Child has been born and is now nine days old. We have given Him the name Jesus."

Elizabeth smiled because of the excitement she heard in Joseph's voice; his behavior was most unusual for she knew him to be a quiet and serious person. Mary came to the entrance without the infant Jesus just as Joseph moved aside the wicker drape. Both Mary and Elizabeth were overcome with joy; tears filled their eyes as they embraced. Joseph, Athalia and Elizabeth's servant were deeply moved by their happiness.
Elizabeth stepped back from Mary and asked, "Where is the Child?"

"Within the cave," Mary answered.

"Take me to him so that I may see Him and caress Him," she demanded.

Mary took her hand and led her to the rear of the cave. The infant Jesus awoke as Mary lifted Him from the manger and placed Him in Elizabeth's arms. With great love and warmth she pressed Jesus to her heart then kissed both of His little hands, His forehead and eyes. Some of her tears ran onto the Child's face. Joseph saw the infant Jesus smile.

Later after having refreshed herself with a change of clothes and something to eat, Elizabeth sat with Mary and Joseph beside the manger. She asked them to describe all the events that occurred prior to her visit. Joseph described to her all that took place beginning at the moment the angel spoke to him in the field of Chimki, the journey from Nazareth to Bethlehem, the difficulties they endured on the road and upon arrival in Bethlehem their vain search for lodgings in an inn.

Mary recounted all that took place the night the Infant was born, her ecstasy at the moment and the miraculous manner of the birth. She told her of the many visitors, especially the visit of the three shepherds, and the wonderful gifts presented to Jesus.

"You have not given birth in the same way as other mothers," Elizabeth exclaimed. "The birth of John was sweet also, but it was not like that of your Child."

Although Elizabeth was fatigued from the journey her desire to adore the infant Jesus caused her to kneel before the manger for sometime, praying and silently adoring. Joseph and Mary knelt beside her; the servants knelt opposite them. When Joseph saw Elizabeth raise her head he began to recite a passage from Isaias.

"In that day shall this canticle be sung in the land of Juda.

Sion the city of our strength a savior, a wall and a bulwark shall be set therein.

Open the gates, and let the just nation that keeps the truth, enter in.

The old error is passed away: you will keep peace: peace, because we have hoped in you.

You have hoped in the Lord for evermore, in the Lord God of might forever.

For He shall bring down them that dwell on high, the high city He shall lay low.

He shall bring it down even to the ground, He shall pull it down even to the dust.

The foot shall tread it down, the feet of the poor, the steps of the needy.

The way of the just is right, the path of the just is right to walk in.

And in the way of your judgments, O Lord, we have patiently waited for You: Your name, and Your remembrance are the desire of the soul."

Elizabeth suddenly fell prostrate before the manger. Joseph at first thought she fainted but realized she had not when she extended her arms forward. With her face close to the floor she declared, "Let us be humiliated and grovel in the dust, while Your greatness is magnified and exalted in all the eternities. How insufficient is human affection, as it cannot adequately give a just return for the love You have for all mankind! You made a solemn promise to David, and You will not take it back: 'I will make one of your sons king and he will rule after you. If your sons are true to my covenant, and to the commands I give them, their sons, also, will follow you as kings for all time."

Mary and Joseph were deeply touched and greatly affected by Elizabeth's love and adoration for the Child. When she returned to a kneeling position Mary presented the infant Jesus to her again.

Her delight which affected her every fiber caused her to exclaim several times, "Praise the Lord!"

After a while, when Elizabeth's rapture subsided, she and Mary sat beside the manger and talked until it was time to retire. In the meantime Joseph and the two servants unpacked all the things Elizabeth brought and stabled the ass in the adjacent cave. Joseph noticed a drastic change in the weather; the wind had increased in velocity and the temperature was close to freezing. He quickly hung a large cover over the wicker screen at the entrance but the cold had chilled the entire cave. Mary and Elizabeth huddled together next to the manger which Mary had covered with two small woolen blankets. Joseph lit additional lamps hoping they would offset the cold; he then retired to his sleeping place. Athalia and the other servant slept near the Holy Family's animal which radiated much body heat. In the morning Joseph was awakened by the sound of an animal climbing the hill; he heard voices but was unable to identify them.

"Who can this be?" he wondered.

He hurried to the entrance, moved aside the cover and screen and scanned the terrain still obscured by the usual morning mist. He saw the outlines of three people and an animal come from behind a row of short pine trees. His heart began to pound; he feared that the spies had returned. But to his surprise he saw that it was Anne, Mary's mother, her second husband Eliud and a female servant who was guiding an ass that had upon its back a cross-seat and several packages. He ran into the cave and woke Mary and Elizabeth. Mary was overjoyed when she learned who their visitors were. Elizabeth, too, was most happy; it had been many years since she and Anne had seen each other. Mary hurried to the entrance with the infant Jesus and waited. Elizabeth stood beside her. Athalia and the other servant who were awakened by all the commotion came to the entrance also.

As Anne emerged from the row of cedar trees she spied Mary with the Babe in her arms. She ran to them and threw her arms around both. So great was her joy that she could hardly breathe and began to faint. Joseph stepped up to her and supported her.

She recovered quickly and asked, "May I hold the Child?"

Mary presented the infant Jesus to her and exclaimed, "We have named Him Jesus, mother."

Anne caressed the Babe tenderly and was filled with a great love. Jesus looked up at her, raised His arms and placed both hands upon her face. Anne was immediately filled with an almost overwhelming Joy.

She declared, "Oh! How beautiful He is! How wonderful it is to behold His face! I thank you Lord with all my heart for allowing your servant to know Him, and to love Him."

Several minutes passed before Joseph suggested they move into the cave where they would be warmer. Once inside the women reclined on Mary's bedding near the manger. Joseph and Eliud sat on the opposite side of the cave and spoke of the events that occurred since they last saw each other in Nazareth. The servants were busy preparing the morning meal and storing things Anne brought. Mary related to Elizabeth and Anne all that took place before the infant Jesus birth and the conditions they now endured.

At a pause in Mary's narration Elizabeth reached out, grasped her hand and pleaded, "Dear cousin, will you share with your mother and I all that occurred when the Child was born?"

"Yes, Mary. Please tell us!" Anne exclaimed.

Mary reflected for a few moments then with her head bowed she began her narrative.

"Joseph and I were cleaning the cave most of the day and part of the evening for their was much debris strewn about. Joseph was anxious about my delivery without the aid of a midwife he wished to secure from Bethlehem. But I assured him I would have no need of her service. Together we prayed for a favorable reception of the Savior's coming then retired to our sleeping places. At once I was no longer aware of anything around me or Joseph's presence until after the Child was born. A wonderful light filled the cave and I suddenly felt elevated above the ground by two angels. An intense longing for the Child came over me which lasted for sometime. It was as if my heart would break apart. All at once I felt an emptiness within me and now a longing for something outside of me. Below and before me I saw a bright light that was much brighter than that which filled the cave. Within the light I saw a child and he seemed to grow before my eyes. The child cried and moved about but I hesitated picking him up because of the light that still shone from Him. He cried again and suddenly I was kneeling upon the rug again and aware of everything around me. I covered the child, raised Him to my breast and He quieted. As I held Him I was filled with an unspeakable love and joy, for the Lord, our God, had sent the PROMISED ONE as the prophets had foretold. And I His lowly handmaid was chosen to be His mother. All generations will surely call me blessed."

Anne went to her knees, then sat back on her legs, very much amazed at what she just heard. She said aloud, so that all present heard her, "I recall now what was said by the prophet Isaiah about a child. 'For a child is born to us, and a son is given to us, and the government is upon his shoulder, and his name shall be called Wonderful, Counsellor, God the Mighty, the Father of the world to come, the Prince of Peace. His empire shall be multiplied, and there shall be no end of peace; he shall sit upon the throne of David, and upon his kingdom; to establish it and strengthen it with judgment and with justice, from hence forth and for ever; the zeal of the Lord of hosts will perform this."

Joseph and Eliud joined them just as Anne finished speaking.

"The holy Feast of the Maccabees begins this evening." Joseph announced. "Therefore I will mount three menorahs on the walls of the cave, one for each of you to light."

"Dear husband," Mary said to him, "when the days of the feast have passed we will be visited by three kings from the East. They are coming to visit our Jesus. They are carrying with them gifts of great value. We must prepare ourselves, this cave and the adjacent caves for them and all in their caravan. Their arrival will cause a great deal of commotion and attract much attention."

Anne saw that her husband was about to ask Mary how she knew this, but before he could speak Mary placed her hand upon his lips and walked away with him. The others realized that Mary had this revealed to her and made no comment. That night Anne announced that she and Eliud would leave the next day to visit her sister who lived near Jerusalem but promised to return after the kings had departed. At the same time Elizabeth declared that she would return to Juta; she was anxious to share with Zachary all that she experienced, and she was concerned for their son John.

CHAPTER FOUR
Journey of the Kings

A small caravan of dromedaries and their riders moved steadily westward through the Valley of Sirhan in the Syrian Desert. The sun was setting behind the hills that lay before them. Moving ahead of them but out of sight on the southern side of the valley was a large band of marauders. The valley was their hunting ground and these travelers dared to enter it. Their band was greatly feared; only large caravans with many hired guards passed through the valley unmolested. They wore animal skins, rode the swiftest dromedaries, carried spears and wore short swords in their girdles. Where the valley narrowed stood the ruins of a once thriving city that was a stopping place for caravans on their way to Jerusalem. The marauders usually attacked their prey from this site.

Arriving at the ruins well ahead of the caravan, they prepared for the attack. A lookout was posted atop one of the several pillars still standing; he was able to observe the entire valley from this perch.

"I can see them clearly," the lookout shouted to the leader. "They are coming directly toward us."

The leader was about to give an order to his men, when the lookout shouted, "There is something strange about this caravan. I have never seen one move so swiftly. Their animals must be the finest in the world. We must take them."

Their leader decided to look for himself; he quickly climbed to the top of an adjacent column. The men below waited for the order to attack. He followed the caravan's movements but could not believe his eyes.

"You are right, Abed," the leader exclaimed. "Look how swiftly they move and there is very little dust behind them. We will have to attack sooner than we planned."

"Be ready men!" he shouted. "They will be here soon."

But to his surprise the caravan's pace quickened. It was too late. Their animals could not overtake the caravan at that incredible speed. The entire band moved out of the ruins, watched their prize race through the valley and wondered about the strange sight before them. The lookout followed the movements of the caravan, which continued westward toward a pass through the hills, but before they were out of sight he spied another caravan, about the same size, moving southward and a third moving northward at the same incredible speed. As they watched in utter amazement, there instantly appeared above the entrance to the pass a large bright disc. Within the disc they saw the figure of a child with its arms outstretched toward the merging caravans. Fear gripped them all. Quickly they mounted their beasts and retreated in the direction they came. The leader and the lookout remained in the ruins and looked back in disbelief once more. They saw the caravans come together, enter the pass and disappear in the darkness. Once in the pass the caravans moved at a slower pace. The pass was narrow and fallen rocks lay along the trail, but none fell while they traveled through it.

Leading the first caravan, upon a dromedary loaded with baggage and small packages, was a man with the look of royalty. His skin was dark, he had dark hair and a short beard. He wore a high cap beautifully embroidered in many colors and with white bands wound thickly around his head. He wore a short surcoat that reached only to his calves. The coat was silken with a few buttons and a multi-colored breast ornament. A mantle, very long and wide covered him and the back of the animal. Behind him rode several other men also finely dressed. Following them was a small retinue of servants, each riding a dromedary that carried many packages, carpets, tents and cages of live birds. The servants were dressed in simple garments and wore nothing on their feet. Their responsibilities were the care and feeding of the animals, erecting the tents and protecting the provisions.

The second caravan was led by a man of similar dress but had much darker skin. He also had a retinue of followers and servants. In this group some carried short swords in their belts. The leader of the third caravan, which originated east of the Caspian Sea, had a yellow complexion. He and his companions dressed somewhat differently. All except the servants wore rounded caps adorned with white pads and had round cowls embroidered with silk thread of various colors and designs. They wore tunics that buttoned from the neck to the knees and were ornamented with laces, spangles, and glittering buttons. Their mantles were brightly colored and short. The leader and his friends wore a star shaped ornament on the right side of their tunic. The caravan traveled through the night. Before them, low in the horizon, was an unusually bright star.

In the morning they halted at a very lush oasis which had a large spring surrounded by palm trees, stables and sheds; it was a resting place for the many caravans traveling to Jerusalem and on to the Mediterranean Sea. The servants quickly unloaded the animals, allowed them to drink at the spring, then poured feed they brought with them into the troughs within the stables and the sheds. Some of the items they unloaded were long slender compartmented cages filled with several pairs of doves and quail which were used as food as they traveled. Oblong chests made of leather and wood were filled with loaves of bread and dried fruit. Several chests, made of wood, contained gold chalices, plates and bowls ornamented with precious gems that were used for eating and drinking. Other chests held gold triangular shaped coins, precious incense and myrrh. A fire was made in the middle of the encampment for the preparation of the food. A dozen birds were killed and roasted then served on small golden, three-legged dishes. The three kings cut up the birds, carved the bread and distributed the food themselves. They also distributed cups of water mixed with balsam to each member of their group. They did not partake of the meal until all were served. This simple, good-natured and humble act of the kings touched the hearts of their followers and several of the people living near the oasis who had brought bundles of wood to sell. The travelers rested until early evening. The sky was clear. Many bright stars could be seen and there in the west was one unusually bright star, shining with a reddish light, as the moon appears when just rising. The people of the area helped them to reload the animals; receiving from the kings a small gift and were told they were welcome to anything left behind. The people were greatly surprised at their generosity; they asked that many blessings be granted to them by their god, and then returned to their homes.

Soon after leaving the oasis the terrain became very difficult for the animals. All the riders dismounted and walked beside them praying with their heads uncovered. When they reached a high plateau that was smooth and clear all mounted again and continued moving at the same incredible speed. To the north was a chain of mountains and to the south was the desert. The star to the west was their beacon and the moon their light. While it was still dark the caravan arrived at a small village comprised of tents on stone foundations. The kings were cordially greeted by the ruler and he ordered a meal to be prepared for them. The ruler inquired about their journey, the reason and their destination.

One of the kings spoke for the others saying, "I am Mensor of Chaldea," turning his head to the others he continued, "My companions are Seir of Media, and Theokeno of Serica in the East. We are each descendants of Job who lived on the Caucasus and ruled other lands far and wide. Our ancestors received from an angel of God that from a virgin the Savior would be born and whom their descendants would honor. They were instructed to watch the stars. Three prophetesses announced a prophecy to the people, five hundred years before our time that a star would appear that they must follow. They foresaw that this star would arise out of Jacob and that an inviolate Virgin would bring forth the Savior, promising that messengers from the Savior would come to their people and lead them to the worship of the true God. They watched not one star alone, but an entire constellation. As they gazed visions and pictures were formed and the details passed on from one generation to the next. We, also, have been granted the gift of these visions and the coming salvation more clearly shown. We have been following the prophesied star these past fifty-six days."

The ruler, who listened intently, interrupted Mensor and begged them. "Tell me of this vision, I beg you. What did you see in the star?"

Mensor continued, "It was not in one star alone that we saw the visions, but in several that formed a figure, and there was movement in them. We each saw the same; a moon over which arose a beautifully colored arch on which was seated a woman wearing the garments of a virgin. Her left leg was drawn up under her and the right hung down and rested on the moon.

To the left of the virgin and rising above the arch was a grapevine, and on her right a sheaf of wheat. Before her was a chalice filled with light that emanated from her. Out of the chalice arose a child, and above the child a bright disc appeared surrounded by radiating beams of light. On the Virgin's right was a temple with a golden door. With her right hand the Virgin placed the child and the bright disk into the temple which grew larger and larger. Above the Virgin was a star which suddenly shot from its place and skimmed along the heavens. A voice announced to us that the Child, so long awaited, was about to be born in Judea and that we were to follow the star until we found him."

"Where may I ask is this star you speak of?" the ruler asked with much skepticism. "Show it to me and my people and we will believe."

The three kings and the ruler left the tent they were in and the ruler called together his people who had been asleep. The sky was no longer clear and the star was hidden behind a large dark cloud. The ruler and his people, who were not at all happy about being roused from their tents, began to ridicule the kings. Theokeno stepped away from the crowd and pointed to the sky.

Suddenly the cloud moved away and the star appeared, brighter now than it had been and with rays seeming to reach down to the earth. The people and their ruler were awestruck and deeply moved.

"I humbly and earnestly beg you to forgive me and my people," declared the ruler. "On your return, please inform us all that you discover so that we might erect altars and offer a sacrifice to the child."

The people pressed around the kings but said nothing; their respect for them had grown quickly. The servants were directed to distribute grain to the poor and small triangular silver coins to all. And at the ruler's bidding the kings decided to remain in the tent village until the evening of the same day. Before their departure the people blessed them and sadly bid them farewell. With the shining brightly before them they resumed their journey star.

Moving rapidly, they passed through several small Jewish villages as they approached the Jordan River and were about one day from Jerusalem. At mid-day they reached the Jordan and crossed by ferry. Only two of the ferrymen who were not Jews helped them across because it was the Sabbath. Boards were laid over the cross-beams of the ferry for the animals to stand on. After several trips, without mishap, all were on the west bank. They could now see the tops of the tallest buildings of Jerusalem. The kings led their groups to an orchard where they rested until evening. When the star appeared they were all very concerned because it did not shine with its usual brightness. The kings drew apart from their groups to discuss what they observed.

"Why is there no excitement in this land?" asked Seir. "Why is there no joy and celebration of the birth of the new-born Savior?"

"And why is the star less bright now that we are in Judea?" Theokeno inquired. "Have we been wrong in our thinking?"

Mensor added, "Perhaps we have made an error and have strayed from our path? Shall we retrace our steps or continue on? What shall we do?"

Seir pondered the situation for a few moments and replied, "Let us continue. The Savior is born and we are to honor Him. It is the will of God. We must travel until the star moves no more."

He spoke with such surety that the others readily agreed and directed their followers to continue on toward Jerusalem. The Sabbath was now over; more people were seen along the way. It was mid-night when the caravan reached the outskirts of the city. As the caravan neared the northeast wall of Jerusalem their guiding star became less bright than it had been the previous night. Each of the kings was disconcerted by this. They expected the Messiah to be in Jerusalem and therefore the star should have been at its brightest, and the absence of any excitement in the people they passed compounded their concern. The people were very curious about them not only because of their appearance but there was no apparent reason for them to be arriving at Jerusalem at that time. The Feast of the Maccabees had ended and no special events were scheduled in the markets. Many people had joined the caravan since they crossed the Jordan because of the gifts the kings were distributing along the way; there were almost two hundred following when they came to a road that led them passed the hill of Golgotha. They entered Jerusalem by the Fish Gate near to the fish markets. Here the wall was circular and it enclosed a large courtyard containing many houses and inns. The wall curved to the southwest and connected to the wall at the Tower of Marianne close to Herod's palace. At the east end of the courtyard was the outer wall of the Temple. Most of the courtyard was on a hill but where David's tomb was located it was fairly level. The caravan moved to this section where the kings issued orders for the tents to be pitched close to the wall. Not far from David's tomb and near the center of the level area was a well with a stone wall, surrounded by several watering troughs and benches. Soon the city inhabitants carrying torches and lamps began to mingle with the servants of the kings as they unloaded their baggage and provisions. The people were amazed to see such a large and rich caravan move into the city, especially at night. Many of them came to watch but asked no questions and the servants asked none as well. Mensor noticed however that several of those that followed them had walked toward the center of the city.

Theokeno called Seir and Mensor to his tent and said, "I see no signs of the excitement we anticipated. Perhaps we should send some of our people into the city to make inquiries."

Seir and Mensor agreed then left to assign two men from their groups for the task; Theokeno called two men as well. When the six men were gathered Theokeno gave them their instructions.

"You are to go to all sections of the city and make inquiries of those that you can identify as being Jews and say to them, 'Where is the King of the Jews, who is born? For we have seen his star in the East, announcing to us his birth and we have come to see him and adore him.' Do this until you find someone with knowledge of the child but if you find no one return here in one hour."

The men bowed low, turned and walked quickly out of the tent. The kings followed them, stood in the courtyard and looked in every direction for their guiding star but to no avail. The sky was clear of any clouds and no unusual star was visible. They could do nothing now but wait for their messengers to return. The wait was short for one of the messengers returned one half hour later followed by an official and four soldiers from Herod's palace. The official welcomed them to the city and asked further about the infant King they sought.

"We have come a long way," declared Seir, "to find the Child revealed to our ancestors many years ago and recently to us. We are to follow a star that would lead us to him but the star has now disappeared. Several of our people were sent into the city to make inquiries but have not returned except for the man you have followed."

"Do you know of the Child?" Mensor asked. "If you have any information at all we will pay you well for it. We wish also to obtain an audience with Herod your king so that we may inform him of our quest."

The official treated them with the respect afforded visiting dignitaries for fear of offending Herod but in truth he was agitated because he thought their story was incredible.

"I have no knowledge of a child being born under a certain star," he replied. "Nor have my men heard anything about this new King. And we have listened to others in the city give the same answer to your messenger. Perhaps Herod knows something of him; he has sources of information from all parts of the city and within his kingdom. If there was a special child born, a new king, the news certainly would have reached him. I will convey your desire for an audience tonight. Wait for my return in the morning."

With that he bowed, turned and left, followed closely by the soldiers. As they walked away they laughed disdainfully and loud enough for the kings to hear. Theokeno was very troubled; Seir and Mensor were dejected. Mensor suggested they spend time in prayer and to trust that they will be directed by God. But their prayers were soon interrupted by the return of the remaining messengers. Each was questioned and gave the same answer. No one knew of a child that was born and declared the king of the Jews. But one messenger received an answer about a promised child to be born in Bethlehem. He stated that this answer came from two beggars they found near a small pool. The kings were now concerned that perhaps they were in error in their calculations and the Child was to be born at another time. Mensor again suggested they pray for guidance; they retired to their own tents and did so.

Herod's official and the soldiers continued to discuss the kings and their quest while they walked toward the palace; the official was concerned about the manner in which Herod would receive the news of a new king. Before reaching Herod's quarters he mentally composed his speech, deciding not to make light of the royal visitors' story. The road to the palace, which was situated at the top of a hill, was lined with torches and lamps. Guards were stationed at regular intervals along the road but the official was not challenged because he was well known by every soldier in Herod's personal guard. The palace was well lit because of the many guests enjoying Herod's nightly celebrations. Several women in dancing costumes were in the hall where the official entered waiting their turn to entertain the guests. Herod usually attended the festivities but this night because of an uneasiness he felt, he retreated to his chambers and left his wife with their guests. The official went reluctantly to Herod's quarters, begged an audience then entered. He found Herod pacing the floor of his private dining area; he appeared to be in a very nervous state.

When Herod became aware of the official's presence he was quite irritated and shouted, "What do you want, Sodi?"

Sodi approached with his head bowed, saluted and replied, "Sire, I am here to inform you that three rulers from the East have entered Jerusalem this night and are camped near the Fish Gate. They request an audience for the honor of meeting you and to discuss their reason for coming to Jerusalem."

"Who are these rulers? And where do they come from?" Herod asked.

Sodi responded, "One is called. Theokeno, he is the oldest, He is from a land east of the Caspian Sea. The second is called Seir of Media and the third is from Chaldea, He is called Mensor. I learned this from their messenger whom I found in the city streets. I learned also that they are very learned astrologers and greatly respected."

Herod became impatient. He signaled for his servant to pour a cup of wine then reclined on several silken pillows situated on the raised portion of the room where he could still look down upon the official! Continue!" he commanded.

Sodi continued, "They claim, Sire, that through a revelation of some kind that a child was born in your dominion that is now the king of the Jews and they are here to greet him and honor him. They also claim to have been guided by a star that will bring them to the new born king."

"A star guides them?" Herod repeated quizzically.

"Yes, Sire, that is what they claim but as they entered the city the star disappeared."

"They say a new king is born, a king of the Jews!" Herod shouted.

"That is their belief, Sire." Sodi replied, now becoming frightened by Herod's behavior and obvious agitation.

Herod's face flushed red; he hurled the wine goblet toward his servant and rose quickly. Some of the pillows were knocked about as he paced back and forth. Sodi was amazed at Herod's response, He knew of Herod's anger; he had been subjected to it before but this was different from all the other times. He was almost insane with rage.

"Bring these men to me at once!" he shouted. "Bring them to me so that I may question them myself."

"Yes, Sire!" Sodi responded nervously then turned to leave. Herod called to him just as he reached the exit, "Wait!"

Sodi turned and faced Herod again; he was much surprised at the change in his composure for he was quite calm.

Herod remained silent for a few moments, pondering some plan, then said calmly, "Disregard what I have just told you to do. I will not see them this night, Convey to them my greeting and my apology for not granting them an audience now, but say that I will see them in the morning. Tell them also I am making inquiries about the child and may have news of him when they arrive."

Sodi now less concerned, said, "I have taken that liberty Sire. I asked them to wait for my return in the morning."

"Well done, Sodi!" Herod declared while reflecting upon his next move, "You may leave now."

Sodi exited quickly and went to his quarters within the palace. Herod paced the floor for some time pondering this development and the action he should take. Unable to decide he called for his chief advisor, Nabat, whose opinions and advice he greatly respected. Nabat, son of Jehu of the tribe of Judah, lived in Hebron from his birth but moved to Jerusalem at Herod's request and took residence with his family within the palace grounds. Aroused from his sleep, he rushed to Herod's quarters and found him pacing the floor and very distressed.

"You sent for me Sire?" Nabat asked. Herod made no acknowledgement; he continued walking with his head lowered and his hands clenched behind him.

Nabat waited a few minutes then repeated his question, "You sent for me, Sire?"

Herod stopped, turned to Nabat and proceeded to tell him about the royal visitors and their search for a newborn king. Nabat saw that Herod was quite concerned about a course of action; he recalled that scripture contained some thing about a child king and a prophecy. He informed Herod and advised him to summon the priests, elders and scribes to obtain from them their interpretation of these signs. Pleased with this advice, Herod dispatched soldiers with instructions that they were to escort all those he named to the audience hall without delay. Within one hour all those he summoned had arrived; the priests came last because they took time to don their priestly garments. Some were very annoyed but others were frightened. They wondered why they were summoned at such a late hour and escorted by the soldiers. Not looking at anyone, Herod walked quickly to a high backed chair located on a terraced part of the hall with a large canopy overhead and silken curtains hanging on each side. Nabat stood before him facing the people; Sodi, who was also summoned, stood to his left. Herod directed him to give in detail a full account of all that he saw and heard that night. The priests, elders and scribes listened intently while two of the scribes wrote down all that was related. When Sodi finished his account Herod commanded the listeners to search the scriptures for any prophecy concerning the Child.

One of the priests stepped forward and said, "We do not need to search the Scriptures. The prophecy is well known to us and where the Child is to be born."

"What is it? Herod demanded. "And where may he be found?"

"In Bethlehem of Judea," the priest replied. "For it is written by the prophet, 'and thou, Bethlehem, of the land of Judah art by no means least among the princes of Judah; for from thee shall come forth a leader who shall rule my people Israel.' "

Herod was greatly agitated but concealed it from them by speaking slow and deliberate about the star that was supposed to be guiding the kings.

One of the scribes spoke out, "These people from the East put great store in the study of the stars and what they see in them. But it is sheer nonsense and superstition. Do not pay any heed to their stories. I have heard many of them from the caravans traveling to Jerusalem, and all have been absurd."

Sodi interrupted and said, "They claim the star led them here to Jerusalem, then lost sight of it as they entered the city."

"Let us go up to the roof," suggested one of the elders, "and see for ourselves."

"Yes," Herod declared. "All of you follow me to the roof."

Herod rushed from the hall and climbed a stairway leading to the roof. Everyone gathered at the center of a large open area surrounded by potted plants and small couches. They scanned the still clear sky in every direction.

"I see nothing unusual," declared the scribe. "It is as I said, nothing but superstition."

Maloch, the elder from the west section of Jerusalem, was standing with Nabat and Sodi, he added, "Sire, if there were any truth in what they said about the Child being born at this time and declared King of the Jews surely the priests of the Temple would have known of it soon after it occurred. They have heard nothing and neither have we, the elders."

Herod appeared to accept his reasoning, dismissed everyone except Nabat and Sodi and returned to his quarters.

Once there he instructed Sodi, "At daybreak return to our visitors. Tell them I will grant them an audience. But do not bring them to the hall, I will question them in the antechamber where we may speak without being overheard."

"Yes, Sire," he answered while bowing low.

"Do you wish me to be present?" Nabat asked.

"Yes," replied Herod, "and have two scribes standby in the corridor in the event I require their services."

Nabat and Sodi bowed, turned and left.

Herod busied himself with some matters requiring his attention for he knew he would not sleep that night. Sodi slept well; as one does who has pleased his master and has little more to do but obey. About one hour before daybreak his servant woke him; without delay he returned to the kings' encampment. He conveyed Herod's message then led the kings to the palace and into an apartment adjoining Herod's private chambers. The rooms were small and lined with flowering plants and small bushes contained in colorful pots. Near the entrance there were two tables filled with various foods, fruit and beverages; a servant stood next to it with a water bowl and small towels. The kings did not eat or drink; they remained standing until Herod entered from his chambers. Nabat was behind him. Sodi per- formed the customary introductions then moved aside. After bowing to Herod the kings presented him with a small silver drinking cup with jewels set along the base. Herod expressed pleasure in their gift.

Theokeno spoke first, "Herod, we have been told by your official that you have many sources of information and that you may help us in our quest. We have come to do homage to the newborn King of the Jews, for we have seen His coming in the stars and have been guided by one until we arrived in Jerusalem. We entreat you to tell us where we may find the Child."

Herod still very troubled and agitated walked to the tables of food and ate a few small pieces of cheese and fruit before answering.

"Last night I summoned several priests, elders and scribes. I questioned them about this and they informed me that of Bethlehem-Ephrata is the Promised One to come."

Nabat added, "Bethlehem is a town located less than two leagues journey south of Jerusalem; it is situated adjacent to the main road to Hebron. Our King David resided there many years earlier. It is his tomb that you have pitched your tents near to."

"Have you had any reports of the Child being born there?" Seir asked.

Herod responded, "Some of my informants related that many of the people were talking about a miraculous birth but found only a simple man living in a cave with his wife and their child. Certainly a king would not be born in such a place."

Mensor asked, "How long has it been since you received the report?"

Herod replied, "I believe the report came to me ten days prior to this day. But I assure you that my informants are reliable and thorough. No king has been born in Bethlehem."

Mensor continued, "We are certain that the Child has been born, but we know not where or under what circumstances. Each one of our visions has been identical to the others. We have been shown a Virgin holding a child on her lap and from the right side of the infant came a beam of light. Upon the beam stood a tower with many gates. It increased in size until it became a city and the Child stood above it holding a sword and scepter. Many kings of the earth came and bowed before Him and they adored Him. His kingdom was to vanquish all other kingdoms."

Herod was impressed by the certainty he heard in Mensor's declaration but at the same time he was filled with fear. After moments of recollection, he said to the kings, "Perhaps you are right. Go quickly to Bethlehem and search for the Child. After you find Him return and inform me of His identity and where He may be found for I too wish to do Him homage and adore Him. Go at once, but say nothing to the people within this city until you return."

Herod bid them farewell and returned to his chambers. Nabat and Sodi escorted the kings out of the palace grounds then left them. The kings returned quickly to their encampment, issued orders for the tents to be taken down and to prepare for another journey.

CHAPTER FIVE
The Kings Arrive

The road to Hebron was wide near the city and lined with cedar and balsam trees uniformly spaced for a distance of half a league; it narrowed where the trees ended. A narrow, rocky steam ran parallel to the road until it reached the Water Gate. The caravan left by this gate followed by many people. As the last animal moved onto the road the people turned back. Mensor's group led the caravan, followed by Seir's then Theokeno's. They were not certain of finding the Child in Bethlehem but nevertheless they decided to go there. After traveling one full league from Jerusalem, Seir and Theokeno joined Mensor at the head of the column. At the crest of a hill they halted and looked about for their guide. It had appeared to them during daylight many times before.

"There is no star for us to follow," declared Mensor. "Should we be traveling in the wrong direction many days may be lost. Let us all pray to our Lord for He will hear us and help us."

Theokeno turned to the remainder of the caravan and asked them all to join in the prayers. While sitting on their animals with their heads bowed and uncovered they prayed. Seir raised his head after several minutes and scanned the cloudy sky. He saw no sign of the star at first then suddenly at a small break in the clouds he caught a glimpse of it.

He pointed skyward and shouted, "There it is! There it is! Do you see it?"

Simultaneously a cheer went up from each of them and immediately they moved in the direction of the star; all were filled with great joy and began to sing. The star appeared differently than it did at night; it was about as bright as the full moon when seen during the day. They could see no rays coming down, but it had the image of a child within it. Now that the census had been completed many people were returning to Jerusalem. Traveling at a rapid pace was impossible because of their number. At a point where the road became narrower the star suddenly changed from a southerly position and appeared directly eastward. The kings did not hesitate to follow it even though they knew this course took them away from the road to Bethlehem. Soon they were in a valley that was thick with plants and trees. An old narrow trail, which was quite level, allowed them to move quickly through the valley to a beautiful grove of fruit trees. A small pond surrounded by much grass was fed by a stream that ran from the high ground where they halted and prayed. They rested near it for a long time before continuing their journey. The star moved again to a southerly direction, guiding them through rolling pastures and groves of fruit trees where they encountered only a few travelers. The caravan continued southward until almost directly east of Bethlehem then followed the star westward; traveling much the same route Mary and Joseph traveled.

At dusk the caravan arrived at the east side of Bethlehem. The star was brighter now with rays radiating from it, longer at the bottom than the sides. Directly ahead was the Custom house. As they entered the courtyard the star suddenly disappeared. Mensor, Seir and Theokeno came together and dismounted.

"Can this be the home of the Child?" Theokeno asked.

"It may well be," declared Mensor, "there seems to be a great deal of activity within and observe the many people in the courtyard."

At once a large crowd gathered around them out of curiosity, and when the kings began to distribute small coins their number increased. Two Roman soldiers moved in the direction of the crowd but said nothing; the commotion had attracted them.

Seir suggested, "Let us inquire of the Child from these people. Surely they should be able to tell us something."

An elderly man who was standing away from the crowd went toward them and without any apparent reason the people moved aside leaving a clear path to the kings. The man was tall, had a moderately long, gray beard, grayish hair and a ruddy complexion; his clothes were modest and he wore no sandals.

Seir spoke to him first, "Sir, we are seeking a new-born Child that is the King of the Jews. We assume the Child to be in this house. Are we correct in our assumption?"

"The One you seek is not here," he replied. "You must travel yet a little further."

"Can you tell us where we may find Him?" asked Theokeno.

"Your search is almost at an end," the man answered. "Continue to follow your guide."

He turned, walked away and moved into a group of people near the house.

Mensor called to him, "How is it that you know of our guide?"

The man did not answer. The group he joined now moved in around the kings but the elderly man had vanished. The press of the crowd increased. With great difficulty the kings made their way to their dromedaries and remounted. Uncertain as to the direction they should take, Seir led them toward the east wall of the city. But as they approached the gate the star appeared above the south end of the wall. Overjoyed at seeing their guide again they turned toward it. Upon arriving at the end of the wall the star moved to the west and grew even brighter. Before them was the trail Joseph followed; they followed it into the valley below the cave. Here the star no longer moved and it began to descend. The kings understood this to be a sign they were to remain there, and gave orders to the servants to erect the tents and to prepare the food for the evening meal. A crowd of townspeople had followed the caravan from the moment it left the custom house but returned to their homes when they saw the kings preparing to stay.

Joseph had been standing at the entrance of the cave when the caravan moved into the valley. He was expecting them. Mary had informed him that their royal visitors would arrive that night. He had worked continuously through the day moving many of the gifts and the sheep to a cave on the opposite side of the hill so that more room would be available for them. Joseph saw their torches and fires; he knew they had pitched their tents and would soon be settled for the night. Below, the servants were busy preparing their food and tending to the animals. The kings planned to meet in Theokeno's tent for consultation but as Seir and Mensor approached it the star began to descend again; it was now perfectly round. Seir called Theokeno out of his tent and the three stood gazing fixedly at the star with wonder and excitement. Suddenly the figure of a child with his arms outstretched appeared within the disc as if beckoning them. The kings were overjoyed. It continued to descend until it was directly over the entrance of the cave. Immediately the kings began to climb the hill.

Their friends and servants saw them leave but did not follow. As they came close to the entrance, the star descended further until it seemed to be absorbed by the earth and a bright glow could be seen emanating from the cave. They walked up to the wicker screen, moved it aside and walked slowly into the cave. The walls and ceiling were glimmering and seemed almost alive. Mensor led the way; Seir was behind him, then Theokeno. When they came around the turn in the cave they beheld Mary holding the infant Jesus in her arms and sitting beside the manger. Joseph was standing beside her. The Holy Family was surrounded by a beautiful light but they could be clearly seen. Immediately the kings recognized Mary as the Virgin they had seen in their visions. They were amazed and filled with great adoration. But they did not approach the Holy Family, instead they bowed low and walked backward out of the cave. Joseph followed quickly and found them standing under the arbor silently staring at each other. Joseph too was amazed; he had not seen anything like these men before. Everything about them was foreign to him. Of course he knew they were rulers; Mary had revealed this to him that day.

Joseph approached them and said, "Peace be with you. I am Joseph, son of Jacob, lately of Nazareth, residing here in this cave because we could find no room in the inns. You are welcome to stay longer if you wish. We have been awaiting your arrival for the past three days and have made preparations to serve you."

Seir responded to Joseph's greeting and invitation, "Peace be with you, Joseph. My companions and I have traveled a great distance to adore the new-born King of the Jews. We have seen His star in our lands in the East and have come to bring Him gifts. But we are not presentable as we are now. We will return to our tents in order to change our clothes and to prepare our gifts for presentation. Will you permit us to do so?"

Joseph was surprised at this humble request from a king. He answered, "The Child, His mother and I will anxiously await your return. God be with you."

Not saying anything further, the kings hurried to their tents where they gave orders to the servants regarding the preparation of their royal garments while they saw to the gifts. One hour later each king emerged from his tent in royal attire of silk mantles, colorful girdles surrounding beautifully embroidered tunics, silk stockings and jeweled shoes. Hanging from their girdles were small golden boxes with gold knobs; they were suspended on fine gold chains. Each one brought along four friends and two servants, each of whom was instructed to dress for the occasion. The servants brought along a small table with folding legs, a silken coverlet with tasseled edges and a long narrow carpet woven by Theokeno's people. In all twenty-one were in the party that left for the cave.

When they arrived, Joseph was waiting for them under the arbor; he welcomed all of them. Now the three kings introduced themselves and their friends; they informed Joseph that each king would enter in turn with their friends and servants. Seir directed his servants to place the carpet at the entrance and lay it down until it reached the manger. They did as instructed then joined the others at the entrance. Mensor was to enter first; he took the small table from his servants then had them remove his sandals. His friends did the same, before stepping upon the carpet. Joseph escorted Mensor and his friends followed.

The cave was again filled with a brilliant light but they felt no discomfort in their eyes; nor were they the least frightened or nervous. On the contrary they felt a warmth flow through them that they had never experienced before. When Mary came into view, she was kneeling next to the manger. The infant Jesus was lying in it wrapped in white swaddling cloths and covered with a small red blanket. Mary picked up the Child as they approached and covered Him partly with her veil which she had drawn around her. Jesus' head and arms were exposed. Mensor approached very reverently and placed the small table near the manger. Mary raised the infant Jesus and leaned Him against her breast. Mensor bowed very low and remained in that position; his heart was pounding and his eyes were filled with tears. He then fell to his knees. The infant Jesus crossed His arms upon His chest then extended them out to Mensor. Mensor was filled with an unspeakable joy; only by a special grace was he able to endure it. He crossed his arms upon his chest in the same manner as the Child then bowed until his head touched the carpet. His friends, kneeling a little further away did the same. Joseph was standing beside Mary with his hand upon her shoulder. Mary reached up and placed her free hand upon his, and did not remove it all the while Mensor was bowing.

Several minutes passed when Mensor raised his head; he looked at Mary and the Child and spoke very humbly these words, "We have seen His star and that He is King over all kings. We have come to adore Him and to bring Him gifts. With grateful affection I place them at your feet."

He removed a bag from the box hanging from his girdle and poured out the contents upon the table. It had been filled with small gold bars about two inches long and one quarter inch thick; on one side a small flower resembling a rose was inscribed.

"Dear and Blessed Daughter," Mensor continued. "I have anxiously awaited this moment for many years; confident always that someday salvation would be mine. Now it is at hand."

Joseph bent down and said to Mary, this is Mensor of Chaldea and these are his companions. They have traveled a great distance to visit Jesus."

Mary was greatly affected by Mensor's love and adoration. She smiled at him, at the same time lying Jesus upon her lap, then nodded her head in a way that Mensor understood her pleasure in accepting his gift. The infant Jesus lay quietly on her lap.

Joseph, too, was very moved by Mensor's display of love. While he escorted him and his companions to the cave's entrance he said to Mensor, "On behalf of the Child and His mother I thank you for your gift but especially for your devotion to Him, Our Savior. I will always remember your visit and from now on I will call you 'Caspar' which means 'He who is won by love'."

Mensor embraced Joseph and left with tears flowing upon his cheeks.

Next, Seir and his companions followed Joseph into the cave after removing their shoes and sandals. Mary had gotten to her feet and was holding the infant Jesus when Seir came. He knelt down with his companions close behind him. He bowed low and said, "We have seen His star and that He is King over all kings. We have come to adore Him and to bring Him gifts. For it is the will of God that all men be saved through Him."

Joseph moved close to Mary and told her, "This is Seir of Media and his companions. They also have traveled a great distance."

Seir removed a small boat-shaped container from his girdle; it was filled with frankincense. He placed the container upon the table, very reverently bowed again and said, "My life has been one of hope that someday I would see our Savior and now God has willed it so. May I always conform to His will and entirely accord with it."

Mary held the infant Jesus beneath His arms and lifted Him so that He was facing Seir. Seir, who was suddenly filled with an unspeakable feeling of warmth, rose to his feet and bowed. He remained that way for awhile then began to walk backward, with his eyes only on the Child Jesus and His mother, until he was beyond the turn of the cave. Joseph and the companions went with him.

As they neared the entrance Joseph said to Seir, "On behalf of the Child and His mother I thank you for your gift and your loving adoration of our Savior. I will always remember your visit and from now on I will call you 'Balthasar' which means 'With his whole will he accomplishes the will of God'."

Seir leaned toward Joseph, placed his face upon each side of Joseph's face then walked slowly out of the cave.

Theokeno and his companions were anxiously waiting their turn. Joseph bid them enter and walked a little ahead of them. Mary was again on her knees but sitting back on her legs; the infant Jesus was in her arms and covered by her veil. As Theokeno approached the light surrounding Mother and Child grew brighter. But there was no fear in Theokeno. He advanced very slowly; his feet were bare and he made several very profound bows. He remained standing; kneeling was very difficult for him because of his age and weight. His movements were very gentle and with profound gesture. He had brought with him a plant, fresh and living, very straight, bearing small delicate green leaves and small white flowers. It was set in a golden pot shaped like a ship used by his people on the Caspian Sea; from the plant they were able to produce myrrh. After placing the plant upon the small table he said to Mary and Joseph as the others did, "We have seen his star and that He is King over all kings. We have come to adore Him and to bring Him gifts."

He bowed very low then stood erect. He remained silent for a long time interiorly adoring the infant Jesus and thanking God for the great honor and privilege of being able to do so. Mary and Joseph could say nothing. It was most difficult for them to speak because of the great joy and emotion that came over them.

Then Theokeno spoke with deep feeling, "All through my adult life I have had to struggle against temptations of idol worship and taking many wives as is customary in my homeland. Now, for whatever time remains for me, I commend myself to Jesus, and all my goods, property and all that I have that is of any value. But most especially I commend to Him my heart and my spirit."

While he was speaking, Mensor and Seir reentered the cave without their companions and stood beside Theokeno.

"We beg Jesus to take all of us, all our actions, our thoughts and our emotions," Mensor added.

"We also entreat Him to enlighten us," Seir continued with very great fervor and humility, "to bestow upon us many virtues and to grant peace, happiness and love to all of us here present and to the entire world."

The kings wept. Mary and Joseph wept also at the honor and recognition paid to their Child and Savior by these royal visitors. Mary silently gave thanks for their adoration and gifts presented to her Son which were brought over great distances, by God's almighty power, in spite of the dangers and difficulties they encountered along the way. She and Joseph joined the kings in adoring Jesus for quite some time then Joseph went to Theokeno, stood beside him and grasped his arm.

He then said to Mary, "This is Theokeno. He rules a people that live near the great Caspian Sea in the East. But from now on we shall call him 'Melchior' which means 'one who uses so much address and approaches so gently'."

Mary smiled at Joseph, stood up and presented the infant Jesus to Theokeno. He took the Child, caressed Him gently and spoke endearing terms in his own language. Jesus reached up touched Theokeno's beard and then placed His little hand upon his lips. Theokeno was enraptured.

Mary presented the Child in turn to Seir and Mensor; both shed abundant tears while their faces were beaming with joy. Mary allowed them to hold Jesus for several minutes then placed Him in the manger. At that, Joseph directed Theokeno's friends to approach the manger. Each one went to his knees, bent low to the ground then gazed upon the Child. Realizing that their visit was a long one the kings decided to leave.

Mensor said to Mary and Joseph, "We are most gratified at this visit, but we have been here long enough for now. We will return in the morning if that would please you."

Mary came close to them and declared, "Your presence has given us great joy and we are most grateful for your loving adoration toward our Child, Jesus. You are welcome to visit Him whenever you wish and a like invitation is extended to all who made the journey with you."

Joseph escorted the kings and their companions out of the cave and accompanied them to their encampment. He was surprised at the beauty of the encampment because of the many fires and the tents which were aglow from the lamps placed within them. Several servants were moving about although the hour was late. He greeted each of them with his usual pleasant and humble manner then returned to the cave. The kings retired to their tents and reflected upon all that had occurred. They realized that the long wait was over; they had lived through the vision their ancestors had longed to see. All the joy and hope of the promise made many hundreds of years before had now been fulfilled. Just after the sun rose above the crest of the hill the kings were awakened by the sounds of people moving about the encampment and the servants trying to quiet them. Many people had come out from the city hoping that the kings would again distribute gifts of coins and clothing. What they hoped for soon took place; the kings came together at the center of the encampment and began to distribute not only coins and clothing but their provisions as well. A great deal of bread which was baked each time they made camp was given away without regard for the depletion of their stores. Some of the servants were concerned because the journey home was long and the provisions would be needed. But the kings called together all their servants, declared that they were now free and that they could remain in Israel if they so desired or return with them. Because they had grown to love these humble and generous rulers most of the servants decided to return. Those who decided to remain in Israel did so with the hope of becoming shepherds or farmers; to these the kings gave some of the animals piled high with provisions and to each was given a small bag of gold particles. Their departure was swift but affable.

During all this commotion Joseph arrived and beaconed for the kings to join him in one of their tents. They had difficulty in doing so because of the press of the people.

"What are you doing?" Joseph inquired. "I have seen your servants leaving and you are giving away your provisions. What will you use on your return to your lands?"

"Joseph, my friend," replied Theokeno, "do not be concerned. We will not need all that we have and now we are able to travel much faster. "

Mensor added, "It gives us great pleasure to share what we have with these good people. Come sit down with us. We have something to tell you."

They reclined upon beautifully woven carpets covered by several silken cushions in the section of the tent used for eating and receiving guests. It was separated from the sleeping area by several layers of fine curtains.

Seir spoke first, "During the night each of us had a similar dream. In it we saw a fine looking young man enter our sleeping quarters. He advised us to leave Bethlehem before midday, and that Herod had designs against the Child. We are not to return by way of Jerusalem but to travel south into the Engaddi Desert along the Dead Sea and to take with us only that which was necessary. He informed us that we would be guided through the remainder of our journey by an angel of God."

"Now, you can see why we are giving away so much," said Theokeno.

"What may I do to help?" Joseph asked.

"Return to Mary and the Child," Theokeno replied. "We will visit with you again before we depart."

Joseph promptly returned to the cave. The kings resumed the distribution of the provisions as well as coins and clothing. In the meantime their servants and followers struck the tents and loaded the animals. When the supply of gifts was exhausted the kings and their companions returned to the cave for a final visit. They brought with them many things: rolls of precious silk, white and red, small carpets, several plants, many dishes and drinking vessels, a basket filled with pots and a dozen boxes of grain. In addition they presented to Joseph their large woolen mantles.

Mary and Joseph accepted all they brought with a deep gratitude but without any great pleasure at receiving them. Their intention was to distribute these gifts to the poor shepherds and city dwellers. Joseph had informed Mary that the kings were about to leave and the warning they received in their dreams, so that when they arrived at the cave she immediately placed the infant Jesus in Mensor's arms, who in turn gave the Child to Seir, then to Theokeno. All of them wept, as did Mary and Joseph. It was a sad parting but yet they were filled with enormous consolation having met Mary and Joseph and held the Savior in their arms.

Just before midday one of the servants entered the cave and at an appropriate moment announced that it was time to leave. Without further delay they said farewell to Mary and the Child then left accompanied by Joseph; he decided to guide them until they were in sight of the road to Hebron. Nothing remained to be done when they reached the encampment; they mounted their animals and started on their way. Joseph walked alongside Theokeno leading them along a trail that wound through pastureland in a southwesterly direction.

At the center of one field was a magnificent cedar with a very wide trunk capped by many spreading branches thick with fine green leaves. It was broad enough to provide shade for many animals without crowding but none were present when the caravan came to it. A few paces from the south side of the trunk a small spring flowed from the ground, and on the north side were two small sheds with a furnace for cooking between them.

"There are no trees in my homeland that can compare with this one," Theokeno declared. "And it appears to be very old."

"A legend exists among the shepherds that Abraham and Melchisdech once met under it and that the waters from the spring have healing qualities." Joseph commented. "At certain times in the year the sick are brought here in the hope that they will be healed. Actually the tree is regarded as sacred by them."

In response to Joseph's explanation Seir said, "I suggest that this would be a good place for us to lift up our prayers in thanksgiving for the great honor bestowed upon us and for a safe journey to our lands."

"Yes," Mensor stated." "Let us begin now."

All in the caravan dismounted, uncovered their heads, knelt facing in the direction of the Nativity Cave and silently prayed. Joseph and the kings were side by side and at times raised their arms while singing songs of praise. Any passerby would have been amazed at the sight. When their praying ended the servants watered the animals and filled every water container they had. They resumed their journey, now moving more toward the south. At the crest of a rather long hill they halted again; ahead of them was the road to Hebron. The three kings dismounted and came to Joseph.

With tears in his eyes he said to them, "Before you is the road to Hebron which leads to the south and west. To the east of Hebron is a pass leading to the Engaddi and the Dead Sea. You will have no trouble finding it."

Joseph felt a profound sadness in his heart; he knew they would not see each other again. Each one of the kings embraced Joseph and many of their companions did the same.

"It is time for me to leave you now my good friends," said Joseph. "The Lord bless you and keep you! The Lord let His face shine upon you, and be gracious to you! The Lord look upon you kindly and give you peace!"

The kings could say nothing; their sadness was so great; they remounted and slowly moved on. As each of the companions and servants passed Joseph they said a few kind words and gave him a small salutation with their hands. Joseph watched the caravan descend toward the road; one of the kings would occasionally turn and wave. Joseph returned their wave and remained on the crest until he could see them no more. He had come quite a distance with the kings; now that he was returning to the Nativity Cave he wondered if he would arrive before dark. Suddenly his sadness was replaced by the joyful thought of being with Mary and Jesus again.

Daylight was rapidly fading when Joseph climbed the hill to the cave. He could see a light shining through the wicker curtain at the entrance, and he heard the infant Jesus crying as he emerged from the row of small cedar trees. Mary and Athalia were at the rear of the cave. Athalia was preparing food for the evening meal while Mary was attending to Jesus. Mary heard Joseph's footsteps and rose to greet him. He grasped her hands gently and placed his face against hers; his usual way of greeting Mary when others were present. He then knelt beside the manger, place his index finger in the Infant's hand and spoke to Him in endearing terms. Athalia greeted him from where she was and continued working.

"Dear husband," Mary said, "while you were gone several of Herod's soldiers came into the valley. They were asking questions about new born children. None came to the cave but the shepherds have said they will return tomorrow."

Joseph replied, "On the way here I spoke to some of the shepherds. They informed me that the arrival of the kings had caused a great commotion in the city, and by drawing many people into the valley an edict was made by the Elders saying the people should not follow them any longer nor should they visit this cave."

"What shall we do?" Mary asked calmly but with a little concern in her voice.

While returning Joseph had considered moving to another cave. "With the help of the shepherds, who will be here shortly, we will move all that the kings and shepherds brought to us into a cave on the opposite side of this hill. We will also move most of our furnishings and provisions. And if it becomes necessary we can go there quickly with the Child."

Mary, reassured by Joseph's plan, continued to attend to the infant Jesus. Joseph went to the spring to obtain fresh water and when he returned the evening meal was served. Following the meal, Joseph, Mary and Athalia knelt beside the manger praying and silently adoring the Child. Afterward Joseph began moving the gifts to the entrance; from there he and the shepherds would carry them to the other cave. Amos and Jorim, two of the shepherds, entered the cave just as Joseph brought up the last box of grain. Joseph explained his plan to them and together they transferred the first load.

The new cave was not as large as the Nativity Cave but was of sufficient size and much brighter; the walls were cut in soft white stone. After several arduous trips Joseph decided to leave the remainder of the work until morning. He knew that Amos and Jorim were tired; they had been guarding their flocks since before daybreak, and he was tired from his journey with the kings. Before departing the shepherds promised to return early the next morning, because they wanted to be finished before the start of the S

In the morning Mary and Joseph were awakened by voices at the entrance. Athalia was greeting Anne, her husband Eliud and another daughter called Mary Heli. They had departed from Anne's sister's house long before daybreak. After embracing Mary and Joseph, Anne spent time kneeling at the manger. The infant Jesus turned toward her when he heard her voice and gave a slight smile. Eliud and Mary Heli stood next to her.

Mary went to her mother and said, "Our royal visitors have returned to their homelands but before leaving they gave much to the poor and left many things for us."

Anne rose to her feet and said, "Yes, daughter, I know of their departure. It was revealed to me in a dream this past night. Where upon, I asked Eliud and Mary Heli to return with me. We left my sister's house before daybreak and came straight here. You must tell us of all that occurred during their visit."

At that moment Athalia announced that the morning meal was ready. Mary and Anne began to talk about the behavior and sleeping habits of the infant Jesus. Eliud listened while Mary Heli examined some of the many gifts; she was amazed by their variety and beauty. Joseph began eating; he knew the shepherds would arrive soon. Mary described in great detail all that took place and all that was said during the kings' visit, and she disclosed the reason for their hasty departure.

Anne was troubled and asked, "What did the angel mean when he spoke of Herod's designs against the Child? And why are his soldiers making inquiries in this area?"

Mary replied, "I know not what is troubling Herod, but fear not Mother, we will avoid discovery. Even now Joseph is preparing another cave for us to live in if it becomes necessary for us to leave. Some of the shepherds are assisting him, and if the soldiers return the others will warn us."

Anne was consoled by what Mary said; she and Mary then reclined near the entrance and ate. Shortly thereafter, Amos and Jorim arrived with two friends. By midday all was moved except that which was needed for their comfort. Anne cared for the infant Jesus while
Mary and Athalia went to the new quarters to unpack and arrange their furnishings. Anne was delighted. She fed the Babe with a fine cereal made from one of the plants that was common to the valley. It was not unusual for Jewish mothers to feed their children at such an early age. Anne carried Jesus all the while Mary was gone except when bathing the child or a change of clothing was performed. Her husband left to assist Joseph; Mary Heli remained to assist her.

One hour after noon, Joda, the third shepherd arrived at the cave excited and short of breath. He had just come from Bethlehem where he saw and heard Herod's soldiers and some officials asking questions about the Child and the kings.

Anne sent him to the other cave where he called Joseph out of the cave and said, "My friend I have called you out so that what I am about to tell you will not alarm the women. I have just come from Bethlehem where I observed several of Herod's spies asking questions of the women who have given birth within the past two months and of the midwives who assisted them. I saw also some official looking men questioning the elders and the priests about the kings that arrived from the East. They now know that the kings came into this valley and of the edict against the people following them. Very soon they will be here to question you and us. I advise you to leave here at once. Herod cannot be trusted for he is very jealous of his throne."

"Thank you, Joda," said Joseph. "I have anticipated this and have moved most of our belongings to this cave with the help of Amos, Jorim and Eliud. The entrance is shielded by several trees and difficult to see from below. I will see that Mary, the Child and our relatives remain here."

Joseph returned with Eliud to the Nativity Cave and said to Anne, "Now that we have moved almost all that we have to the other cave I think it would be best for you to go there with the Child. Mary Heli will accompany you. Eliud and I will bring the remainder of our belongings. I would like all to be settled in and everything moved before the Sabbath begins."

Anne sensed urgency in Joseph's words; she surmised that the soldiers were again asking questions.

Without hesitation she picked up the infant Jesus and said to Mary Heli, "We must leave here now. Joseph wishes us to go to the other cave. Will you help me to carry Jesus' garments and the manger?"

Mary Heli did not question her about the sudden move; she promptly did as Anne wished. The walk to the new quarters was difficult because of the narrow trail to it and the steep grade. Anne was sad about leaving the Nativity Cave and hoped they might return to it soon. Joseph remained behind with Eliud and began to remove the furnishings he had built. He told the shepherds they could take the partitions he had hung around the sleeping places to the other cave; they would be needed again. By mid-afternoon the Nativity Cave was empty except for the ass stabled in the rear and the wicker curtain at the entrance. Joseph wanted to leave it in good order. Now alone in the cave, he stood near the center and looked about; he too was sad about leaving. He felt it was a special place and would be from then on. Many memories raced through his mind about the Child's birth, the wonderful events surrounding it, the many visitors they received, first the shepherds, then the kings with their marvelous retinue and gifts. He thought of Elizabeth and Anne and their excitement about the manner of the Child's birth. And he thought of the quiet moments he and Mary had together and the love and adoration they showered upon the infant Jesus. With a few shelves that he removed from the wall under his arm he started for the other cave. As he opened the wicker curtain four soldiers came and stood before the entrance. Joseph was momentarily surprised but did not lose his composure.

"Are you Joseph, son of Jacob?" asked one of them.

"I am," replied Joseph. "What may I do for you?"

"Nothing," snapped the leader. "We are here to ask you some questions."

Joseph made a low bow and remained silent; he waited for the first question.

"Have you a wife and child?" the leader asked.

"I do," Joseph answered.

"How old is the child?"

"Less than a month," Joseph replied.

"Do you live in this cave?"

"We did, but have just moved to a new dwelling."

The leader shoved Joseph aside and entered the cave followed by two others. One soldier remained with Joseph. Once inside they looked about for signs or evidence of the quality of the inhabitants. They saw the ass stabled in the rear, straw piled against the wall where Mary slept and a few lamps still hanging on the walls. The cave had lost its warmth and coziness now that everything had been removed.

One of the soldiers declared, "How can anyone live in a place like this; it is so dark and barren. Surely a king would not be born under these conditions."

"I agree," said the other soldier. "Why do we waste our time here? Let us go to the houses in the valley or return to the city. These people are very poor. They can be no threat to Herod."

Their leader pondered their remarks for a few moments, took one last look about the cave then walked to the entrance. Joseph was standing under the arbor; the fourth soldier was seated upon a large rock near the cedar trees. As the leader emerged he jumped to his feet.

Turning to Joseph the leader asked, "Where are you from?"

"My wife and I have recently traveled here from Nazareth. I am a carpenter by trade and I hoped to find more work here in Bethlehem."

"A carpenter!" exclaimed the leader.

"Yes," Joseph answered humbly.

"You are right," the leader said to the other soldiers. "We are wasting our time here. We shall return to the city."

Without saying another word to Joseph they walked through the cedar trees and descended toward the trail to Bethlehem. Joseph watched them for a few minutes while silently saying a prayer of thanksgiving then proceeded to the new quarters. When he arrived Mary was busily preparing sleeping places for everyone. Athalia was attending to Jesus and Mary Heli. Anne was giving directions to Eliud and the shepherds on the placing of the furnishings and the partitions. Joseph decided not to tell them of his encounter with the soldiers to spare them any anxiety. He quickly hung several lamps upon the walls and helped to erect the partitions. In a short time their new quarters were in good order and fairly comfortable. As the sun dropped low upon the horizon, the shepherds left to prepare for the Sabbath.

CHAPTER SIX
Simeon and Anna

The Sabbath had just ended when Simeon, a priest of the Jerusalem Temple, announced to his family that he would return to the temple. The next day was expected to be a busy one; several women were coming with their children to make the prescribed sacrifices during the Presentation and Purification ceremonies. Though walking was becoming very difficult for Simeon, he visited with his wife, his three sons and their families as often as possible. He lived within the temple, spending most of his time in prayer and studying the Scriptures. He was well into his seventy-eighth year and had been a priest since his twenty-first. His face was thin and wrinkled, his gray hair was moderately thick, as was his beard which he kept short and neatly trimmed. Simeon was of average height, had a dark complexion but his eyes were light in color; his voice was strong yet not deep.

While crossing the bridge to the west gate of the temple he stopped, looked up to the star-filled sky and repeated a short prayer he often said.

"What else do I have in heaven but you? Since I have you, what else do I want on earth? My mind and my body may grow weak, but God is my strength; He is all I ever want!"

He then continued across the bridge. In order to reach his cell, which was built into the thick temple walls, Simeon had to pass through a long narrow passageway with an occasional lamp lighting the way. His room, which was stone throughout and approximately nine feet square, contained only the barest necessities. A small table upon which he placed a red woolen coverlet and his prayer book, a pitcher of water and a small bowl were on the floor near the door. His bed consisted of a mat filled with animal hair which he kept rolled against the wall until he retired. A small window on one wall afforded him a good view of the Temple floor two stories below. At night he was accustomed to kneeling on the cold, stone floor reciting the Psalms or speaking to God in a friendly but respectful manner. This night was no exception. Nearly an hour had passed when Simeon realized he was no longer alone in his cell. Turning to the corner of the room where he slept, he saw an unusually beautiful young man dressed in a gown of delicate material, golden in color and without a girdle. Simeon could not speak, and while he gazed upon the youth a light began to emanate from his body. Immediately the old priest went into an ecstatic trance; he could not move nor was he aware of anything in the cell except the vision before him. The young man came to Simeon, placed the index and middle fingers of each hand upon Simeon's forehead, stepped back and began to speak with a voice unlike any Simeon had ever heard.

"Peace be with you, Simeon. I bring you tidings of great joy. The Messiah whom you have awaited so long has come into the world. God, the Most High, has heard your prayer; you will soon behold the Promised One. Pay particular attention to the first child brought into the Temple for presentation, for that Child will be the Savior. Soon after you will be taken from this world."

The light slowly faded; in an instant the young man disappeared, and Simeon's faculties returned. But his face and eyes remained aglow from the joy he felt within. He looked around the room but saw only the usual furnishings; he remained on his knees unable to speak or even think for several minutes. When fully recovered, he looked upward, extended his arms toward the ceiling and recited some of his favorite Psalms.

"Lord, your mercy is in heaven, and your truth reaches even to the clouds.

Your justice is as the mountains of God, your judgments are a great deep.

Men and beasts you will preserve, O Lord: O how have you multiplied your mercy, O God! But the children of men shall put their trust under the cover of your wings.

They shall be inebriated with the plenty of your house; and you shall make them drink of the torrent of your pleasure.

For with you is the fountain of life; and in your light we shall see light."

He ended his prayers with a Psalm of praise; "Sing joyfully to God, all the earth: serve you the Lord with gladness. Come in before his presence with exceeding great joy. Know you that the Lord he is God: he made us, and not we ourselves.

We are his people and the sheep of his pasture. Go you into his gates with praise, into his courts with hymns: and give glory to him.

Praise you his name: for the Lord is sweet, his mercy endures for ever, and his truth to generation and generation."

One week passed since the Holy Family moved into their new quarters; much of their time was spent making it more habitable and comfortable. Anne, Eliud and Mary Heli remained with them until midweek then returned to Nazareth. Athalia went with them. Joseph did not go to Bethlehem again following the soldiers visit; the shepherds obtained for them what food they required. And at Joseph's direction distributed to the poor and widows nearly all the things the Holy Family received as gifts. While it was still dark on the morning of the next Sabbath Joseph received instructions in a dream that the time for the Child's Presentation and Mary's Purification was at hand. He was told to take Mary and the Babe to the Temple in Jerusalem, and their offering was to be two doves and a basket of fruit. They were to leave after midnight so as to arrive at the Temple before daybreak. Upon awakening Joseph informed Mary. Soon after the Sabbath ended he first brought the ass to the cave then placed the cross seat with a small footboard he added and their provisions on the animal. Mary prepared a small bundle of clothes for them and asked Joseph to place two covers upon the seat. About an hour passed midnight they set off for Jerusalem, traveling around the west side of Bethlehem. No one saw them leave except the three shepherds who were standing watch on a hill not far from the road. The moon was almost full and very bright; the sky was clear. As they came near to Jerusalem, Joseph saw that Mary was uncomfortable and he knew the infant Jesus would need some attention. So he stopped at a small house next to a large inn. He hesitated to knock upon the door; it was still dark and no light was visible from within, but he did so. A man about middle age opened the door slowly; he was holding an oil lamp and was dressed in his nightclothes and a robe. He looked at Joseph, saw Mary and the infant Jesus behind him and declared, "At last you are here! We have been anxious about you. Come in! You are truly welcome."

Joseph, greatly surprised at this greeting, asked, "But how did you know we were coming?"

The man answered, "During the week some of your relatives stopped here and asked us to take you in for you would need rest and care. Their names were Eliud and Anne; they had a daughter and their servant with them."

At that moment the man's wife came to the door greeted the Holy Family and then helped Mary to dismount. Once inside they introduced themselves; his name was Jothra and his wife was called Leah. Jothra told Joseph that he was a gardener working for the inn next to their house and he was also responsible for the trees and plants along the road from the Cedron Brook to Jerusalem. Leah brought Mary to the rear of the house where she changed Jesus clothing and nursed Him. The couple had two children but they did not awake when Joseph knocked. Jothra brought a basin of water to Joseph, washed his feet, gave him some cold well water to drink and some food. Mary saw to her ablutions, changed her clothing, ate some fruit and bread then sat and talked with Leah. The couple sensed the holiness of their guests and out of pure love waited upon them as they would an important visitor.

When Joseph announced that it was time to leave, Leah went to her room and brought out a small wicker cradle which was lined with a pale-blue cotton quilt; she presented it to Mary as a gift for the infant Jesus. This act of love deeply touched Mary; she embraced Leah and kissed her. Joseph also embraced the good couple and thanked them for their hospitality. Jothra helped Mary to remount while Leah held the Babe. Joseph tied their gift to the basket containing the doves. It was still dark when the Holy Family continued their journey. Mary spent the remaining time in prayer preparing herself for the coming ceremonies.

In a cell very much like Simeon's, located on the opposite side of the Temple, knelt a very old woman, praying through the night as she often did. Anna, considered a prophetess, was the daughter of Phanuel, of the tribe of Aser. Her husband had passed away in the seventh year of their marriage; she was now in her eighty-third year. Soon after his death she received permission to move into the Temple to assist with the training of the young maidens. From that day onward she remained in the Temple praying and fasting night and day. Anna was much revered by the priests and all the people in Jerusalem because of her austere life and her great devotion to God.

Very early in the morning while it was still dark Anna knelt facing the interior of the Temple. Her prayer was one of sincere supplication, "Lord, you are my patience my hope, O Lord, from my youth. By you have I been confirmed from the womb: from my mother's womb you are my protector. Of you I shall continuously sing. I am becoming unto many as a wonder, but you are a strong helper. Let my mouth be filled with praise, that I may sing your glory; your greatness all the day long. Cast me not off in the time of old age when my strength shall fail, do not forsake me."

Suddenly the room was filled with light and before her stood the same young man that appeared to Simeon. Anna became frightened and covered her eyes.

The vision spoke to her, "Anna fear not I come from God with news of the Promised One."

Anna raised her head slowly and at the instant her eyes beheld the youth's face she became enraptured.

The young man continued, "Before dawn the Promised One will be brought to the Temple for Presentation to the Most High God. The first child carried to the place where the ceremony is to take place will be the long awaited Savior. You and Simeon shall announce His arrival to all present. Before the year is finished you will be taken to Abraham's bosom until His kingdom is established"

He vanished in an instant and the light faded until the cell was illuminated only by a small lamp hanging from the ceiling. Anna bowed her head, crossed her arms upon her breast and wept.

In his cell, Simeon was pacing back and forth anxiously awaiting the time for the ceremonies to begin. Overcome with a strong desire and impatience, he hurried to the women's passageway into the Temple and waited. Anna left her cell at the same time and went to Noemi's quarters. Noemi was a woman dedicated to service at the Temple and assigned the training of the young maidens also dedicated to Temple service. She was Mary's instructor while she lived at the Temple until her betrothal to Joseph. Anna assisted her with their training as much as she was able. The two of them waited for the Child but near the porch where the ceremonies were to be conducted.

The Holy Family entered Jerusalem through the Water Gate in the section of Jerusalem called Ophel and proceeded to the south entrance into the Temple's outer courtyard. There they were met by an old woman carrying a lamp who instructed Joseph to stable the ass in a small shed near the wall then led them to a covered walkway leading to the Temple proper. At the end of the walkway was the women's passageway; Joseph left them and went to the men's entrance. Mary, carrying the infant Jesus, followed closely behind the old woman to the inner courtyard. The light from the woman's lamp which illuminated the exit from the passageway alerted Simeon of their approach. He quickly moved to greet them.

"Praise the Lord God Almighty for He is all good and merciful!" he declared aloud. "The redemption of Israel is at hand."

Mary was very surprised by this greeting and responded, "Peace be with you."

"Peace be with you, daughter," Simeon replied. "May I take the Child?"

When Mary placed the infant Jesus in Simeon's arms, he was almost overcome with joy. He pressed Jesus to his heart, turned and walked toward the other side of the Temple. Mary looked after them for a few moments then followed the old woman to the porch where she was met by Anna and Noemi. Mary was overjoyed at seeing Noemi again; she was like a mother to her during her service at the Temple. Anna embraced Mary warmly but said nothing.

Joseph came forward, handed the cradle and baskets containing the doves and fruit to Anna then returned to the area for the men. Anna carried the articles to the altar rail and laid them upon the first step leading to the altar. She then rejoined Mary and Noemi. Just then two men entered the hall carrying a chest which they placed before the altar; two more men entered and placed a marble slab upon the opened doors of the chest. The slab matched the size of the altar and when a red cloth was placed over them it became a large square table. The hall was well lit by many lamps hanging from the walls and by the menorahs placed on the four corners of the altar. The cradle was placed in the center of the table; priestly garments taken from the chest were laid beside the cradle. On either side of the altar rail were several rows of seats filled with priests swaying from side to side as they read from their prayer books. Simeon entered the hall with the infant Jesus cradled in his left arm. Mary had dressed Jesus in a sky-blue dress and a white coverlet. She, too, was wearing a sky-blue dress, a thin white veil and a pale yellow mantle. Simeon asked Mary to accompany him to the altar and together they placed the infant Jesus in the cradle. Mary was then conducted to the area designated for the women. Simeon commented to one of the other priests about Jesus' good behavior because he had not cried out once. Three priests came to the altar and began to don the priests' garments. Simeon removed the plain brown mantle he was wearing and handed it to a man standing outside the altar rail. The tunic he was wearing was green with long narrow sleeves and tied tightly around his waist by a broad white girdle wrapped around him several times. He draped a very beautiful white mantle with brown designs, which was sleeveless over his shoulders. It hung loosely around him; a gold clasp set with jewels held it together. His feet were bare except for two thin straps holding a thin strip of leather at the soles. When their vesting was completed Simeon and the three priests positioned themselves on each side of the altar. Anna came to Mary, escorted her to the altar rail, handed her the two baskets of offerings and directed her to the altar. Simeon came down to meet her and walked to the altar beside her. Mary placed a basket on either side of the cradle; the doves on the right and the fruit on the left. One of the priests directly opposite Mary and Simeon removed Jesus from the cradle, raised the Babe above his head, pointed Him toward the four corners of the Temple and began to pray in unison with Simeon and all the priests present. After a few minutes of prayer the priest then handed Jesus to Simeon who in turn laid Him in Mary's arms. Simeon removed a small parchment from the altar, unrolled it and prayed over Mary and Jesus. When he finished the prescribed prayers he escorted Mary to the railing where she was met by Anna, who escorted her to the place reserved for the women. While Mary was at the altar several women had entered the hall with their first born. Their husbands stood with Joseph as two priests at the altar began a service using incense and prayers.

    Simeon surprised the priests when he left the altar. He went to the women's area and asked Mary for the infant Jesus once more. He turned toward the altar and raised the Child above his head. Everyone's attention was upon him; he then recited a psalm familiar to all present.

    "Give to the king your judgment, O God: and to the king's son your justice: to judge your people with justice, and your poor with mercy. Let the mountains receive peace for the people: and the hills justice. He shall judge the poor of the people, and he shall save the children of the poor: and he shall humble the oppressor. And he shall continue with the sun, and before the moon, throughout all generations. He shall come down like rain upon the fleece; and as showers falling gently upon the earth. In his days shall justice spring up, and abundance of peace, till the moon be taken away. And he shall rule from sea to sea, and from the river unto the ends of the earth. Before him the Ethiopians shall fall down: and his enemies shall lick the ground. The kings of Tharsis and the islands shall offer presents: the kings of the Arabians and of Saba shall bring gifts: And all kings of the earth shall adore him: all nations shall serve him. For he shall deliver the poor from the mighty: and the needy that had no helper. He shall spare the poor and needy: and he shall save the souls of the poor. He shall redeem their souls from usuries and iniquity: and their names shall be honorable in his sight. Let his name be blessed for evermore: his name continues before the sun. And in him shall all the tribes of the earth be blessed: all nations shall magnify him. Blessed be the Lord, the God of Israel, who alone does wonderful things. And blessed be the name of his majesty for ever: and the whole earth shall be filled with his majesty. So be it. So be it."

    Simeon lowered the Child, cradled Him in his arms and continued speaking but only those near to him could hear.

    "Now you may dismiss your servant, O Lord, according to Thy word, in peace; because my eyes have seen your salvation, which you have prepared before the face of all peoples: a light of revelation to the Gentiles, and a glory for Thy people Israel."

    Still holding the infant Jesus, he escorted Mary to the foot of the altar again; he called for Joseph to join them and gave his blessing.

    With tear filled eyes he placed Jesus in Mary's arms, looked directly at her and said, "Behold this Child is destined for the fall and for the rise of many in Israel, and for a sign that shall be contradicted. And your own soul a sword shall pierce, that the thoughts of many hearts may be revealed."

Although the occasion was one of great joy, Mary felt a very deep sorrow when it was instantly revealed to her the sufferings and death her son would endure. She saw also how Jesus was to be a stumbling block to the Jews, accomplish the salvation of the Gentiles and establish His Church throughout the world. Anna, the prophetess, joined them at the altar rail, placed her hand upon the infant Jesus, raised her eyes to heaven and spoke loud enough for all in the Temple to hear.

"Now that my eyes have seen your salvation, your Son made in our human nature according to your infinite wisdom, I shall realize true joy and find true peace. Now, O Lord, you have brought into the world your divine light so that it may shine upon all mankind and receive from it the way of salvation. For this is the light which is revealed to the Gentiles for the glory of your chosen people of Israel."

No one was startled by her speaking out; she had done so many times before, but they were all amazed at the words spoken about this child whose parents made such a humble offering. Following a second blessing by Simeon, Anna and Noemi escorted the Holy Family out of the hall toward the exit to the main courtyard. Many of the people demonstrated a reverence toward Jesus and reached out to touch Him as the Holy Family walked by. Once in the courtyard, Joseph informed Noemi and Anna that they would return to Nazareth. He then gave Anna several gold triangular shaped coins, gifts from the kings, and asked that the gold be used to help the young maidens who wished to serve at the Temple but were unable to present a suitable dowry. Joseph then left them to retrieve their animal. When he returned Anna blessed the Holy Family and declared that she would not see them again for she would soon die. With tear filled eyes Mary placed the infant Jesus in Anna's arms. She pressed Him to her heart; holding Jesus was for her a most precious gift. Noemi, too, held Jesus for a few moments. Then she and Anna stood side by side and watched the Holy Family leave the courtyard and disappear beyond the Temple's outer wall. Because it was yet early in the day only the fishmongers were moving about preparing their booths for the daily shoppers. Joseph was relieved when he saw none of Herod's soldiers about. Now only a few people would be aware of their departure. The sun was just rising above the crest of Mount Olivet as the Holy Family passed through the Fish Gate and turned onto the road to Bethhoron, a small village on the way to Lydda near the west coast of Israel. Joseph had decided to travel northward through the coastal lowlands where it was much warmer than the hill country, it was now the middle of winter. He was greatly concerned for Mary's comfort on the return to Nazareth; he recalled how much she had to endure on their journey to Bethlehem. He knew that Herod's spies were everywhere so they traveled parallel to the road but out of sight of it. For three days they saw no one. It was the morning of the fourth day when Joseph led the ass onto the road leading to Nazareth, and as they came near the south side of the village several people greeted them and inquired about the infant Jesus; some were relatives of Mary. They passed quickly through the village and came to Anne's house. Anne, Eliud, Mary Heli, another daughter Mary Cleophas and Athalia were there to welcome them. The Holy Family received much attention, especially the Child, but there was no excitement or commotion. Several neighbors heard of the arrival and brought gifts. Anne quickly arranged for a small feast and invited some of the priests and elders. Later that evening Anne and Athalia escorted the Holy Family to their own house and helped them to unload their animal and another loaded with gifts received at the feast. Mary and Joseph were overjoyed to be home again and to be with those they knew and loved. When the unloading was finished and all their belongings were stored away, Mary asked if they would join her in prayer. She covered a small table near the fireplace with a red tasseled coverlet, placed a roll of parchment upon it and a lamp. Anne, Athalia and Mary knelt at the table while Joseph knelt in his sleeping area. It was the custom of the men to pray apart from the women.

After several minutes of silent prayer Mary, with her arms crossed upon her breast, prayed aloud: "I rejoiced at the things that were said to me: We shall go into the house of the Lord. Our feet were standing in your courts, O Jerusalem. Jerusalem, which is compact together, for there did the tribes go up, the tribes of the Lord: the testimony of Israel, to praise the name of the Lord. Because their seats have sat in judgment, seats upon the house of David. Pray you for the things that are for the peace of Jerusalem: and abundance for them that love you. Let peace be in your strength: and abundance in your towers. For the sake of my brethren, and my neighbors, I spoke peace of you. Because of the house of the Lord our God, I have sought good things for you. To you, who dwells in heaven, have I lifted up my eyes. Behold as the eyes of the handmaid are on the hands of her mistress: so are my eyes unto you Lord my God."

After a long time devoted to prayer and meditation, Joseph left the house to stable the animals. Anne, Athalia and Mary saw to their ablutions then retired. When Joseph returned all were in their beds asleep. He too was tired but did not retire. Instead he walked about in the courtyard and pondered all that had taken place in Bethlehem and Jerusalem, and the prophecies of Simeon and Anna at the Temple. He recalled the sorrow he saw come over Mary when Simeon spoke of the sword that would pierce her soul. His love for Mary was so strong that he was very troubled when he saw her so tearful at an occasion which should have brought joy to her heart. He thought of Herod, the warning received by the kings and their hasty departure. Concerned and afraid he turned his eyes toward heaven and. prayed.

"Hear, O Lord, my justice: attend to my supplication. Give ear unto my prayer, which proceeds not from deceitful lips. Let my judgment come forth from your countenance: let your eyes behold the things that are equitable. You have proved my heart, and visited it by night, you have tried me by fire: and iniquity has not been found in me. That my mouth may not speak of the works of men: for the sake of the words of your lips, I have kept hard ways. Show forth your wonderful mercies; you who saves them that trust in you; from the face of the wicked who have afflicted me."

Suddenly he felt confident that they would be in no danger and retired to his sleeping place.

During the next three days Mary and Joseph busied themselves with their daily chores and setting simple furnishings. Anne had returned to her home but left Athalia to assist Mary. Joseph obtained large strips of bark from which he made a screen to cover the ceiling in order to make the house warmer. Mary spent some of her time making knitted garments for the infant Jesus from the wool given to them by Anne. While Athalia saw to the housework and preparing the food.

Not long after the Holy Family left Jerusalem the words spoken by Simeon and Anna spread throughout the city. The accounts reached Herod and his fears were again disturbing him. He had almost forgotten the kings and the Scripture prophecies when the royal travelers did not return with the information he expected. Once again he summoned the priest and scribes, and with Nabat and all of his advisors present he asked many questions about the prophesied king. He commanded them to once more search the Scriptures, and they reaffirmed their belief that the new king, the

Promised One, was to come from Bethlehem-Ephrata. Herod was close to losing control of himself when Nabat wisely ordered everyone to leave. Many thoughts raced wildly through Herod's mind as he paced back and forth before his throne. One particular idea caused his heart to pound and the blood race through his veins. "The only way to be certain the child is no threat," he thought, "is to kill him. But which child? No one has identified the family and surely no one will betray them. All the new born males must die! It is the only way! But should this be done, how will the people react? This must be done in such a way as to avoid an uprising. The Romans may lose confidence in my ability to rule and have me replaced or assassinated. I have it! I will dispatch soldiers to the region and wait. Perhaps while they are garrisoned there they will learn the family's identity."

He turned to Nabat and said, "Nabat, summon the commander of my personal guard and have him come to my chambers."

Nabat bowed and left to do as he was ordered. Herod returned to his quarters but continued pacing the floor.

After a short time Nabat returned with the commander called, Bezech. Herod dismissed his servants and motioned for the two to follow him to the terrace which was completely isolated from any other rooms in the palace. Nabat and Bezech watched Herod closely; both knew that he was greatly disturbed about the prophecies and was about to take action. Herod had a great deal of confidence in Bezech for he had never failed to do as he asked and could be trusted to keep silent in any confidential matter. Bezech had no liking for Herod but he would remain loyal as long as he was paid well.

"I have a most important assignment for you, Bezech," Herod declared. "News has come to me that a king has been born recently within my domain. I wish to learn of the child's identity but my informants have been unable to determine who the parents are or where they reside. I want you to select one hundred and fifty of the best and most reliable soldiers in my guard; dispatch fifty to Bethlehem, Hebron and Gilgal with orders to garrison themselves and gather information about all families who have had a male child born within the past year. They are to do this in such a way as to avoid alarming the people. You will be responsible for the list and you are to report to me at the end of sixty days. See to it immediately. Nabat will give you the funds you will require from my treasury."

Bezech bowed low and replied, "Yes, sire. I will attend to this with all speed."

He and Nabat left.

Herod felt certain his plan would work and soon the threat to his kingdom would be no more.

CHAPTER SEVEN
The Flight to Egypt

While in a restless sleep one night Joseph saw the same angel that appeared to him in the field of Chimki beside his couch surrounded by a brilliant light. He awoke and sat up, but the angel touched his forehead and he fell softly back upon the bedding; he went into a deep sleep and dreamed.

"Arise, and take the Child and His mother, and flee into Egypt," the angel commanded, "and remain there until I tell thee to return to Nazareth. For Herod will seek the Child to destroy Him."

At sunrise Joseph awoke and a great sorrow swelled within him. Their time at Nazareth was filled with happiness and security but now they must leave. And he knew how much sorrow this would bring to Mary and her family.

"But it must be done for the safety of the Child," he thought.

He could see the sky getting brighter in the east as he entered Mary's sleeping area. The Babe was asleep next to her. He woke her gently and motioned for her to follow him to the other end of the house.

"What is it?" Mary asked. "What is troubling you?"

"Mary," he replied sadly, "an angel of the Lord has spoken to me in a dream. He announced that it is the Lord's will that we must suffer yet another journey. We are to flee to Egypt and remain there until we are told to return because Herod is seeking to destroy the Child. Beloved, please fortify yourself to bear the discomfort of this journey for it will be long and dangerous. But tell me what I can do for your comfort, and the Child's. My life and my being are dedicated to the service of the Child and to you."

Mary placed her hand upon Joseph's cheek and replied, "Dear husband, it is the Lord's will that we endure this hardship. We should do so gladly because of the great blessings we have received. We have with us His only Begotten Son, what harm shall befall us with Him so near. Not even the power of Herod can touch us. The Lord, our God, is our guide and light. He is our defender, protector and provider. Of what shall we fear? Let us hasten to do His will."

Together they returned to Mary's sleeping place and stood gazing upon the infant Jesus asleep in His cradle. Mary gently lifted Him and pressed Him to her heart. Joseph placed his hand upon Jesus' head and with tear filled eyes kissed Him upon the forehead.

Mary spoke softly to her little son, "Who among men can think of taking your life, sweet Jesus? You have come to bring them eternal life. Why should they wish to end yours? Awake little one for it is time for us to leave."

Joseph wasted no time getting ready. He made a wicker screen to cover the cross seat and placed it at the stable until it was time to leave. He then filled three long cylindrical shaped baskets with loaves of bread, fruit and live birds. He also filled the leather bottles with fresh spring water. Later that morning Anne returned with Mary Heli.

"Mother, Joseph and I are preparing to leave for Egypt," Mary declared.

"Why, Mary?" Anne asked. "What is wrong?"

Anne knew they would not leave on such short notice unless there was a serious reason.

An angel of the Lord came to Joseph in a dream," she replied, "and instructed him to take the Child to Egypt for He is in danger. Herod is seeking to take His life. We must leave immediately and not return until we are instructed."

Anne and Mary Heli were visibly upset by the thought of danger to the Child Jesus and the thought they may never see each other again. Anne began to weep and embraced Mary several times; Mary Heli and Athalia wept also.

At that moment Joseph entered the house and announced that all was ready and it was time to leave. Mary brought the infant Jesus from His bed; she gave Him to Anne, then to Mary Heli and Athalia. Joseph asked Anne and Mary Heli to accompany them as far as the southern edge of the village. Athalia was to remain behind to close the house. For added comfort Mary placed the infant Jesus in a sling that came around her shoulders and hung upon her breast. She wore a large pale yellow veil which hung down on each side of her face and covered the Child as well. Her mantle, which was made of wool and colored pale blue, was large enough to drape over the crossseat. Joseph wore a gray colored woolen tunic, strong leather sandals and carried a walking staff.

The long journey was now begun. Anne and Mary Heli watched the Holy Family move on until they disappeared over the first hill. Mary and Joseph did not look back but remained in silent prayer. Joseph's plan was to travel as they did on the journey from Jerusalem to Nazareth following Jesus' presentation; they went south through the western lowlands staying just off the main road leading to Lydda. The sky was overcast and the temperature quite cool when they left Nazareth but as they entered the Plain of Esdraelon the weather improved. Legio was the first town they passed; it was located at the crossroad leading to Haifa near the great sea, and it had many merchant shops and inns catering to rich travelers and vacationing Roman soldiers. Joseph knew that many of Herod's soldiers came there for rest and entertainment; he decided to pass one league east of the town limits and did not stop until they came upon a lean-to like shed two leagues beyond. While they rested beneath the shed and had some refreshments, Joseph informed Mary that soon they would arrive at a small Samaritan village called Nazara where he knew a family that would give them shelter for the night. He remembered the owner and his wife as being gentle in nature and charitable toward travelers. Many years earlier Joseph had made new doors for their house and helped erect a stable. Mary was comforted by Joseph's words and was anxious to reach the house where she could better attend to the infant Jesus.

Shortly before sunset they arrived in Nazara and went directly to the house Joseph spoke of Issachar, a shepherd of late middle age, and his wife Emerentia who was a robust but very sensitive woman greeted Joseph and Mary with warmth and joy: Emerentia gave Issachar three sons, now all married, and had seven grandchildren. She gave to Mary and the Child the most kind attention not entirely in charity but because she sensed the holiness of the Mother and Child. Joseph and Issachar remained outside the house reminiscing about the years gone by. Mary bathed the infant Jesus and attended to her own ablutions within. Following the evening meal Joseph unloaded their belongings while Mary placed the infant Jesus in his cradle at the side of the bed she was to use.

When the Infant was asleep Mary, Joseph, Issachar and Emerentia spent an hour praying and singing psalms. After which Mary and Emerentia retired. Joseph and Issachar continued to talk about many things.

Early the next morning Mary awoke when she heard Jesus give out a short cry .She nursed Him, changed His clothing then knelt before Him to say her morning prayers. Emerentia was already awake preparing food for her sons who were about to come by on their way to the pasture lands. Joseph, too, was awake; he brought the ass now reloaded to the front entrance. Issachar was drawing water from the well for the animals watering trough and to fill the leather bottles Joseph gave to him.

Issachar came to Joseph and said, "You are welcome to stay longer if you wish. We are very pleased to have you with us, and Emerentia has offered you our own room."

Joseph knew that his offer was a sincere one, and with difficulty he replied, "You are very kind Issachar, but it is most important that we leave for Egypt as quickly as possible. Upon our return we will visit with you again. But now we must be on our way."

The gracious host did not understand the urgency but acceded to Joseph's wishes. They then entered the house for the morning meal.

As the Holy Family departed a light fog moved down from the nearby hills; the ground and all the plants were soon covered with moisture. Mary pulled her mantle tightly around her and the Child. Issachar and Emerentia accompanied them until they reached the end of their pasture lands then returned to their house.

Traveling became more difficult for the Holy Travelers because of the dense plants and thickets in this area. Several shallow but very cold streams had to be forded and at one place they crossed a small river on a raft. Joseph had traveled through this area several times before; he knew it well and was at all times aware of the distance to the road. About midday the Holy Family arrived at a grove of young umbrella-shaped trees where they stopped to eat and refresh themselves. While Mary and the infant Jesus rested Joseph climbed to the crest of a nearby hill to survey the land around them. To the north was Antipastris a moderate size trading city; to the east he was able to see the top of a tall building located in the city of Gophna which was about four hours travel north of Jerusalem; to the south he could easily see the buildings in Lydda a busy city located at the crossroads between Jerusalem and Joppa on the coast. Joseph planned to go around Lydda as he did Legio. Less than two leagues beyond Lydda was a small village called Anim which Joseph hoped to reach before dark. He knew of an inn there he remembered as clean and comfortable which was owned by two camel drivers with a lucrative trade between Israel and Egypt.

Mary was well rested when they resumed their journey; she had slept for a short time after nursing the infant Jesus. The cross-seat was small but fairly comfortable and the wicker screen protected Mother and Child from the constant wind. Joseph usually walked a little ahead but occasionally he would walk along side Mary to pray with her. The long hours of solitude allowed Mary much time for prayer and contemplation.

There was still enough light to travel when they arrived at Anim. The village was quiet. Joseph went directly to the inn which was situated on the east side of the village alongside a road between Lydda and Herbron. Their lodgings were modest, clean and private, and the inn keeper provided them with fresh bedding and enough water for their baths. The innkeeper's wife, a kind woman, brought them fruit and a small bowl of cereal for the Child. Mary and Joseph were most grateful for their kind attention. Joseph retired soon after their evening meal and prayers; many hours of walking had tired him. Mary sat upon her bedding with the infant Jesus on her lap and sang to Him the lullabies Anne had taught her until He was asleep. She placed Jesus in the cradle, extinguished the lamp mounted on the wall above her bed and began her nightly prayers. The room was dark except for the light coming under the door from the corridor lamps. She reflected upon their hasty departure from Nazareth and the sad parting from her mother and sister. She wept softly with her hands upon her face and her head bowed. But soon her thoughts turned to the cave at Bethlehem, the wonderful manner of Jesus' birth, the visit of the shepherds and the kings. She longed to return there for a visit and resolved to ask Joseph if they might do so before going on to Egypt. Suddenly the room was filled with a brilliant light. Mary immediately went into an ecstatic state with her arms crossed upon her breast and her head lowered. Before her appeared the angel that announced Jesus' conception. Mary saw and heard only the angel.

He said to her, "Dear Queen and Lady, Mother of the Savior, it is most important that you continue on your journey to Egypt without delay. On account of the kings' departure without returning to Jerusalem and because of the prophecies and words of Simeon and Anna many people have begun to say that you are the Mother of the Promised Messiah. There is much talk of the kings' visit to Bethlehem and of a miraculous birth. Herod has been informed of all these things and has ordered a search for the Child. His intention is to kill Him. The Most High God commands you to fly to Egypt with great haste."

"Let it be as the Most High wills," Mary humbly answered.

"Herod will search in vain," the angel continued, "and on account of his anger will command that all male children within Bethlehem, Gilgal and Hebron less than two years are to be killed."

Mary at once thought of her cousin Elizabeth and her child John and was concerned for his safety.

Knowing Mary's thoughts, the angel assured her, "Fear not for John's safety. Elizabeth has been warned and even now is preparing to take him to a place of safety."

The angel left her and the room was again dark. Mary's heart was deeply saddened by the thought of Herod's vicious scheme to murder innocent children; she began to pray that he would not issue the terrible order and no longer seek to take the life of her Son. She resolved not to tell Joseph of Herod's plan against the innocents until they were settled in Egypt. She then went to her bed.

In the morning Joseph was awakened by the grunts of the camels anxious for their feed. He was pleased that they woke him for the trip to Gaza was yet nine or ten hours travel and he wished to arrive before the start of the Sabbath. He woke Mary and asked her to prepare to leave as soon as possible after their morning meal. She rose from her bed at once, knelt with Joseph next to Jesus' cradle and said their morning prayers. The innkeeper's wife heard them moving about and prepared a simple but hardy meal for them of cereal, fruit and goats milk.

Warm, moist air carried by the west wind brought with it the smell of the Mediterranean and the sky was overcast with grayish clouds as the Holy Family departed. Joseph expressed a concern that it might rain before they could find shelter. He set a brisk pace so that they would arrive at Gaza before the Sabbath began.

Near midday they came to a small rock filled brook with balsam trees on each side where Joseph stopped to rest. While Mary nursed the infant Jesus he filled their water bottles and prepared two bowls of fruit and bread for Mary and himself. The sun had not shone through the clouds since they left the inn at Anim but suddenly it broke through giving them a welcome warmth.

Mary's concern for Joseph caused her to ask, "Dear husband, how much further is it to Gaza?"

"We have done well to have come so far at this hour," Joseph replied. "If we continue at the same pace we should arrive well before the start of the Sabbath, and I am confident we will find lodgings for Gaza has many inns."

Several times they came within sight of the road. On the east side were small houses used by merchants catering to travelers; on the west side they saw much sand spotted by small groups of date trees and low plants. Few travelers used the road this day.

The sun was low in a reddish sky when they arrived at Gaza. Joseph found lodgings at an inn owned by a large, boisterous man who with his wife and two sons also sold camels and dealt in stolen goods. He and his family were known thieves and pillagers, but were deeply affected by Joseph's and Mary's humility and the infant Jesus' holiness. Young children used as servants were ordered to attend to whatever Joseph and Mary required. It was a welcome rest but the behavior of the owner and his friends who drank and cavorted as if at a pagan wedding feast was appalling. Reluctantly the Holy Family remained there for the Sabbath and the day following to allow Joseph and their beast enough rest before continuing the journey; the remainder of the trek would be the most difficult.

Before them lay a large, dry desert upon which Joseph had never before traveled. There were no roads or trails to follow and little or no water. The innkeeper volunteered his advice, that they join a caravan traveling to Egypt, but he gave them no direction. And he had no idea how long it would be before a caravan would come by the inn. Joseph knew they should not wait any longer. He purchased additional provisions and filled the water bottles. They departed early the second morning, crossing the brook called Bezor about an hour beyond Gaza and came to a trade route village called Raphia. On the east side of the village, which consisted of a few small houses surrounded by large corrals, they came upon a small grove of palm trees and a well covered by a small shed. Joseph received permission of the owner to use the well and rest under the trees. Again Joseph was advised to join a caravan because it was the safest way to travel in a land of marauding bandits and wild animals. He was grateful for the advice but departed without further delay.

Soon their pace was slowed by the deep sand and large dunes; by night fall they had traveled only two leagues. Joseph hoped to find shelter from the desert cold in a cave or the tent of a nomadic tribesman but found only open desert. Clouds obscured the moon's light causing it to be totally dark. Joseph lighted a small oil lamp and walked beside the ass with his hand upon the beast's neck; he could see nothing beyond twenty feet on all sides. Without any apparent reason the ass came to a sudden halt; she would not move no matter how much coaxing Joseph gave her. Joseph was baffled by her behavior. He walked forward several steps but found nothing of concern. He did notice, however, that they were now on a narrow trail of hard ground. Joseph coaxed the animal once more but to no avail.

"Perhaps this good beast is in need of rest," Mary declared. "Should we remain here for the night?"

Joseph replied, "But there is no shelter for us, Mary. You and the Child will become very cold and there is no wood available to build a fire."

Mary was about to answer him when she saw in the distance a light moving from side to side as if on the mast of a ship.

"Joseph, there is a light ahead," she exclaimed, "and it is moving."

Joseph realized at once that the light was not moving closer nor further away.

"I believe it is a lamp hanging upon something," he replied. "We will go to it. Perhaps it is the tent of a tribesman."

He turned the ass's head in the direction of the lamp hoping that she would now move. To his surprise she moved directly toward the light and continued without coaxing. Joseph raised the oil lamp above his head and silently prayed that shelter would be granted by whomever they encountered. When they arrived at the light Joseph saw that it was suspended from a long, slender pole swaying from the wind.

"Is anyone here?" Joseph called out.

There was no reply.

"I am seeking shelter for my wife and child." he called out again. "They are cold and tired. Will you help us?"

Again there was silence.

"Perhaps the light is only a beacon for those that live here," Mary suggested.

"You may be right, Mary," Joseph replied. "We will wait here until someone returns. Let me help you to get down, then sit under the lamp while I look about for something to burn. We must have a fire for warmth."

Mary did as Joseph asked and waited while he walked in a circle about the area. After a short time he returned with a few small bushes and several dried camel droppings. He had a fire going in a few minutes; the warmth of it was most welcome to Mary and the child Jesus. Joseph took food and a water bottle from their baggage and his mantle to cover Mary and the Child, then sat beside them. Except for the crackling of the fire and Joseph's mantle rustling in the wind the desert was quiet. Soon Mary and Jesus were asleep, comforted by the warmth of Joseph's mantle and the fire.

Suddenly and without the slightest sound two men brandishing swords and a young boy came out of the dark. Joseph was startled by their appearance; his sudden moves woke Mary. She covered her face and remained silent.

Joseph rose to his feet, stepped away from Mary and spoke to them.

"Peace be with you. We are happy to see you for we are in need of shelter. We have a young child with us."

"How did you get here?" one of the men asked.

"We have walked here from Gaza," Joseph answered. "We are on our way to Egypt."

"Did you come directly to this light?" the other man asked. "Yes we did," Joseph replied. "My wife spied this light when we were on a trial not far from here."

Joseph wondered at these questions. The trio turned to each other and spoke in whispers. Joseph and Mary were baffled by their behavior.

One of the men turned to Joseph and said, 'You must be highly favored by the Most High God. It is a miracle that you came this far. We have several pitfalls along the trail and more around this pole. It is impossible for anyone to get by them in the dark."

"Why do you have pitfalls?" Joseph asked.

The trio laughed.

"We have them to trap travelers as yourself. And when they are trapped we take their belongings, their money then send them on their way. If they are wealthy we sometimes hold them for ransom. We are robbers as our fathers were before us and as our children will be after us." he said this in a proud manner at the same time placing his hand upon the boy's head.

"We are poor," Joseph said. "But you are welcome to whatever we have. You need not take it from us."

The men were amazed at Joseph's offer and his sincerity. They glanced at Mary and the Child then turned to confer again. The young boy seemed to be insisting upon something; the men finally agreed with him, then turned to face Joseph.

"You may keep what you have," one of the men said. "We do not want any of your belongings, and you are welcome to remain with us for the night. Come follow us. We live in a small village not far from here."

After lighting torches the trio led the Holy Family passed the pitfalls placed around their lure. None of them spoke until they were close to the village; then a password was given. It was answered by another voice from the dark.

Joseph caught a glimpse of a few palm trees at the edge of the darkness and assumed these people lived at an oasis. Several men armed with lances and swords appeared before them and congratulated the trio for their capture. But the same man who gave the password shouted that the man, woman and Child were to be guests at his home and treated accordingly. When no one challenged him Joseph realized that he was their leader and they were in no danger. As they approached one of the houses a door opened. A woman stood in it silhouetted by the light from within. No other light shone from the house; the windows were covered by wooden shutters without openings. Once inside, the men behaved very cordially to the Holy Family. This greatly surprised the woman for she was used only to their rough and rude behavior. Mary and the infant Jesus were led to another part of the house where she could wash and change her clothing in privacy. Joseph sat and talked with the men.

The leader spoke first, "You are now in my home. I am Mosoch, the leader of my people. This is my brother Japhet and his son Heber. We are Jews that once lived in Bethhoron but for reasons that I cannot tell you we moved here several years ago. My wife is called Derketo. She is an Egyptian from the city of Memphis and we have a son now two years old. Now tell me who you are and where you are going."

"I am Joseph, son of Jacob of Bethlehem. We have traveled from Nazareth of Galilee. Our destination is Egypt but I know not where we will settle. My wife is called Mary and the Child is called Jesus. We have been traveling three days now and the journey becomes more difficult as we go on. I am most grateful for your hospitality to us. May the Most High God bless you and all in your family."

"Why are you going to Egypt?" Japhet asked.

Joseph responded, "I too have a reason that cannot be told."

Mosoch and Japhet glanced at each other and smiled. They liked Joseph's answer. But Mosoch had a feeling about his guests which was troubling him.

"What is it about these people that brings such warmth and peace?" he whispered to Japhet. "Do you not sense something unusual about them?"

"I like this man," replied Japhet. "But I feel nothing unusual about him. He is just a poor traveler and a man concerned for his wife and child."

"I know that," Mosoch said in return. "I cannot explain to you my feelings but I have not felt like this since my childhood. It is the feeling I had when I was with my parents and I had complete trust in their love for me."

At that moment, Derketo asked the young boy, Heber, to bring in water from the well for the Child's bath. Heber did as he was asked and returned with two wooden buckets full of cold water. Derketo warmed the water in the hearth of their fireplace so that it would not chill the infant Jesus. In the meantime Mary had refreshed herself, removed the Babe's clothing and wrapped Him in a small coverlet. From a partitioned part of the house used for sleeping came the cry of a young child. Derketo went to it. Mary heard her speaking softly to the child and it quieted. She then returned and poured the warmed water into a small, wooden tub close to the hearth. The men watched as Mary uncovered Jesus and slowly lowered Him into the water. Joseph was more than a little surprised by the attention Mosoch gave to this little act. He saw a small tear form at the corner of his eye and he made no attempt to wipe it away. Japhet and Heber who were beside him were unable to see his face. They paid little attention to what was happening; they were hungry and the food Derketo placed before them was their favorite.

When Jesus bath was finished, Mary returned with Him to the rear of the house. Derketo asked Japhet and Heber to carry the tub of water out of the house and get rid of it. But Mosoch stood up and commanded them not to remove the tub. He then walked into the sleeping area and returned with their child which was wrapped in white cloths from the middle of his chest down to his feet. His small arms were tightly wrapped as well.

"What are you going to do?" Derketo asked.

Mosoch did not answer but turned to Joseph and said, "This is our son. He is called Dismas. He has leprosy which is spreading over his body. I do not know why but I feel I must wash him in the water used for your child."

Mosoch gently removed the cloths. Joseph saw the sores plainly and an unpleasant odor filled the room. At that moment Mary returned with the infant Jesus. She saw Mosoch on his knees lowering his child into the water. She, too, could see the leprosy which had caused large putrid sores on the child's arms, legs and torso. Silently she and Joseph prayed that a healing be granted the child. Mosoch slowly lowered the little boy into the water. Derketo stood next to him holding the cloths; she was crying. With his eyes closed Mosoch turned his face toward the ceiling. His lips were moving but he could not be heard. A few minutes passed before he opened his eyes and began to lift the child from the water.

"Look there! The sores are falling from his body," Mosoch shouted. "O Lord! He is healed! He is healed! Praise the Lord of Israel for He is kind and Merciful! Praise the Lord!"

Mosoch raised the child above his head and wept. His joy was so great he could say nothing more. Derketo, Japhet and Heber stood staring with their mouths open wide. Mary and Joseph wept also. The infant Jesus turned His face toward the child; at the same time reaching out to him with His little hand. Mosoch and Derketo embraced their son several times; bestowing many kisses upon his face, hands and feet.

Mosoch turned to Mary and with great joy and emotion said, "My joy is so great that I feel that I could die from it. I never thought the Most High God, blessed be His name, would be so compassionate toward this sinner. What may I do for Him in return?"

Mary replied, "Reform your lives, live according to the law given to us by Moses, and be compassionate toward all who pass this way."

Mosoch resolved at that moment to do as Mary suggested.

"I will be eternally grateful to your God and to you," Derketo declared. "For we thought we would lose our child but now he is healed. We will never forget you."

"And we will never forget you nor that which has happened here tonight," Joseph exclaimed. "I promise that we will pray for you and visit you upon our return from Egypt."

"You have a most difficult journey before you," said Mosoch, "There are many dangers in the desert and little water between here and the Nile. Why not stay here with us. We would be greatly pleased if you did so."

Joseph smiled, placed his hand upon Mosoch's shoulder and replied, "Your offer is a very considerate one, Mosoch. But it is imperative that we continue our journey for we are in grave danger as long as we are near Herod's domain."

"But why do you fear Herod?" Mosoch asked somewhat surprised? He thought to himself: "What threat can these people be to Herod?"

"I can not tell you now," answered Joseph. "But someday you and your people will know. In the morning we will leave before sunrise so that we will be able to travel several hours before the warmest part of the day. Will you escort us until we are safely passed your snares?"

Mosoch assured Joseph he would accompany them until they were beyond all the traps. He then directed Derketo to set aside food for the Holy Family to take with them. Japhet and Heber who silently observed all that occurred now left for their own homes. Their account of the night would cause a great stir among the villagers. Derketo brought Mary to a sleeping place which was near to her own. Joseph retired to a place near Mosoch's bed and prayed for Mosoch and his people. His prayer was for them to turn from their ways.

CHAPTER EIGHT
Egypt

As they prepared to leave the next morning Mosoch again advised Joseph of the many dangers they would encounter in the desert. Joseph assured him they would arrive safely at the place God chooses them to be and he promised once more to visit them upon their return. Mosoch accompanied the Holy family for almost an hour before returning. It was an emotional farewell for him.

At the end of the day Joseph reckoned they had traveled only two and one half leagues from Mosoch's house; many dunes of soft sand made traveling slow and difficult. And more than the usual amount of water was consumed by their animal because of its increased effort. Although the desert was hot during the day, the nights were uncomfortably cold. Mary and Joseph huddled under their mantles on the leeward side of a large dune as protection from the wind, and without a fire; there was nothing to burn. The night was long. By dawn Mary was shivering but her concern was for Jesus and Joseph. When there was enough light to see by they resumed their trek. Mary walked alongside Joseph for a while to regain her warmth.

Because he could find no trail or road Joseph became concerned about their direction. He moved in what he thought to be a southwesterly course using the sun as a point of reference, but he was unsure. Nevertheless they continued, trusting that the Lord God would not allow them to become lost. They encountered no people nor saw any animals the entire day. That night, after traveling a little more than three leagues, they slept in a shallow gorge with only the light and heat from a small oil lamp. This night was colder than the last, and they could do nothing but huddle together for warmth. The infant Jesus was wrapped in a warm woolen cover between them but after several hours He, too, was feeling the cold.

In the morning Joseph took stock of their provisions and saw that not much remained. He told Mary that the food was very low and that they must eat only once each day until they could find more. Their water supply was greatly diminished by midday. Joseph was very troubled about their situation; he knew Mary would need more bodily nourishment in order to nurse the infant Jesus. And he knew their animal could not travel much further on the small amount of water and fodder he could give it. Late in the afternoon when they stopped to rest Mary saw how grave Joseph had become.

She asked, "Dear husband, how much longer will our food and water last?"

He replied, "There is very little water left, but I think it will last one more day. All that remains of the food are two small loaves of bread and a few figs. The fodder for the ass is almost gone. Without nourishment the poor beast will be unable to carry you and the Child. We must find water and food soon."

"Perhaps we will come to an oasis or find a well tomorrow," Mary said. "We must hope for the Lord's help."

That night Joseph removed the wicker screen over the cross-seat and fashioned a tent-like shelter by covering it with their mantles. It gave them added protection against the cold and the relentless wind. They ate their first food since morning, had a little water with it then huddled under the makeshift tent. They spent much of the night praying and taking short periods of sleep. Before daybreak they were awakened by unusually strong gusts of wind that threatened to blow away their shelter. Joseph quickly surrounded the bottom of the mantles with sand and placed the ass on the side facing the wind. After a while the wind subsided allowing them to continue on. But by midday the wind shifted from a westerly direction to the southeast; it was warm and strong. Joseph had heard of these sudden desert storms; he feared that one was beginning. Before long it was very difficult to walk or see because of the wind's fury and the sand stung their skin. Joseph helped Mary to dismount and he erected their shelter on the leeward side of a rather high dune. He brought the animal to its knees next to the shelter then tied a cloth over its head for protection and to prevent it from wandering.

Mary, holding the infant Jesus beneath her veil, and Joseph sat with their backs against the wicker screen with the ends of their mantles tucked under them. In a short time the sand piled high around them. Mary and Joseph grew fearful and were at the same time saddened because of the hardship inflicted upon the Child. Yet the infant Jesus made no complaint, crying only when hungry .At the height of the storm a choking dust began to fill the shelter no matter how tightly they held the mantles closed. Mary became very concerned about Jesus breathing in this dust and the affect it might have. Anxiously she asked Joseph to join her in prayer that the storm would subside. She began to weep. Joseph tried to comfort her by placing his arm about her and pressing her against his side.

With her eyes closed and her head bowed Mary prayed most earnestly, "Eternal, great and powerful God, our Protector and Provider, with your mighty strength you created all things on earth. You made the day and night; you set the sun and the moon in their places; you set the boundaries of the earth; you created the seasons. Everything you do is holy! None are as great as you! You are the God who works miracles; you have shown your might among all peoples. You gave us life and preserved us in it though we are but dust and useless creatures. How can we give you satisfactory thanks for all these magnificent gifts? Heavenly Father, smile down upon us and look upon your Only Begotten Son. Please provide that which my spouse and I need for sustenance so that we may live according to your will and serve Him who has come into the world for the salvation of mankind. Command the elements to cease afflicting Him and grant that I may suffer their violence instead."

Immediately the wind subsided and the dust settled so that the tent was completely clear. Within a few minutes the wind was reduced to a gentle breeze and the sky cleared. Joseph left their shelter, ran to the crest of the dune and looked about. He could see no dark clouds or dust blowing about; it was as if the storm never occurred. He returned to Mary who was now standing beside the tent holding the infant Jesus out before her at the same time singing hymns of praise and thanksgiving.

Joseph lifted his hands and face toward the bright blue sky and prayed aloud, "With all my heart I thank you Lord. How wonderful are the things you do. Lord, your constant love reaches all the ends of the earth, the skies above and the depths of the sea. You care for men and the beasts. How precious is your love Lord. We call to you Lord; we begged for your help and you answered our plea. Lord you are our God; we will give you thanks always."

Joseph then set about clearing away the sand that covered almost the entire wicker screen. The storm had begun at midday and it was now close to sunset; they were hungry and thirsty. All that remained of their provisions was a half loaf of bread and nearly a cup full of water which they ate and drank to regain their stamina. Now it was urgent for them to find food and water; without it they would perish in a few days. When it was fully dark except for the star-filled sky, Mary and Joseph sat outside the tent and talked about the storm, its fury and the miraculous ending of it, and their situation. Joseph had no way of knowing how much further it was to the next village or if one existed along their route. He was greatly concerned for Mary and the Child but tried to show confidence that they would obtain food and water very soon. As they talked the moon rose above the dune; it illumined everything about them; it was three-quarters full. A thought came to Joseph that they could travel at night to make up for the distance lost due to the storm; he felt they might be able to travel further without the heat of the sun sapping their strength. Without complaint Mary prepared herself and the infant Jesus while Joseph replaced the wicker screen above the cross-seat and collected their few belongings. Using the stars for reckoning they proceeded in a southwesterly course. This night was not as cold as the two previous because of a warm wind from the south. The moon was high before they stopped to rest, but they found nothing to eat or drink. For several hours more they traveled until the moon was obscured by thick clouds. They were now forced to stop because it was totally dark. Again they huddled under their mantles. When the sun rose Joseph looked about from the top of a nearby dune and to his surprise he saw a long row of palm trees and low bushes a short distance to the west. He rushed back to tell Mary.

"There are trees and shrubs not far from here," he exclaimed. "There must be water present. Perhaps we will find something to eat."

"I will pray there will be, Joseph," Mary declared. "Let us go now."

When they reached the oasis they found it to be a long narrow gathering of date palms and several groups of balsam plants. At the extreme end they found a well covered by a heavy wooden platform, but secured by a large lock with three key holes. Joseph became quite concerned when he could find no way to open it. Mary in the meantime was walking through the plants below the palm trees that had clusters of ripe dates high in their branches. Joseph saw that climbing the smooth trunks was impossible.

"We have found food and water but we are unable to obtain either of them," Joseph declared dejectedly. "If we remain here perhaps someone will come along that can unlock the well but that is uncertain or we can continue on hoping we will find another oasis or a village. The choice is a difficult one. Let us pray for the Lord's guidance."

They fell to their knees in the soft sand and Joseph began, "Save us, O Lord. We have no water or food. Our throats are parched and we feel the pangs of hunger. Our eyes burn from searching the desert. We look to you Lord for help at all times and you rescue us from danger. Turn to us now, Lord, and be merciful because we are alone and weak. We pray to you, Lord, because you answer us. Reveal your wonderful love, O Lord."

Mary rose to her feet, looked upward and prayed silently for a few moments; she then approached one of the heavily laden date palms and raised the infant Jesus above her toward the tree. Immediately the tree began to bend and continued until its uppermost branches were touching the ground. Joseph rose quickly to his feet, grabbed a basket from the back of the animal and filled it with as many dates as it would hold. Mary stood nearby giving thanks and praise for this wonderful miracle granted through Jesus her son. It was several minutes before Joseph realized what had happened; when he did he fell to his knees and praised God. Mary in the meantime had returned to the locked well.

She found that the lock was open and calmly called to Joseph, "Dear husband, bring our water bottles here. The well is now unlocked!"

Joseph rushed excitedly to the well with the bottles, pushed aside the wooden cover and using a rope left hanging in the well lowered the bottles into it. Because the well was deep the water was crystal clear and quite cool. Mary used some of it to clean the infant Jesus and her own face, neck and arms. Joseph poured some over the dates then filled the leather bag he used to feed the ass. The good beast emptied it quickly then began to eat the plants near the well. After more prayers of praise and thanksgiving the Holy Couple sat beneath the leaves of the tree that bent to the ground. They ate just enough to satisfy their hunger then slept with the infant Jesus in His cradle between them. The day was warm but a gentle breeze blowing through the shade cooled the oasis; they slept soundly and comfortably.

The sun was low when Joseph awoke. He sat up quickly and looked about. The ass was close by chewing clumps of dry grass. Mary and the Child were still asleep. He took this opportunity to gather bunches of dry grass and small plants as feed for the animal. He filled the water bottles and placed all their belongings in one place until it was time to reload. When Mary awoke he had just finished filling two baskets with dates. He was certain they would last until they reached a village in Egypt. Mary nursed the Babe then walked about the oasis praying and singing psalms. Joseph loved to listen to her soft, gentle voice. The infant Jesus listened intently at the same time staring at her. When they resumed their trek, Joseph moved steadily westward toward the setting sun. They would again travel as long as there was enough light, and then wait for the moonrise before continuing.

The next two days were uneventful. They encountered no people and saw only an occasional bird flying high above them. On the morning of the sixth day Joseph spied a small village about the size of Nazareth from the top of a large dune. The village was situated between two wide canals that were connected to a branch of the Nile. The canal walls were made of stone and many palm trees were on each bank. Near the center of the village steps led down to the water where a few women were washing clothes and bathing their children. Next to the steps was a raft which was used to ferry passengers across the canal. Two large, bare chested black men with long wooden poles sat upon the raft waiting for customers. Joseph helped Mary to dismount then approached the two men and inquired about the fare. He gave them what they asked then brought Mary and the Child on to the raft. Mary sat on a wide plank used as a bench. Joseph led the ass on to the raft and into a wooden tub reserved for animals; he then stood near Mary. The raft moved slowly across the canal and docked at another set of steps on the opposite bank. Joseph learned from the men that the village was called Lepe and that it was a stopping place for barges carrying cotton and lumber to cities along the Nile. .

The village streets were wide and dirty. Several dogs ran freely through the streets eating the garbage thrown from the houses. None of the inhabitants greeted the Holy Family nor did they offer them any shelter when Joseph inquired about lodgings. And they heard boisterous men cursing at their slaves whose pace did not please them. Joseph saw small statues of a half human creature in the windows of many houses and on the roof of a wide building that appeared to be an inn. Because of their rough nature and coolness Mary asked Joseph to take them out of the village and to seek shelter elsewhere. Joseph did as she asked. Soon they were at the second canal which was even wider than the first. Again they were ferried across but this time the ferry was propelled by four women that were slaves belonging to the ferry owner. They, too, were black and could not understand Joseph when he spoke to them.

    The terrain beyond the opposite bank was flat and very fertile from the Nile flooding each year. For as far as he could see there were no houses. He saw only a small grove of trees about a quarter hour walk south of the village. Joseph decided to take shelter among them. As they approached the grove Joseph saw several herds of cattle to the west and a group of men tending them. The men were dressed in white tunics with wide turbans upon their heads; each one carried a staff with knobs of different design at the top and a wide hook at the bottom. They remained motionless as if asleep on their feet while the cattle grazed or rested on their sides. Not far from the grove of trees several people were cooling themselves in the canal. The Holy Family moved into the grove without being noticed and to their surprise they found a large replica of the idol they had seen in the village. It was a stone image of a creature with a human body and the head of an ox. Its arms were outstretched before it and the image of a child wrapped in cloths lay in its hands. The idol was surrounded by stone benches and tables used for worshippers and their sacrifices. The Holy Family continued on until they came to a broad tree with wide branches and heavily laden with long narrow leaves. Joseph could not recall seeing this type of tree before. He and Mary settled under the tree and began to eat more of the dates while reclining comfortably on the ground which was covered by a layer of moss and leaves. A short time later a group of men, most of them short and plump, dressed in white garments draped over one shoulder and barely covering their knees entered the grove; they came to pay homage to their god. Suddenly the earth shook violently. The men fell to the ground and cried out in fear. They looked to the idol and it began to sway from side to side. The swaying increased until the idol toppled over on its side. The men cried out even louder; they were more frightened now that their god lay on its side. The people in the canal and the cattlemen heard their cries and came running toward the grove. All of them stood near their fallen god wondering why it had toppled. At that moment Mary and Joseph rose to leave.

    They had not gone far when one of the women spied them and shouted to the others, "Look! There are two strangers trying to escape. Their presence angered our god and brought this upon us."

    The others turned quickly toward the Holy Family and began to shout threats and curses at them. Mary and Joseph heard them but continued walking away. Joseph pulled at the rope around the neck of the ass to quicken the pace. The crowd continued their threats and began to run after them. Joseph heard them coming and was frightened by their anger. He and Mary prayed for God's protection. Just as the crowd reached the large tree the ground began to heave and shake; the tree swayed violently and fell to the ground before them. The ground continued to heave until a large hole opened under the tree's roots, and a strong flow of water gushed out of it flooding the area between the crowd and the Holy Family. It was impossible for them to follow any further. A small lake formed around the idol and it began to sink into the softened ground. While the crowd watched the entire statue disappeared beneath the water until only a corner of the pedestal was visible. The water continued to rise until the people were forced to retreat to higher ground. During the excitement the Holy Family slipped away and continued in a direction leading to the great city of Heliopolis.

Almost an hour had passed when they came within sight of the city. Near to the north wall was a long and very high bridge spanning the branch of the Nile which circled the city on the east side. The bridge ended at one of the gates which was large and wide; many people were passing through it. Joseph pointed out to Mary another stone image identical to the one that sank into the muddy waters. It was a short distance from the gate and was also surrounded by many benches. No one was near the idol when the Holy Family passed through the gate. A loud noise, like that of a tree split by lightning, was heard and the head of the idol split in two. Each half fell to the ground crushing the benches. The people became very excited and perplexed; they could only stare in disbelief. Mary and Joseph moved quickly toward the city so as not to arouse the anger of the people again. But several men and women were aware of their presence and began to stir up those around them. Before the mob could organize the Holy Family disappeared into a narrow street that led toward the center of the city.

Heliopolis was densely populated by Egyptians, merchants from the north, many Jews and slaves. The buildings were large with stone exteriors and had large columns. There were several towers on the roofs of the buildings but they were unoccupied. The Holy Family passed a large temple with two outer courts and ornate columns supporting a sloping roof. It was without walls and Joseph saw that the center had a floor of smooth black stone surrounding another stone idol which was smaller than the others and mounted high upon a white stone pedestal. The pedestal began to sway as they passed by causing the idol to crash upon the stone floor and break into several pieces. Some of the priests who were in the temple fell prostrate upon the floor and covered their heads with their clothing.

Not far from the temple was an elevated road supported by columns about twice the height of a man and of varying shapes. Beneath the road were many dwellings with only three walls; they once were small shops and booths now abandoned. Joseph selected the cleanest and largest for their quarters. It was large enough for the ass to be stabled at the rear. After Mary was settled in with the infant Jesus, Joseph searched the area for material to build a wall for their privacy. In another building nearby he found coils of rope and bundles of wicker which he quickly used to construct a wicker screen similar to the one he made for the Nativity Cave. The weave was tight enough to afford them privacy yet it would allow air to pass through for ventilation. Before dark he found a fountain used for drinking water; he also found a small table in another of the abandoned shops. Mary covered it with a red cloth, placed a transparent white cloth over the red cloth and a small oil lamp in the center. It was to serve as their prayer altar.

Within the temple there was much excitement and concern about the destruction of their god; several priests and many people gathered around it and discussed what they must do. One of the priests, called Helichar, asked for silence and spoke to them.

"People of Heliopolis listen to me! I know you are perplexed at this tragedy. So are we your priests. I recall a passage in our ancient writings about a prophet of the Jews that traveled throughout Egypt. His name was Jerimicha of Jeremias. He spoke of a God that was jealous and angry about our gods. He foretold of a King of the Jews that would someday come into Egypt and many temples and idols would be destroyed."

A great stir arose among those listening; many of them shouted curses and threats against the Jews.

Helichar moved to the top step before the idol and raised his arms and shouted, "Be quiet! I have not finished."

The other priests moved among the crowd and ordered them to be silent. After several minutes of chaos order was restored.

Helichar continued, "I believe that the prophesied King has come into Egypt, and he may be here in Heliopolis or with the Jews in Goshen. There can be no other explanation for the destruction of our idols. A king cannot move through a land without notice. If any of you know of a rich caravan that has crossed our borders speak now so that we may find this king and destroy him. Come forward if you have seen such a caravan or anything that may be helpful."

One of the men shouted back, "I was present when the idol near the canal fell over earlier today. It sank beneath a small lake that formed from a stream of water that gushed forth from a cavity below the roots of a large tree. The tree mysteriously fell to the ground, but the only strangers present were a poor family wearing Hebrew garments."

"Where did they go?" Helichar inquired.

"I did not follow them but they were traveling toward the bridge leading to this city," the man answered.

"How do you know they were poor?" Helichar asked.

"Their clothing was of poor quality," the man replied, "they had only one animal, an ass, and the woman carried an infant in a sling."

"That does not sound like a king's caravan." Helichar quipped. "Listen to me! All of you are to spread this throughout Heliopolis and the surrounding villages. A foreign king has entered Egypt, a king of the Jews. Anyone who finds him is to report to me. They will be handsomely rewarded. Now leave here and do as I have commanded."

The people dispersed quickly, still murmuring and speculating about the king's whereabouts. Some recalled seeing the Holy Family enter the city and the idol splitting in two as they passed by; they began to search the city for the Hebrew visitors.

The Holy Family did not leave their new quarters for the remainder of the day; they prayed before the altar for a long time giving thanks for their safe arrival and the shelter they found. They ate the last of the dates and some bread Joseph had purchased in a shop near the fountain. Afterward Joseph continued to clean the shelter and put their belongings on shelves left by the former resident. As he worked he thought of their journey through the desert, the hardships they endured, their entry into Egypt, the idol and tree that fell to the ground near the canal and the idol that split in two as they entered the city. He reflected upon all these things and recalled a passage from Isaias.

He turned to Mary and said, "I was truly astonished when the idol fell to the ground at the canal and when the idol split in two near the gate. Now I recall that which Isaias foretold about the idols of Egypt. 'Behold the Lord will ascend upon a swift cloud, and will enter into Egypt, and the idols of Egypt shall be moved at his presence, and the heart of Egypt shall melt in the midst thereof.' We must rejoice that we belong to Him and serve Him, and when we return to Nazareth we must tell everyone the wonderful things the Lord, our God, has done."

Mary listened intently, thought about the many things that took place during their journey and said aloud, "He, the Lord, is our God; his commands are for all the world. His promises for so many generations have been fulfilled."

She then knelt before the infant Jesus in His cradle; Joseph knelt beside her and together they prayed and adored Him in silence. The infant Jesus was very much pleased by their love and devotion. He smiled but tears filled His eyes and flowed down the side of his face. He raised His right hand and with only two fingers extended pointed toward his beloved Mother and her loving spouse. Mary and Joseph remained in prayer for quite some time then at Joseph's suggestion they retired. The night was warm but a gentle breeze blew through the wicker screen to cool them. Because there were no people living near them it was quiet and they slept well. In the morning, after their usual prayers and a breakfast of bread and water, Joseph left the shelter in order to find work. He saw that the houses were in good condition and well made. He therefore, sought work among the shops providing articles, such as, furniture, cabinets and carts. While he was gone Mary occupied herself with cleaning and mending some of Joseph's garments. She sang most beautifully as she worked. Several people heard her that were passing by and began to gather before the shelter's entrance. They watched and listened as Mary moved about but said nothing. Suddenly Mary became aware of their presence, moved to the rear and remained near the infant Jesus.

One of the women called to her, "We will not harm you, my child, come forward we wish to speak with you and your husband. Some of us were near the gate when the statue of our god split in two just as you passed it. And yesterday the priests saw another statue fall to the floor of the temple. We are curious as to the reason for these things happening when you and your family are present. Please come out to us."

Mary was reassured by the tone of the woman's voice. She covered her face with her veil and moved slowly to the entrance but did not go out.

"My husband is not here." Mary said. "If you wish to speak with him return this evening."

The woman responded, "Could you not speak to us child for we are anxious to see you and to know you."

Mary hesitated for a few moments, prayed silently then opened the screen and stepped out. She kept her eyes lowered and her head slightly bowed as she approached the small group. Mary's appearance was so pleasing to them that several sighed and wondered why they had such feelings of warmth toward this young stranger. The others remained silent, waiting for someone to start the questioning.

Another woman asked, "Where are you from child?"

"My husband and I have journeyed from Nazareth of Galilee," Mary answered.

"So, you are Jews," she declared. "And where is your husband?"

"He is seeking work. He is a carpenter and can do many things well. Do you know where he might find work to do?"

The woman ignored Mary's question and countered with her own, "Why have these strange things happened to the statues of our god when you are present? What power do you have?"

Mary thought about her question for a few moments then replied, "We have no power to make these things happen. But we are children of the One and Only God who is our Creator and our Lord. He alone is to be adored and honored as God. The statues you worship are false. They are made of silver, gold or stone and formed by human hands. They have mouths, but cannot speak, and eyes, but cannot see. They have ears, but cannot hear, and noses, but cannot smell. They have hands, but cannot feel, and feet but cannot walk; they cannot make a sound. They have no power; any man that made them can destroy them when he pleases. Therefore, man is more noble and powerful than they. The priests and prophetesses that attend them are directed by lying and deceitful demons who are avowed enemies of the one True God."

Jesus was aware of what was taking place and through His intercession a knowledge of the True God was instilled in their minds; they suddenly became aware of their errors and a great sorrow filled their hearts. Mary's words were so clear and her manner of speaking so gentle that all the listeners were filled with a love for her. They remained silent for several minutes pondering over the things that Mary said.

Jesus again interceded on their behalf, and they received a grace to accept what Mary said, to believe that only one True God existed and at the same time became repentant and overjoyed. One by one they returned to their homes and families. Soon the account of what took place spread throughout the city and to the Jews living in Goshen and many surrounding communities. When Joseph returned after several hours of a futile search for work, he was exhausted, depressed and hungry. He had visited many shops from one end of the city to the other, and had not eaten since their meal together that morning. But there was nothing to be had nor could they purchase any. He had used the last few coins for the bread he bought the day before. He and Mary would go without food again.

"We must trust that our Lord will provide for us," Mary said, "though we must suffer this now. And we have an opportunity to offer these sufferings and deprivations to the Lord our God who considers them as a wonderful gift and a treasure for the giver. Be patient, you will find work soon. But let us be thankful for what we have now."

Joseph smiled and let out a sigh.

"You are right Mary," he said. "I had forgotten for the moment how the Lord our God provided for us in the desert. I will seek work again tomorrow at a place I heard of today. There they construct small shelters for the soldiers as a protection against the sun. These shelters are also in demand by the people with gardens and bathing pools. I am sure they will need a carpenter."

Mary provided water for Joseph to wash himself and a fresh garment to wear. While he performed these ablutions Mary cared for and nursed the infant Jesus. After awhile they had an opportunity to sit and talk. Mary related all that had occurred when the people came to the shelter. Joseph was greatly pleased at the outcome but at the same time concerned. Mary assured him that there was nothing to fear.

At first light Joseph awoke; he felt the pangs of hunger and was saddened knowing that Mary too would be without food one more day if he did not find work. He left without waking Mary. The shop he intended to visit was at the opposite end of the city. Two branches of the Nile must be crossed before he would enter the section of the city heavily occupied by Jews. He prayed fervently that he would be given work and with the day's wages buy food, mats for their beds and a small chest for their belongings. Along his route he saw many people placing offerings of snakes and small four legged creatures upon the idols. Many of the idols were made of stone but two were of dark marble. He asked for directions at an intersection of several streets but was rudely ignored. Joseph assumed they did not understand him and continued on trusting that he would be led to his destination. He glanced at each street then chose one leading to the west and walked quickly through it. The homes were poor and in need of repair; they were attached but their roofs were at different heights. The streets were littered with garbage and animal excrements. Only a few people were in the streets and they appeared to be beggars. The pavement was very irregular and rough; it ended at a small canal then turned northward. Along the canal were several homeless families struggling to survive on the alms they were given and the food they were able to steal at the markets. Those unfortunate enough to be caught in the act had the first and second fingers cut off their right hand, even the children suffered this cruel punishment. On the opposite bank was a long stone building with heavy wooden bars in the windows. The depraved and possessed inmates stared at the passerby and occasionally a wild scream was heard from within. Joseph was deeply saddened at this sight and asked God's blessing on all of them.

A sickening smell filled the air as Joseph passed slaughter houses and animal pens crowded with bleating sheep. Beyond the slaughter houses were yards filled with cut stone used for the exterior of the homes in the more affluent section of the city. He saw no lumber yards or fabrication shops; in desperation he stopped a large man carrying bags of wool upon his back and sought directions.

"Not far from here," the man said "you will find a bridge across the canal. Cross it and go to the right along the edge of the canal. The shop you seek is about one quarter hour further, but I advise you to hurry for there are many men searching for work."

Joseph thanked him and hurried off.

CHAPTER NINE
Heliopolis

Mary was not surprised to find Joseph gone when she awoke; she knew how anxious he was to arrive at the shop before any others looking for work. As always, she began the morning with prayers of thanksgiving and supplication. This morning she especially asked for Joseph to find work and receive fair wages. After attending to the infant Jesus, Mary continued to clean the shelter until she saw the people gathering near the entrance. Within a half hour there were nearly one hundred gathered. Some came because of their curiosity about these foreigners, some were among the first visitors who wished to listen to Mary again, while others came to object to their presence. Mary observed the people through the wicker screen but did not go out to meet them. A middle aged woman came to the entrance with her daughter who was about Mary's age and called out to her.

"Young woman, I am the sister of Sephima who visited you yesterday. I, and most of these people with me, have come to hear you speak of the one true God. Your words yesterday have been spread throughout the city and the surrounding villages. And the destruction of the statues has drawn much attention. Will you come out to speak to us?"

Mary was touched by the sincerity in her request; she moved the screen aside and stepped out. Her face was veiled, her head covered, and Jesus was in her arms.

"Good people," she began, "I spoke yesterday of the One and Only true God and the falsity of your gods that are created by man and may be destroyed by man whenever he wishes. The One true God is the Creator of all things. Heaven and earth belongs to the Lord alone, but He gave the earth to man."

The people were stirring and murmuring. One of the young men called for attention.

"Why do you come to this woman?" he shouted. "She is but a sorceress who used her powers to topple over our gods in order to draw attention to herself. You should ask our gods for forgiveness and leave here."

Another young man jumped to his feet and shouted, "Be quiet! We have come to hear her not you. Can you not see the loveliness of this girl and sense the sincerity in her speech. Our gods say nothing to us. Be quiet and let her go on. And if you do not agree with her then leave content that you are loyal to your god."

Mary stood with her eyes lowered and her head bowed. Some of the children went to their knees so as to see her face then sat before her. When the people quieted Mary continued. "There are demons who are avowed enemies of God and man. Their influence has caused you to worship idols and to believe the false directions spoken by your priests and oracles. Many of you have lived evil lives and committed most serious offenses by their inducement. Do not put your trust in worldly things or in human advice, or anything else that cannot save you. Happy is the one who has the God of Jacob to help him and depends on the Lord, the only God, who created heaven, earth, and sea and all that is in them. Trust in the Lord, people of Egypt, He helps you and protects you."

The people moved closer but not close enough to touch Mary. Some of the children pushed forward and began to struggle for a position close to Mary and the Child. A young boy was pushed aside and fell to the ground; he could not get up because he had lost the use of both arms and much of the strength in his legs when afflicted by one of the many diseases rife in Egypt. Mary moved toward the boy and reached down to him, her veil fell from her face and the boy saw her warm, sweet smile. She reached out to him with her free hand and the boy raised his hand to grasp hers. The crowd gasped, they were aware of his paralysis, and moved back a few steps. The boy's mother rushed forward and fell to her knees close to Mary. Mary helped the boy to his feet; he turned to his mother raised his arms and embraced her. Tears flowed from the eyes of those who were able to see their embrace. Those in the rear who did not see the miraculous healing became very excited when told of it. Many believed and began to shout praises for the one true God that Mary spoke of. The young man who accused her of sorcery was speechless yet a doubt remained in him.

The boy's mother looked toward Mary and Jesus, lifted her son and said aloud, "With all my heart I thank the One and Only true God. How wonderful are His works. There is no one like the Lord who lives in the heavens above. He raises the poor from the dust; He lifts the needy from their misery."

Mary restored her veil, turned to the people and said, "Good people, now let us give thanks to our Creator. Join me in prayer. Kneel before Him who is all love and mercy."

Mary knelt next to the woman still crying and clutching her son. Most of the people knelt, as Mary asked; they said nothing and kept their eyes fixed on Mary and the Child. Those that did not kneel turned and walked away. The young man who spoke against Mary was the last to leave.

Mary bowed her head and began her prayer; her tone and words were strong and confident. "O God, You have been merciful to us and blessed us; You looked upon us with kindness, that all here may know Your will; that all nations may know Your salvation. May these people praise You, God; may all people praise You."

She stood up, walked to the entrance, turned once more toward the people, moved the screen aside and entered. The people remained on their knees for several minutes then departed in groups of two and three; some who had food with them left what they had at the base of the screen. Two women left their veils and a large leather flask of water. The children turned their heads to look back hoping Mary and the Child would appear again. Word of the healing spread quickly, but not everyone who heard accepted it. Many of the city's inhabitants were angry about the destruction of their gods and began to plot ways to drive off the strangers. When all had gone Mary placed the infant Jesus in His cradle then brought in the food and gifts left at the screen which consisted of a small bag of flour, a jar of olive oil and a few pieces of fruit. While she hung the flask on a peg and draped the veils over a small stool near the cradle, Mary thought of Joseph and how tired and hungry he would be when he returned.

For the remainder of the day Mary occupied herself with cleaning the shelter and caring for the infant Jesus. She sang and prayed as she worked. Some passersby heard her lovely voice and did not continue on until she was silent. When long shadows of the buildings opposite darkened the shelter she lit the oil lamp then sat with the infant Jesus in her arms and prayed. Time passed slowly; she was anxious for Joseph's return. The sun had just set when Joseph returned; he was tired but excited. And he was carrying two bundles.

"I found work, Mary!" he exclaimed. "At the shop I was directed to. I was paid for each shed that I was able to finish and extra for the improvements I made to some of the sheds already completed. The manager, a fair man, liked the work I did. He asked me to return tomorrow for there is much work to be done. Look, here! I have food and mats for our bedding."

He unrolled the mats, laid the bundle aside then embraced Mary and the child Jesus. He looked about the shelter noticing its cleanliness and remarked, "Well, you have been busy. The space is clean and our belongings are placed neatly on the shelves. What is this?" He picked up the bag of flour. "Flour," he declared, "Where did it come from?"

Mary smiled; she had not seen Joseph behave like this before.

"We had more visitors today, Joseph. They left the flour, some fruit and a jar of oil. And the lovely veils upon the stool. A most wonderful thing occurred while the people were here. I will tell you about it while we are eating. Here, I have filled a basin with water for you to wash with. But first light a fire so that I may make bread for your meal."

Joseph left the shelter and with some cuts of wicker made a fire. He then removed his outer garment and washed while Mary mixed the flour with water and small amounts of salt Joseph purchased. She made several small balls of dough, flattened them until they were about the size of her hand then cooked them in a small amount of oil. During the meal Mary recounted all that took place when the people were there. Joseph listened intently and began to praise God when Mary told him of the miraculous healing of the crippled boy.

When Mary finished her account Joseph said to her, "No doubt this will be spoken of throughout this city and those nearby, and tomorrow many more people will come bringing the crippled and ill. You must be prepared for this and for attacks by the Egyptians and their priests, which may be the beginning of many attacks against the Lord our God, blessed be His name, and we will be harassed because we were present when their idols were destroyed. Perhaps I should remain with you tomorrow."

"Dear husband," Mary replied, "you need not worry about our safety; there is no power on earth that can harm us for we have the Son of God in our care."

That evening the young man who spoke against Mary went to their temple where he related to Helichar, the priest, all that occurred and the words Mary spoke.

"She is a sorceress," he declared. "How else could these things happen?"

"Are you certain the boy was healed?" Helichar asked. "Or was he part of a plan to fool the people?"

"No!" replied the young man, "I know the boy and his family. He was stricken with a high fever which lasted several days. When the fever left him he was unable to move his arms and barely able to walk. I believe he can hear in only one ear as well. This happened about two years ago. He was healed; there is no doubt in my mind. But how?"

"We shall determine that," Helichar responded. "I want you to visit these strangers everyday that people gather there and observe all that happens. I will send others to do the same. Here are some coins for your service. Remember, report to me only. Leave now!"

The young man bowed low, turned and left, shaking the coins in his purse. He thought: "Perhaps I will earn much more."

Helichar summoned four of the temple priests and divulged his plan to them. From that night on a persecution would grow against the Holy Family which would cause them much suffering.

In the morning Joseph again left before Mary awoke. While on his way a heavy rain fell for a quarter hour causing him to seek shelter. When the rain stopped and the sun appeared a light mist rose from the ground and the air became heavy with moisture. Joseph quickened his pace in order to make up for the delay; he was anxious to arrive at the shop before anyone else. Near the point where he was to cross the canal he again saw the poor families, drenched by the rain, carrying their belongings away from the canal bank and hanging their sleeping mats on the cattle pen fences. Joseph wondered why they chose to live in the open when there were many vacant shelters under the roadway.

Only Merichat, the manager of the shop, was present when Joseph arrived. He greeted Joseph in a friendly and respectful manner. "Joseph you are here before the others. That is good for I wish to speak to you alone. Come with me to my office."

Joseph followed him to an extension of a large building in which the lumber and finished houses were stored. Merichat was well into his fiftieth year; he was tall and muscular. His hair was short, slightly gray and his face was clean shaven. Once inside Merichat sat upon a long narrow table covered with several rolls of paper and turned to Joseph who remained near the entrance.

He smiled at Joseph and said, "I have had many carpenters working in this shop during my fifteen years as manager, but I have not seen one with your talents, Joseph. The sheds you built yesterday were excellent and in so short a time you have won the respect of the others. I am more than pleased with your skills and your attitude. Continue as you are and I will see that your wages are increased. The owners listen to any suggestions I make as long as they continue to reap good profits."

Joseph was not a little embarrassed by his compliments and replied, "It pleases me that you are satisfied with my work. I enjoy working here. The others are friendly and helpful and you are a good man. Whatever wages you pay will be fair I am sure."

"I must warn you though," Merichat said very seriously, "you are an Israelite working in a Egyptian city. The Gentiles, as you call us, are not tolerant of the Jews, who were once our slaves, and have restricted them to live in the poorest sections of the city or in Goshen. Try to remain out of trouble and do not attract attention to yourself outside of this shop. There are many who would welcome the opportunity to persecute you."

Joseph thought of the crowds that would come to visit Mary at the shelter and the ensuing commotion.

"You are most kind, Merichat," Joseph said. "Thank you for the warning. I will try to do as you suggest."

"Good!" Merichat responded. "But now it is time to work. You may return to your position."

Joseph left quickly. He went directly to his station, removed his tools from a small wooden box and began his labors. Once more his thoughts were of Mary and Jesus. He knew that the growing crowds would create a stir but he could think of no way to prevent it. He prayed all the while he worked.

Mary left the shelter with the infant Jesus following her morning prayers. She took with her one of the leather bottles to fill at a nearby fountain and some of the bread she made they day before. Along their route were several homes with idols placed on the window sills and a few with larger statues in their gardens. As Mary and the child Jesus passed them every idol fell over and broke in pieces. The heads of the larger idols cracked down the middle and the halves fell to the ground. Many people came out of their homes shouting and cursing; all were very much agitated about the destruction of their gods. Their behavior greatly disturbed Mary. She walked by quickly keeping her head lowered and her face covered with her veil. Several women and children were at the fountain when Mary arrived; none of them had been in the crowds that came to the shelter and took little notice of Mary and her Babe. She filled the bottle and returned to the shelter.

As she approached the beginning of the elevated roadway she could see small groups of people walking toward the shelter. Mary knew that they had come to see her. As she came near to the entrance the crowd was dense; the people were maneuvering for a place to sit close to the shelter. There was no pathway for Mary.

Suddenly one of the women saw her and shouted, "Here she is. The Hebrew woman that we spoke of."

The people rose to their feet and crowded around Mary and the Child. They pressed forward but no one touched her. Mary stood still with her head lowered and looked upon Jesus' face. Silently she asked for His help. No sooner was her prayer finished when the people began to move aside until there was a clear path to the entrance. Nearest to the entrance was the woman whose boy was healed; he was standing beside her. Behind the woman was the youth hired by the priest, Helichar.

Mary walked up to the woman and said, "I must attend to my child now. Please ask everyone to sit. I will speak to them shortly."

The woman nodded affirmatively and held the screen as Mary entered the shelter. She then turned to the people and raised her arms. The crowd quieted.

"You must be patient a while longer," she shouted. "The young mother must attend to her infant then she will speak to us. Be seated and try not to create too much noise."

Everyone did as she asked except the young man and the other spies sent by Helichar; they wished to remain standing so as to be able to see all who were present and all that took place. Within the shelter Mary stood in the darkness and looked out upon the crowd through the screen. She saw a man supported by crutches among them and some others lying on stretcher-like beds. She pressed the infant Jesus against her breast, kissed His forehead and hands, placed Him in the cradle then knelt before Him with her arms crossed upon her chest. The shelter was dark and cool and the people were quiet. Mary dreaded the thought of going out to them; she preferred to be apart from the worldly minded and to speak little. But her charity toward them compelled her to go out. She changed Jesus' clothing, wrapped Him in a small blue coverlet, cradled Him in her left arm and walked to the entrance. The people were sitting quietly but the spies moved among them. Everyone knew their purpose when they recognized them as the temple hirelings who did anything the priests paid them to do. Mary went to the screen but before moving it aside she bowed her head and prayed.

"Lord, You guide me in all ways as You have promised. You hate those that worship false gods; You love those that honor You and You protect those that trust in You. I am not afraid now because You are with me. Help me to remember all the instructions You gave me that I may explain

Your law to them and will You grant them the grace to accept and obey it. I am Your servant, Lord. Give me understanding that I may know Your testimonies."

She moved aside the screen and stepped out. Immediately those that were ill or crippled where calling to be healed. Their friends or relatives brought them as close to Mary as the crowd would allow. The woman whose son was healed placed herself between Mary and the people.

She raised one arm and shouted, "Listen to me! Listen to me! Be still! All this noise and excitement will frighten this young girl and the child. Sit down! Let her speak and if any of you will be healed, her God will do it."

Their shoving ceased and they again sat down but their minds were occupied with the desire to see a miracle.

Mary went to the woman, placed her hand upon her arm and asked, "What is your name?"

"I am called Thaina," she answered.

Mary said to her, "Thaina, I am grateful to you for your assistance in calming these good people. Now with the guidance of my Lord I will speak to them."

Mary turned to people with her head bowed slightly and her eyes fixed upon the children sitting before her. The people were still murmuring but quieted when they saw that Mary was about to speak to them.

"Look about you!" Mary began. "See how much the natural things of the world reveal God's glory. How clearly they show what He has done. The entire world and all that is in it, and in the heavens above belong to Him. He alone created all things, the one and only God.
No mere man created any of these things, nor could man create Him. But here in Egypt you create your own gods. They are made of many materials, shaped by human hands and surrounded by man made adornments. You may destroy them at your pleasure. Who then has the greatest power, the gods you made or the God Who made you? He is the Lord, our God and His commands are for all the world. He has made a covenant with Abraham, His servant, which He will honor for a thousand generations."

Mary went on to speak to them, of the exile of the Jews from their country, the time when Joseph was a great one in Egypt, how when Jacob came to Egypt and settled there the Lord blessed them with many children and how the Egyptians came to hate them. She spoke of the slavery of the Jews, their great suffering, of Moses and Aaron through whom God did mighty acts and performed great miracles in Egypt. She told them of the people's wickedness and rebellion against God in the desert in spite of all that He did for them; of their golden calf at Mount Horeb made by them and worshipped as a god, of Moses' intercession that turned the wrath of God from them and kept Him from destroying all who turned from Him, of the land that they were given and the many tribes defeated so that they would obey His laws and show their love by obedience.

"Give thanks to the Lord," she declared. "Because He is all good and His love is eternal. I cannot tell you of all the good things He has done, but I can tell you this. You are seduced by the evil one, he speaks to you through the temple priests and the oracles in order to promote worship of your false gods and wickedness. The evil one and his demons are God's avowed enemies. All of Egypt has fallen prey to his influences. Many vile and impure acts are accepted and practiced without restraint. Now, the True and Eternal God has sent into the world the Savior, the Redeemer, the Repairer of all ills who has been promised as it is written in Holy Scripture. He will overcome the evil one and his demons as it is written. And if you do not believe what I tell you, the signs you are about to see will confirm what I say. The Lord, our God will heal the sick that are present; the lame will walk; if there are any with leprosy they will be cleaned; if there are some possessed by the demons, they will be set free. Through my intercession and in the name of the Promised One, let it be done."

Mary lifted the infant Jesus with a hand under each of His arms and presented Him to the people. She moved Him first to the left, then to the right so that He looked upon all who were there and they also looked upon Him. At Mary's feet was an elderly woman on a litter who had been suffering with dropsy; her limbs were swollen with fluid and she was in great pain at all times. Mary reached down with her right hand, touched the woman's right arm and moved into the crowd. Immediately the swelling was reduced and the pain left her; she sat amazed and dumb struck. Mary then moved to a man sitting upon a small wooden crate; he had crutches lying across his paralyzed legs. At the moment Jesus looked at him he felt a warmth flow throughout his body. His legs began to tingle as a limb will do when the circulation is restored; he grabbed his thighs and began to bend his legs.

The old woman, who had been healed, shouted "I am healed! Look at me! I am healed!" Everyone turned their eyes toward the woman.

The paralyzed man now had strength enough in his legs to stand erect.

"And I am healed!" he shouted. "I can stand! I can walk! Praise the God of the Jews! I have been unable to walk since my youth, now I am restored. Praise the God of the Jews!"

The people were very excited. Those that could came to their feet and pressed toward Mary .The temple spies were pushed aside several times but managed to get to the center of the crowd. Mary moved slowly to the right where another woman was propped against a square column. She saw that the woman was very ill; her eyes were partly closed and she was sweating profusely. The woman's son and daughter, both in their late teens, had carried their mother from Goshen a journey of several miles. They, too, were Hebrews that traveled to Egypt to find work and refuge from Herod.

Mary approached the woman and asked, "Are you Hebrews?"

"Yes," the son replied. "We have come here from Goshen. We have heard of you and of the boy who was healed. Will you heal our mother? She has been ill with a fever for several days. The physicians have not helped her and I am afraid she is dying."

Mary was so touched by the son's plea that she wept. The daughter reached out and touched Jesus' hand but said nothing. Mary was aware that something flowed from Jesus to the young girl.

"How are you called?" Mary asked her.

"I am called Arbela. I am a twin of my brother Themeni and this is our mother. Will you heal her too?" she pleaded.

Mary replied, "The Lord, our God, will heal her through my intercession. He alone can heal, I am but His instrument. You will now see His mercy and His power."

Mary placed her hand upon the woman's forehead, closed her eyes and silently prayed. When she removed her hand the woman's eyes opened wide and her color greatly improved. She had not known where she was because of the stupor she was in from the fever.

"She is healed," Mary declared. "Touch her. You will see that the fever has left her. Praise God, the Almighty and the One He sent."

Themeni did as Mary directed; he placed his lips upon his mother's cheek and saw that she was of normal temperature.

"The fever has left her!" he said softly. "The fever has left her!" he said louder. He then turned to the people and shouted, "The fever has left her! My mother is well again."

Themeni turned to Mary and Jesus, fell to his knees and declared, "Oh! Thank the Good God, the Almighty. His mercy endures forever."

He bowed his head and wept unashamedly; his sister Arbela began to weep also. She knelt beside her mother and they embraced.

Suddenly a shout was heard from the opposite side of the crowd; it came from a well dressed man who was brought there by two of his servants.

"And I am healed!" he declared. "I have been healed of the scourge of leprosy. My arms were covered with sores, now they are clean. Look!"

He raised the sleeves of his outer garment and raised his arms. "My servants begged me to come here," he continued, "because of their love for me. I resisted their pleas, but I came and I am healed! It is true, I swear. Praise the God of the Jews. Praise His Holy Name."

The press of the crowd was increasing, making it difficult for Mary to move among them; she moved back toward the shelter.

Themeni turned to the people and shouted, "Wait! Stop! Do not move any closer to her! You are frightening her! How can she move through this crowd if you continue to press toward her? Go back to your places and wait. She will then be able to come to anyone who is in need. Go back! I beg you."

Arbela raised her arms and nodded her head; the people quieted. They realized the young man was right. Several men and woman turned to each other and nodded in agreement. After a few minutes of moving about all were seated and quiet.

Themeni came to Mary and said, "Now you may move among them. I will remain near you in the event they become excited once more."

"Thank you, Themeni," Mary responded, "you are very considerate."

Although Mary spoke to him she did not look at him; she kept her eyes lowered and her face veiled. Arbela returned to her mother. Mary now moved to the opposite side of the gathering; the infant Jesus was quiet but fully aware of all that was occurring. A path opened for her when those before her moved aside. Without warning a young woman, in her early twenties, jumped to her feet, screamed and fell to the ground. She began to shake and convulse violently. Mary was nearly twenty feet away from her but she shrieked, "Woman, stay away from me! I know who you are and the One you hold in your arms. Why do you torment me?"

Her voice changed from one of a high pitch to a very strong guttural sound, "Woman! Stay away!"

Mary stopped where she was and stared at the woman with great pity and compassion. The people watched in awe; they considered this woman to be possessed by something evil; her life was one of many evil acts. She was feared by the children in the area because she struck them whenever they came close to her.

"Do not go near her," one of the men called out. "She can be very violent. She may harm you."

Mary paid gave no heed to his warning and walked directly to the woman still writhing on her back.

"Stay away!" she screamed at the same time raising her hands toward Mary and the Child; her fingers were bent like the claw of an animal about to strike.

Mary bent over her so that the infant Jesus was directly over her head. Mary realized the woman was terribly afraid and about to run off. Mary turned Jesus' face toward her; a small amount of saliva flowed from Jesus' mouth and fell upon the woman's head. In an instant her convulsing ceased and she appeared to be unconscious.

Someone shouted, "Look! She has died."

"She is not dead!" another declared. "See! She is breathing as one does when sleeping."

The young woman had her knees pressed into her chest and her arms wrapped around her legs. Mary reached down and grasped her hand. Immediately the woman's legs straightened and she opened her eyes. She wore no veil as the other women did; her face was very beautiful but covered with too much makeup. On her right cheek there were small painted stars, her dark hair was long, and held in place by jeweled clasps. She would have had many admirers if not for her bizarre behavior. Mary once more touched her hand. The woman smiled at Mary, sat up and looked about; she was unaware of where she was or what had taken place. Two men helped her to her feet then escorted her away from the crowd toward her home. The people were now very quiet. All eyes were fixed on Mary and the infant Jesus. Mary continued to move among the people until all the sick or lame who were present were healed and those in need of spiritual healing received special graces to accept the God of Israel as the One true God. Mary then returned to the entrance of the shelter, turned to the people and asked them to listen to her prayer. No one moved nor did they speak to each other; all were pondering the miraculous healings they just witnessed.

Mary prayed, "My God and King, I will proclaim Your greatness to all. Every day will I thank You; I will praise You forever and ever. The Lord is great, and must be highly praised; His greatness is beyond understanding. Lord, what You have done will be praised from one generation to the next; they will proclaim Your mighty acts. Men will speak of Your glory and majesty, and I will meditate on Your wonderful deeds. You Lord are loving and merciful, slow to anger and filled with love. You are good to all and show compassion on all You made."

Mary entered the shelter and once inside watched the people through the screen.

The temple spies came together beyond the roadway near the temple; they were completely astounded by the events. Of the ten sent by the priest Helichar, five felt that Mary was speaking the truth and the miraculous healings were the acts of her God. The other five were of the opinion that she was a very powerful sorceress.

"What are we to do?" one of them asked. "If she truly is a sorceress we may be subject to her powers if we speak against her, and if her God has done all these things we may be subject to His wrath."

Another declared, "We were hired only to report what we saw and heard, nothing more. Forget your opinions and let us go at once to Helichar. He shall decide what must be done. Therefore, if anyone must suffer, it will be he."

"You are right!" exclaimed another spy. "Let us go quickly before we forget some of the details."

With that they walked away without speaking any further on the matter.

At the shelter Mary continued to give praise and thanksgiving to God; she prayed also for all who witnessed the healings and heard her speak. She asked that those who worshipped false gods would now deny them and worship the One true God. Outside the shelter, the people remained in their places for some time after Mary left them. Those that were healed were the center of attention. Many questions were asked of them concerning their feeling, and how they were before they were healed. After a while, they grew tired of the questions, gathered their belongings and returned to their homes. The wealthy man and his servants left for Matarea, a city not far from Heliopolis. The man who was paralyzed left for his place at the canal that Joseph crossed on his way to the shop. The woman healed of the fever left with her children with the intention of giving thanks in the Synagogue at Goshen and relating all that occurred to their priests.

Helichar was discussing the repairs required to restore the fallen idol with a craftsman when a servant announced the arrival of the ten spies; he was annoyed by the interruption.

"Have them wait in the hall near my quarters," he snapped at the servant. "I will finish with this man first."

The servant went to the entrance where the spies were waiting; he ushered them through a narrow passageway bare of any furnishings but well lighted by oil lamps suspended from the ceiling. They passed several closed doors and saw none of the temple residents. Helichar's quarters were situated at the south east corner of the temple; the rooms were large but not lavish. He presented an image of austere living but in truth he hoarded a great deal of money and jewels left by the worshippers. Almost an hour passed before Helichar arrived. Some of the spies had fallen asleep; they were given a sharp kick against their calves as Helichar appeared.

"Well, you are a sorry lot!" he declared. "What have you to report?"

Four men began to speak at once hoping to receive his attention first.

"Silence!" he commanded. "How am I to listen to you all at once. I will listen to each of you in turn but as I direct."

One by one he interrogated them. Each one gave his version of what took place but offered no opinions. Those that believed Mary to be a sorceress spoke in a manner of ridicule and disdain while those that believed the cures were performed by her God were very descriptive and excited.

"You have done well," Helichar declared. "I wish you to continue your surveillance and to report to me each day."

He opened a small jeweled box placed on a table by the servant, removed a bag of silver coins and gave three pieces to each spy. The young man who spoke against Mary was ecstatic; he had not received such a sum before in his life. Helichar dismissed all of them but the young man.

"What is your name?" Helichar asked. "I am called Abdel," he answered.

"I have listened to your report more intently than the others," Helichar said, "because yours was more factual and you spoke calmly. But I am puzzled by something. I have heard no mention of the women's husband. Does she have one?"

Abdel reflected for a moment then replied, "I am not sure. I have not seen a man with her in their shelter nor have I seen anyone that might be her husband."

Helichar turned away from Abdel and walked to the entrance of his chambers. Without turning around he said, "I want you to determine if she has a husband and if so, what does he do each day. Be at their shelter before daybreak. Follow him and learn all you can about him. Return to me as soon as you learn something:"

He entered his chambers leaving Abdel in the corridor where he stood staring at the silver pieces; he shook them in his fist, placed them in his shirt and walked jauntily out of the temple.

CHAPTER TEN
Miracles and Persecution

It was early evening when Joseph was told to put aside the small shelter he was building.

"Joseph, the sun is setting," Merichat said to him, "it is time for us to stop working. You can finish that shelter tomorrow."

"The day has passed quickly," Joseph answered. "As it does when one is busy."

Merichat smiled and thought: "If I had three more like this man the business would more than double and the owners would be very pleased."

He and Joseph walked together to the shop's exit. Joseph informed him that the Sabbath would begin the following day.

"I must leave the shop early enough tomorrow so as to be home before sunset."

"Why?" Merichat inquired.

Joseph replied, "It is a day of rest that we Hebrews are obliged to take. It is a law of our people handed down to us by Moses. We are to spend this day in prayer and reading sacred scripture. I will not report to the shop the following morning but will return the next day."

"Ah, yes! I recall now the day of rest you speak of," said Merichat. "I do not object to this, Joseph. I wish we Egyptians did the same. Your work has been more than satisfactory and production will increase I am sure. Enjoy your day of rest. Leave now and remember my advice, draw no attention to yourself."

Joseph left with his wages and went directly to the market to purchase additional food and some cloth for Mary. As he was crossing the canal he thanked God, in silent prayer, for the opportunity to work and to provide for Mary and Jesus. At the shelter Mary prepared several small balls of dough and washed the fruit Joseph brought the day before. The people were gone and it was quiet. But Mary felt a dread within her, and she longed for Joseph to be home.

The light was failing when Joseph came to the elevated roadway. He was tired but his spirits were good; he would soon be with Mary and Jesus. As he approached the shelter Mary lit the oil lamps. The light shone through the wicker screen illuminating the area before the shelter and the nearby columns.

"Mary!" he called out.

Mary's heart leaped with excitement at the sound of his voice. She went to the screen and opened it. Joseph entered with a package under each arm. He quickly placed them on the floor and embraced Mary.

"It is good to be with you again, Mary, "Joseph said softly. " And how is little Jesus today?"

"Jesus is fine, dear husband," Mary replied. "Come visit Him for He loves to hear your voice and for you to hold Him."

They walked to the cradle at the rear of the shelter; Joseph saw that Jesus was awake. He lifted Jesus, held Him high before him then drew the Babe to his breast. Joseph kissed Jesus' forehead and each cheek. The joy he felt was almost more than he could bear. Mary stood next to Joseph smiling yet her eyes were filled with tears.

"You are growing quickly little Jesus, and getting heavier," Joseph said endearingly. "I will hold you for a while, while your mother prepares our dinner."

He then walked from the rear of the shelter to the screen and back again several times. He spoke to Jesus as a father does to an infant. Mary carried the packages to the table and opened them.

"The cloth is for you, Mary," Joseph declared. "I know how much you want to make new garments for us. There are rolls of cotton and wool but I could purchase only white and brown."

"These are fine, Joseph," Mary responded. "I will begin sewing after the Sabbath. The day is very long with little to do. Making new garments will help to pass the time until you come home."

"There is a large piece of cheese in the other package," Joseph said. "May we have some with our meal this evening?"

"Yes we will," Mary replied. "I have need of another fire for the bread cakes. Will you start one, please?"

Joseph placed Jesus in His cradle and did as Mary asked. The fire was lit quickly but Joseph realized that not much wood was available now.

"I will search for more wood in the other spaces before retiring," he thought to himself. He then returned to the cradle, sat beside it and continued to talk to the infant Jesus. Mary filled two small bowls with bread, fruit and cheese and set them upon the small wooden stool. Under the stool she placed two goblets of water. During the meal Joseph talked about his day at the shop, his conversation with Merichat and the repeated warning about attracting attention. Mary enjoyed listening to him but the feeling of impending trouble remained within her; especially now after hearing Merichat's warning. When Joseph finished speaking, Mary related all that occurred when the people came. She spoke of their number and the prodigious healings.

Joseph pondered these things for a few moments then said, "I am afraid that we cannot avoid the excitement created by these wonderful things Our Lord has done. This will spread quickly throughout the region, and I am sure that certain Egyptians will be angered by them, especially the pagan priests."

Mary perceived the concern Joseph had for their safety and said, "Dear husband, Our Lord God Almighty has brought us to Egypt in order to escape Herod's wrath; surely we will not be in danger of physical harm now. We may suffer trials and tribulations as we did in the desert but we must trust in His protection. Fear not, Joseph."

Joseph reached for Mary's hand and while gently squeezing it said, "Yes, we are under His protection. I know I should not be concerned. Whatever occurs will be as God Almighty wills it. Blessed be His name."

Following the meal Joseph said the prayers of thanksgiving then he and Mary knelt before the infant Jesus silently adoring Him for more than an hour. With darkness approaching Joseph left the shelter in search of wood, carrying one of the oil lamps. The light from the lamp illuminated only a short distance around him. He entered several spaces but found no abandoned furniture or loose wood. As he exited from one of the spaces he saw something move near one of the columns. It appeared to be a human being but he was not sure. He approached the column cautiously. Suddenly a form moved quickly toward one of the abandoned spaces and entered it. Joseph realized now that it was a man and followed after him.

"Wait!" Joseph called out. "I will not harm you. I want to speak with you."

There was no reply. Joseph continued to search the space. It was larger than the others and the floor was covered with straw. At the rear he found a large pile of straw and behind it was Abdel, the young spy.

"There you are," Joseph said. "Come out into the light so that I may see you. Have no fear. I will not harm you."

Abdel hesitated for a few moments then got to his feet and walked toward Joseph.

"What do you want of me?" he asked.

"I want nothing from you young man," Joseph replied. "I wish only to talk with you."

"About what?" Abdel snapped back.

"Do you live here? And what is your name?" Joseph responded.

"That is none of your concern," Abdel said sarcastically. "You are determined to steal from me. Are you not?"

"No! My friend you are wrong, "Joseph exclaimed. "I have been searching for wood to burn. The nights are cool and our shelter is open."

Joseph saw that the fear was leaving him; so he continued to ask him questions.

"If you do not live here then tell me where you are from. Have you had your evening meal? If not I will return to my shelter to bring you some of our food."

Abdel was hungry. He had not eaten since early morning before he went to the Holy Family's shelter, and he had forgotten to purchase food before the markets closed.

"Yes, I am hungry," he answered. "But I will pay you for whatever you give me."

"That is not necessary," Joseph replied. "I will gladly share our provisions with you. I hope you will not be offended by them. I will return shortly. Remain here."

Joseph left the oil lamp with Abdel, returned to the shelter and gathered together a plate of bread, cheese and fruit. He brought along water as well. Before leaving he informed Mary about the young man then left carrying the provisions in one hand and another oil lamp in the other. He found Abdel lying upon the pile of straw.

"Take this my friend," Joseph said as he handed him the plate of food. At the same time he removed the bottle of water from his shoulder and laid it at Abdel's feet.

"This water is fresh," Joseph said.

Abdel was a little nervous and uncomfortable when he took the plate and said. "Thank you, sir. You are most kind."

"Now tell me your name," Joseph demanded in a friendly manner. "And where are you from?"

"I am called Abdel and I have lived here in Heliopolis for as long as I can remember."

"Do you have relatives in the city?" Joseph asked.

"I have no family. I do not have parents. I live wherever I can and survive by whatever means I can."

"What is your age?" asked Joseph.

"I am not sure," Abdel replied, "I think I am close to twenty years."

Abdel became impatient, turned away from Joseph and began to eat hurriedly. Joseph left him without speaking further and returned to Mary and Jesus .He took with him an armful of straw for their ass and decided to move more of it to the shelter before the Sabbath began. Abdel paid no attention but he noticed the light grow dim. He sat down, ate and drank and thought of the kindness just shown him.

He thought: "At last I have been treated with kindness and consideration. All my life I have had to endure callousness and indifference from my own people. Now a man I do not know, a foreigner, treats me as his brother. He is a good man. I must do something for him in return. After this assignment I will have much silver. I will purchase a fine gift for him."

He finished eating then lay down to rest.

"I must be awake before dawn," he said to himself, "if I am to follow the woman's husband."

He slept and dreamed of the priest Helichar, piles of silver being presented to him and a fine house with servants that was his own.

At the shelter Mary had changed the infant Jesus' garments, nursed Him and placed Him in the cradle for the night. Joseph returned and related to her his conversation with Abdel.

Mary's countenance became very grim.

This caused Joseph to ask, "Mary, you are troubled about something. What is it?"

"Dear husband, I have a feeling of dread within me and I cannot understand what is causing it."

"It is this strange land," replied Joseph. "You are lonely when I am away and you miss your mother and your brothers and sisters. Perhaps if you come to know other families here and visit them you will feel better."

Mary smiled and nodded her head. With that Joseph came to Mary and embraced her, to render to her some comfort, and Mary asked him to join her in prayer before retiring. They knelt next to the cradle where Jesus slept. Mary prayed softly so as not to wake the Babe. Joseph listened until he became quite drowsy then retired to his sleeping place near the screen. Mary went to her couch next to the cradle but continued praying until the hour before sunrise.

At the moment Mary fell asleep, Abdel woke with a start; he was afraid he overslept. He moved to the entrance of the space, leaned against the wall and waited for the first rays of light. Within the shelter, Joseph awoke, dressed quietly then carried water and a basin outside where he washed. He felt the chill of the morning air. The light given off by the oil lamps became weaker as the rays of the sun illuminated the morning sky. Joseph returned to the shelter, placed some cheese and bread in a small pouch which he intended to eat on the way. Before leaving he went to Mary's couch, stood over the cradle and asked God's blessing for Mary, the Child, and himself.

In the meantime, Abdel left the space he was in and moved stealthily around the columns until he was close to the shelter. He was able to see a figure moving behind the screen but only in silhouette. When Joseph left the shelter, Abdel was not able to see his face. He allowed Joseph to travel thirty paces before following him. Each time that Joseph turned his head or changed direction Abdel tried to see his face but could not. At the canal Joseph slowed his pace while looking upon the people still asleep nestled against the stone walls. Abdel came closer. When Joseph reached the bridge the sun had risen above the horizon, it was fully light now. At the center of the span he stopped for a moment and turned to look once more at the poor lying along the canal. Abdel was able to see his face clearly.

"Oh!" he said aloud. "It is the man who was so kind to me."

He did not move onto the bridge as Joseph continued walking along the opposite bank.

"What shall I do?" he asked himself. "What shall I do?"

He crossed the bridge quickly so that Joseph would not get out of sight. His mind was in a turmoil.

"How can I betray this man who helped me?" he thought. "But I must, for his wife is a sorceress. They will do nothing to him. He is only her husband and has done nothing."

He thought of the silver he would receive and resolved to do as he was directed by Helichar. He continued to follow Joseph until he saw him enter the shop; he knew the shop well; he had sought employment there several times but was always rejected by the manager because of his inexperience. When he was sure Joseph would remain within, he returned to the temple where he was allowed to enter the priest's quarters but was ordered to wait in the corridor until Helichar would receive him. After two hours passed without any sound from Helichar's chamber he became impatient. In anger he rapped hard upon the wooden door.

"Who is bold enough to disturb me at this hour," he heard Helichar shouting from within.

"It is Abdel, your servant. I have the information you wanted concerning the woman's husband."

A young boy dressed in a short white tunic trimmed with gold braid opened the door and motioned for Abdel to enter. Once he was inside the boy ran off to another room.

"Come here," Helichar called from his sleeping area. Abdel moved nervously into the room and bowed low.

"Now, tell me what you know," Helichar ordered as he rose from his couch.

Abdel related in detail all that happened from his encounter with Joseph the night before to the moment Joseph entered the shop. Reluctantly he gave the name of the shop and the manager's name.

"I know the shop you speak of," said Helichar, "and I know the owners. You have done well."

Helichar opened a small jeweled box, removed a purse bulging with coins and tossed a bag of coins to the young spy. His eyes opened wide at the sight of so much money.

"You may leave now," Helichar commanded. "Continue to watch this family but report to me in the evening only. I do not wish to be disturbed at this hour again."

"Yes," Abdel said. "I will do as you ask."

He bowed low again, turned and exited clenching the silver coins tightly. Many thoughts of how he would spend them raced through his mind.

Following her morning prayers and after attending to the infant Jesus, Mary busied herself making garments for Jesus and Joseph. While she sewed people began to gather around the entrance. Many more crippled and sick were brought by their relatives or friends. Mary was aware of them but continued with her sewing. No one called for her to come out; the people were patiently waiting for her to appear. Helichar's spies moved among the crowd in order to identify as many visitors as possible. Abdel was there but did not move about; he leaned against the column closest to the shelter and observed the happenings.

It was almost noon when Mary finished an outer garment she made for Joseph that could be slipped over the head and was light enough to be worn in the Egyptian climate. She folded the garment and placed it upon his sleeping mat. Mary saw that the number of people waiting was much greater than the day before. She took Jesus from the cradle, placed a coverlet around Him, held Him against her breast and prayed for several minutes. With Jesus on her left side and her veil pulled tightly across her face Mary left the shelter. All those that were able rose to their feet as Mary and Jesus appeared. The crowd was dense. Mary was concerned about how she would move among them. She bowed her head, prayed silently then moved forward. Without any difficulty a path was made for her in whatever direction she moved.

All the crippled or sick were healed when they looked upon Mary and the infant Jesus, when she came near them or when she touched them. For propriety she touched only the women. A great noise went up from the people. Many began to praise the God of Israel; others began to dance about and sing songs. The din was heard for some distance and was heard within the temple. Several pagan priests left their quarters and with their servants went out to determine the cause. There was a great deal of crying by those that were healed and their relatives, but only tears of joy. Mary wept also. Many Jews from Goshen were present; they shouted praises to the God of Abraham, Isaac and Jacob. The Egyptians listened to the shouts; they wanted to pay tribute to the same God but did not know the words to say. Mary realized this. She moved to the entrance of the shelter and raised her right hand out before her until all were silent. She asked the Jews to join her in prayer and the others to listen intently to the words. She then recited part of the psalm praising the Lord with song and instruments.

"All you that are righteous be glad because of what the Lord has done; praise Him, all you that obey Him! Give thanks to the Lord with the harp, sing to him with stringed instruments."

The older Jews who attended the Sabbath services recognized the Psalm; they accompanied her.

"Sing a new song to Him, play the harp with skill, and sing aloud."

Now the younger Jews who recalled the words joined them.

"The words of the Lord are true, and all his works are dependable. The Lord loves what is righteous and just; His constant love fills the earth. The Lord created the heavens by His command, the sun, the moon, and the stars by His spoken word. He gathered all the seas into one place; He shut up the ocean depths in storerooms. Fear the Lord all the earth! Fear Him all peoples of the world! When He spoke, the world was created; at His command everything appeared. The Lord frustrates the purposes of the nations; He keeps them from carrying out their plans. But His plans endure forever; His purposes last eternally. Happy is the nation whose God is the Lord; happy are the people He has chosen for His own!"

Several of the Egyptians came together near the column where Abdel was standing; they were murmuring among themselves while the Psalm was recited.

"Who are His people?" one of them shouted. "The Jews no doubt!"

"If this is true," another shouted "then we are not heard, nor can we turn to Him in our need!"

Everyone stared at Mary when the man spoke out. Mary was silent for about a minute which seemed a long time to those waiting for her response.

She exclaimed, "God looks down from heaven and sees all mankind. From where He rules He looks down on all who live on earth. He forms all their thoughts, and knows everything they do. All may put their hope in the Lord; He is our Helper and Protector. You will be happy because of Him; trust in His Holy Name."

One of the women gathered at the column interrupted Mary.

"You Jews know the Lord, you know His ways and He listens to you. How could he be good to us who worship another god?"

Mary looked directly at the woman for a moment then with her head slightly bowed answered, 'Find out for yourself how good the Lord is! Happy are they who find safety with Him! Fear the Lord, all you people; those who fear Him have all they need. Even lions lack food and go hungry, but those who obey the Lord lack nothing good."

Abdel was very agitated by the answers Mary gave and disturbed by the healings he witnessed. He stood erect and asked, "Why should we fear your God? What will it gain us?"

Mary answered quickly, calmly and with charity in her voice, "Come my friend, and listen to me, and I will teach you to fear the Lord. Would you like to enjoy life? Do you want long life and happiness? Then keep from speaking evil, from telling lies and worshipping false gods. Turn away from evil and do good; desire peace and do your best to keep it. The Lord watches over the righteous and listens to their cries; but He opposes those who do evil, so that even their own people forget them. Righteous men call to the Lord and He listens; He rescues them from all their troubles. The Lord is near to those who are discouraged; he saves those who have lost all hope."

Her words penetrated Abdel deeply; he could not answer back; he was thinking of the many times he was in despair and had no one to turn to for help.

At the rear of the crowd an elderly man raised his hand seeking recognition then said aloud, "My daughter has been healed by your God, young woman! She was unable to walk for the past seven years. I am not a Jew nor have I ever sought after their God. But deep within me I knew that the Egyptian gods were not truly gods but only man made images. Now I want to know your God and His ways. I intend to seek the truth."

Mary nodded her head toward the man, looked at the infant Jesus and silently gave thanks. She then turned her head from left to right and looked upon all the people.

She looked straight ahead and said, "We must always thank the Lord. We must never stop praising Him. Let us praise Him for what He has done here today. And may all who are oppressed listen and be glad! Proclaim with me the Lord's greatness. Let us praise Him together."

Everyone stood up and faced Mary.

Mary continued her prayer, "I will praise You, Lord, with all my heart. I will tell all the wonderful things You have done. I will sing with joy because of You. I will sing praise to You, the Most High."

Her prayer ended, Mary turned and entered the shelter before the people could move toward her. Once inside she went to the rear, kissed the infant Jesus upon His forehead and eyes and laid Him in the cradle. She knelt beside it and continued to give thanks and praise for the healings and the words given to her.

Outside the people continued to discuss all that occurred. Many of the Egyptians sought out the Jews and asked them many questions about their God. The spies moved among them for a while then at a prearranged signal left for the temple. Abdel went with them.

Mary's prayers were interrupted when a young girl called to her through the screen; it was Arbela the daughter of the woman healed of a persistent fever the day before. Mary came to the entrance when she recognized her.

"My mother sent me to you," Arbela began. "She asked me to invite you and your child to be with us for the Sabbath. Will you come to our home and synagogue in Goshen?"

Mary invited her into the shelter; they walked to the cradle where Arbela looked upon the infant Jesus and spoke endearing words to Him. She suddenly felt something within her that she had not felt before. She turned to Mary, who was staring at Jesus, then looked again at the Child. Arbela sensed the love that passed between them.

He is very beautiful," Arbela said, "and so are you, dear one. Please tell me your name."

"Yes! He is beautiful," Mary responded. "I thank you on His behalf. I am called Mary and I thank you for your invitation. I accept on behalf of my husband Joseph who is of the family of David. We will come to your home early on the Sabbath morn. Tell me how we are to find your home for this is a strange land to us."

Arbela could not give her adequate directions so she said "I and my brother Themeni will meet you at the first ferry that you will come to north of the city. We will guide you from there to our home. Now I must leave so that I may assist my mother with the Sabbath preparations. But before I leave may I kiss the Child?"

"Yes, you may," Mary replied. "His name is Jesus."

Arbela knelt beside the cradle, grabbed the sides, bent over and kissed Jesus' forehead.

"I look forward to the visit," she said to Mary. "The blessing of the Almighty God be upon you, your husband and your child."

"And upon you," Mary responded.

She walked with Arbela to the entrance and watched her walking away until she was out of sight. Mary then began to prepare the evening meal. When the preparations were finished, she was startled by a figure on the other side of the screen; it appeared to be that of a large man. She returned Jesus to His cradle, covered Him then stood in front of the cradle. She did not speak; she was frightened by this dark, silent figure. A few very long moments passed before the person spoke.

"I wish to speak to whomever is in there. Come out so that I may see you."

Mary said nothing; she walked to the screen and stood very close to it so that she could be seen.

"There you are," the man said. "But where is your husband I wish to speak to him."

"My husband has not returned yet," Mary answered. "He is at work in a shop on the other side of the city."

"When will he return?" he asked.

"Just before sunset," Mary replied. "Will you wait until then?"

The man turned to his left and shouted to someone out of sight, "He will return just before sunset."

"Then give the message to the woman," another man ordered.

Mary grew more concerned now; she sensed that these men were there to cause trouble.

The man at the screen looked down at Mary and asked, "Who gave you permission to live in this space?"

"No one," Mary answered, "it appeared to be abandoned when we moved in."

"Well, you are using private property without the owner's approval," the man blustered. "You will have to leave!"

"But there are no other lodgings available," Mary replied. "And we have an infant to care for. Could you ask the owner to allow us to pay rent?"

"No one may use these spaces. The owner plans to build new shops here. He will accept no rent; you must leave. I am instructed to allow you to stay until the morning. If you are not gone by then I and some others, who are not very pleasant, will see that you do leave. You must be gone before I return with them."

"We will do as you say," Mary replied sadly.

The man walked into the shadows of the roadway and disappeared. Mary wept as she walked to the rear of the shelter; she thought of Joseph and how disappointed he would be.

It was nearly three hours passed noon when Joseph was summoned to Merichat's office by one of his fellow workers. He was puzzled by the interruption and even more concerned when he entered the office. Merichat was busy writing on a long roll of paper and did not look up when he heard Joseph enter.

"You sent for me?" Joseph asked.

Merichat turned slowly and stared at Joseph for several seconds.

"Joseph, what have you done?" Merichat asked.

"I do not understand," Joseph replied. "What are you talking about?"

Merichat answered excitedly, "The owners left here a short while ago. They have given me orders to dismiss you, and they say that you will not be hired in any other shop or business in Heliopolis. What have you done to anger them so?"

"I have done nothing to warrant my dismissal," Joseph replied. "Have I not worked satisfactorily?"

"That is not the reason for their action," Merichat responded. "Something else has caused this. What is it?"

Joseph thought of the many people visiting Mary and Jesus and the prodigious healings; he thought also of his words to Mary about the temple priests.

"Merichat, you are a fair man," he said, "and a good man. I appreciate your concern for me. In spite of your warning about attracting attention, it has happened. A great many people have come to our lodgings each day to visit my wife and our child. Many of them have been healed of their illnesses or freed of their possession. This has caused a great commotion in and around the city. I believe the priests are behind this act against me. It was not the owners; they are only doing as they are directed, as you must. I am sad at leaving for now I can no longer provide for my family and we must leave Heliopolis."

Merichat came to Joseph, placed several coins in his hand and said, "I am paying you for what you have done until now and a little extra. I know you can use it. I am sorry to see you go but it must be. Perhaps someday we will meet again."

Joseph objected to the extra wages but Merichat insisted he keep them. He thanked him for his generosity, returned to the shop for his tools and said farewell to the other workers who were very surprised at his dismissal. As he walked away from the shop he thought of the difficulties they would face in search of new lodgings and new employment. But as he did in all situations, both joyful and sad, he earnestly praised and thanked the Lord. This helped him to put aside his anxieties; he felt a peace within that comes only from the Lord and he trusted that all that happens is as the Lord wills it to be.

When Joseph arrived at the shelter, he found Mary sitting beside the cradle with Jesus upon her lap. Jesus was asleep and Mary appeared to be but she looked up quickly when she heard him enter.

"Dear husband, you have returned early today," Mary declared. "How kind of Merichat to allow you so much time before the Sabbath. Come, sit near Jesus and me for we missed you."

Joseph came to Mary, grasped her hand and sat beside her. He then placed his other hand gently upon Jesus' head, bowed and prayed silently.

After a few minutes passed he looked up and said to Mary, "Mary, I have been dismissed. That is why I am here at this hour. Merichat was ordered by the owners to let me go, and they declared that I will not be hired by anyone in this city. It is as I feared, the Egyptian priests have acted against us because of all that has occurred since we arrived. Now we must leave here to find work and lodgings in another place. We shall leave the day following the Sabbath."

Mary perceived how unhappy Joseph was to tell her this. Unhappily she told him of their eviction, "We cannot remain here until the Sabbath passes, Joseph," Mary declared, "we have been ordered to leave this shelter by the owner. We must leave in the morning before they return."

"Well," Joseph sighed, "it seems that the Lord, our God, would have us leave here in haste. It is well that I returned early, I will pack our belongings now and load them on our animal before the Sabbath begins. Now let us pray for all those who have acted against us, and that we may find a place to settle until we are to return to our home."

Following their time in prayer and meditation, Joseph packed all their clothing, food, utensils and water. Only a few items to be left behind and used that night remained on the shelves. When the Sabbath began Mary placed two lamps upon the small stool which was covered by a red cloth and a white cloth placed diagonally over it. Joseph recited from scripture and together they sang psalms. After the Sabbath meal Mary told Joseph of their invitation to the home of Arbela and Themeni in Goshen and that they would be their guides. Joseph was pleased that they would be with other Jews during the Sabbath and he hoped Mary would come to find friends among them. Joseph retired early. Mary washed and nursed the infant Jesus then continued to pray with Jesus in her arms. It was well passed midnight before she lay down to sleep.

CHAPTER ELEVEN
Matarea

The land of Goshen was a large region north of Heliopolis situated between two large branches of the Nile. It was a flat, fertile area that was annually flooded by the river during the heavy seasonal rains. The Jews had dwelt in this region in the time of the Pharaohs but were expelled at the time of the Exodus. Now it was once more occupied by many Jews who left Israel and Judah hoping to find a better life. But they were again despised by the Egyptians who used them only for menial labor and paid them less than all others they hired. Their houses were small, simple and made of mud walls and thatched roofs. Those that farmed their own land ate well and sold their crops in Ramases, the royal city to the north, and Heliopolis and Memphis to the south. They transported the produce on barges along the Nile and via the many canals into the cities.

Arbela and Themeni left their home early; they were concerned that their guests would be anxious if they were not at the ferry to meet them. About an hour after sunrise the Holy Family left the shelter and traveled north along the east bank of the river. Joseph knew the location of the ferry; they passed it on their way to Heliopolis. Once again they came to the place where the idol fell and sank below the water; a small portion of its pedestal could still be seen. The ferry was less than two leagues ahead. Joseph was reluctant to travel on the Sabbath but he was anxious to find new shelter for Mary and Jesus.

They arrived at the ferry well before noon. Arbela and Themeni were on the opposite bank waving and shouting. Joseph waved in return then arranged for the ride across. This branch of the river was wide but shallow enough to allow the ferryman to propel the craft using long poles. Arbela and Themeni were overjoyed when the Holy Family came ashore; they jumped about as younger children do. Mary was happy to see them again and greatly relieved; she knew that soon they would be in their home. Joseph had not met the twins when they came to the shelter but now that he had his heart was warmed by their affection to Mary and Jesus. He explained to them the reasons for having to leave Heliopolis and inquired about lodgings and opportunities for a carpenter in Goshen.

"You must speak with our mother," advised Themeni, "she has been selling our crops in many parts of Goshen since our father died. She knows many people and of many businesses. Arbela and I only farm the land."

"Let us leave here," Arbela added, "our mother is anxious to see you again and to share the remainder of the Sabbath with you. We will be at our home in one hour. There you may refresh yourselves and rest."

The road they used linked the cities of Heliopolis and Ramases; it was used by Egyptian royalty and many caravans. Along the way they passed several inns and resting areas with tables, benches and wells clustered at well traveled and busy crossroads. As Arbela promised they arrived at the edge of their village, Nejel, named after a village in the northern part of Galilee, an hour later. Joseph saw that it was a poor village with houses of mud and stone and straw roofs. The twins' mother saw them coming when they were nearing the center of the village; she hurried to meet them.

Seraphia, as she was called, was tall, slender, dark skinned, had prematurely gray hair and dark eyes. She had celebrated the thirty sixth anniversary of her birth one month earlier. Arbela and Themeni were her first born; three other children were still born. Her husband, Isaac, was ten years older; he collapsed and died in a field he was clearing for planting. Because she had children Seraphia remained an unmarried widow. Their house, which was built by Seraphia's grandfather, was situated at the crest of a small rise at a point where the road turned to the east just outside the village. It was one of the few unattached houses and was made largely of stone covered by several layers of mortar. Its roof consisted of timbers taken from a barge that sank at the edge of the Nile and palm branches which were replaced annually before the rains.

Seraphia greeted the Holy Family warmly; she happily escorted them to her home and assisted Mary with her unpacking. Themeni saw that Joseph received the customary cleansing of the feet then left to unload their belongings and to stable the ass within a large open shed near the house. Arbela stood by Mary while she attended to the infant Jesus. She begged Mary to allow her to hold the Babe. Mary placed Him in her arms and allowed her to hold Him for several minutes. A wonderful, warm feeling flowed through Arbela which caused her to sigh.

"My heart is about to burst! What joy I feel! This Child is not like other children."

Seraphia came to her and gazed upon Jesus, Who was aware of all that was happening; she too felt something within her which she was unable to describe.

"How beautiful He is," she declared, "you are very fortunate, my dear, to have such a child as this. My heart is filled with love for Him and a longing for another child but I fear that I will have no more. My husband died three years ago while working in the fields. He was a good man who loved and feared the Lord, and he was often charitable toward our neighbors and travelers. I miss him very much."

After Mary and Joseph were refreshed Seraphia brought them into a room which was used only during meals and for reading Holy Scripture on the Sabbath and feast days. Seraphia had learned to read shortly before her husband's death; he taught her numbers also so that she could assist him with the trading. Arbela reclined upon the floor near Mary; Themeni sat at the other side of the room with Joseph. Seraphia removed a roll of parchment from a trunk-like box that was kept on a long narrow table on the side of the room facing their tabernacle which was one league north of the village. She handed the roll to Joseph then sat with Mary and Arbela.

Joseph unrolled the parchment scanned the lines for a few moments then read aloud, "Blessed is God, Who gave the Torah to His people Israel. Blessed is He, Who will grant us days that will be all good. Blessed is He, Who makes us worthy of seeing the days of the Messiah and life in the world to come. He is a tower of salvation to His king and shows kindness to His anointed, to David and his seed forever. Eternal God, by your grace, keep us in your commandments, especially in the observance of the Sabbath, this great and holy day. For it was given by You in love for rest and peace. May it be Your will, Eternal God, to give to us such comfort that there shall be no sorrow, tribulations or sighing on this day of rest."

Joseph glanced at Themeni who had his head lowered and his eyes closed. He touched Themeni lightly on the shoulder and presented the scroll to him.

He smiled at Joseph, looked toward Mary and Jesus, opened the scroll and continued reading, "Blessed are You, Eternal God, Ruler of the universe, God our Father, our King, our Mighty One, our Creator, our Redeemer, our Maker, our Holy One, the Holy One of Jacob, our Shepherd and Shepherd of Israel, the good King Who does good to all. As He has daily done good to us forever. As He has dealt bountifully with us, so may He bestow on us with boundless grace, loving kindness and mercy, help, prosperity, blessing, salvation, consolation, sustenance and support, in life and peace and all that is good. And may we never lack of anything good."

He closed the scroll, turned to Joseph and together, as if rehearsed, they said, "So be it."

There was a great deal of joy evident in the faces of Seraphia and her children which caused Mary and Joseph to be lifted in mind and heart to the Eternal God and His Son in Mary's arms. In unison all began to sing psalms and other songs traditionally sung on the Sabbath. It was a most joyful time for Mary and Joseph; they had not been in the company of other Jews since they left the home of Mosoch and Derketo.

Joseph ended the Sabbath prayers with a blessing upon Seraphia, her children, their home and their fields. After which Seraphia and Arbela assisted Mary with the bathing of Jesus and her own ablutions in Seraphia's room. Joseph, too, changed his garments, saw to his ablutions, then sat and talked with Themeni at the entrance to the house. While they talked, Mary, Seraphia and Arbela prepared the food for the second Sabbath meal. The infant Jesus slept in Arbela's bed, which was an open couch in sight of the area, they were working. Mary enjoyed being with Seraphia and assisting with the preparations. She listened as Seraphia spoke of their life in Egypt, their everyday routines, the farming and the selling of their produce. She spoke of her family's migration to Egypt when she was a young girl, her marriage, her parents death during a pestilence that spread throughout Goshen fifteen years earlier, the birth of Arbela and Themeni, her three still born children and the death of her husband Isaac. She spoke at length about him, how much love there was in their marriage and how difficult life was for her after his death.

Mary felt a great deal of compassion for her, embraced her and said, "I know your heart is sad when you think of the past, but do not be sad or troubled. Put your hope and trust in the Lord, our God. Once again you will find joy and praise Him, our Savior and our God. He is our defender, protector, shelter and strength, always ready to help in times of trial. Because He is your defender, no disaster will strike you, no violence will come near your home. And if you wish to honor Him, giving thanks is the sacrifice that will do so."

Seraphia was greatly comforted by Mary's words; she wept as she embraced Mary but they were tears of joy. During the meal Seraphia, Arbela and Themeni continued to talk about life in Egypt for the Jews, the subtle and not so subtle persecution they suffered. The worst being inflicted by the pagan temple priests because of the Jews' denial of their gods. Joseph related to them the persecution they had to endure in Heliopolis and his concern for the well being of Mary and the child Jesus.

"We are now in need of lodgings and I am without any means to provide for our needs,"

Joseph declared. "Where may we go that we will not come to the attention of these priests?"

Seraphia answered quickly, "They watch us very carefully here in Goshen for we are great in number here. But in Matarea there are only a few Jewish families and my husband's sister has a modest house that is vacant. It is in need of repair but I am sure it can provide adequate shelter for you. If you wish I will accompany you to Matarea and speak with my sister-in-law. She is a kind woman and her husband is a good man. They and their children will help you to settle in. As for labor, I do not know what your trade is."

"I am a carpenter," replied Joseph.

"Ah! Then you will have no trouble finding work," Seraphia declared, "there are many shops in Matarea where furniture is made. I recall that many of their cabinets and tables and also couches are sold in Heliopolis. They are always in need of carpenters and so are those that live in Matarea who engage in building new houses or extending them."

"Yes," added Seraphia, "Matarea is the place for you. When you are ready we will leave. It is an easy journey. We will travel by barge along the Nile."

"But stay with us for awhile," Arbela added, "Themeni and I will be very sad when you leave."

Joseph smiled warmly at Arbela, went to her, placed his hand upon her cheek and said, "Your heart is so full of love Arbela, surely you are most pleasing to the Lord, our God. Blessed be His name. We will remain with you for two days more. Then we must leave. If we remain longer word of our presence here may reach the ears of those who act against us. You and your family may suffer even more trials. And you may come to visit us as often as you please. Because you have brethren in Matarea no one will wonder about your traveling there."

"You are right, Joseph," said Seraphia, "and I have business there on occasion. I will try to increase it. We will leave on the morning of the third day but now let us enjoy the time we will have together here."

She began to sing a song well known in Galilee that her mother had taught her. Her voice was strong but she always sang softly. Arbela and Themeni listened with great pleasure; it was their favorite song. Mary and Joseph were pleased also; they had heard it sung many times in Nazareth. Yet it caused Mary to be sad when she thought of her mother, her sisters and all their brethren and neighbors. Joseph saw the sadness in Mary's face and her eyes filling with tears; he knew that Mary was thinking of those they left at home. He began to sing one of Mary's favorite Psalms, which gave much thanks and praise to the Eternal God for the coming Savior. Mary realized his intention, smiled at him then joined in the song. For the remainder of the Sabbath they stayed in the room, praying, singing and reading scripture. When the sun set Seraphia lit three additional lamps and placed them on the narrow table. All recited the Sabbath closing prayers. Joseph and Themeni prayed aloud; the women prayed in silence. Later that night when all had retired, Mary arose from Seraphia's bed; she was asked to sleep in Seraphia's room; it was at the rear of the house where there would be less to disturb the infant Jesus' sleep. Joseph and Themeni slept in a room at the front of the house. Seraphia slept on a couch next to Arbela in the largest room. Mary knelt beside the bed; the cradle was on the same side. Far into the morning she prayed and meditated. When the morning was darkest, the room was suddenly filled with a brilliant light which radiated from the infant Jesus. Mary entered an ecstatic state; her eyes were fully open and fixed upon Jesus. A communication began between them, not of spoken words but interiorly, a locution. Mary, too, became illumined as if reflecting the light coming from Jesus. Her face gave off the most brilliant light but less than the light coming from Jesus. She remained in this state for almost an hour when there appeared before her the angel that announced the Incarnation. He reminded Mary of the awful event about to take place in Israel, the murder of the innocents. But he asked Mary not to tell Joseph until the day of the slaughter which would occur when Jesus was six months old. Mary was again deeply grieved at this announcement; she began to weep bitterly. Just at dawn the light subsided and Mary returned to her normal state. Her heart was heavy when she thought of what the angel told her; she did not sleep.

The Holy Couple spent the next two days in the house, venturing out only to obtain water or to care for their animal. Joseph used his skills to repair parts of the house most in need and he made wicker screens for the windows facing the south and west. Mary assisted Seraphia with her daily tasks and with the preparation of the meals. Arbela and Themeni performed their usual routines in the fields in order to avoid inquiries about them and their guests. When asked by their closest neighbors about the Holy Family, they said their guests were friends who came for a short visit and would be leaving soon.

On the morning of the third day, Joseph and Themeni loaded the Holy Family's belongings on the ass while Mary and Seraphia stored food and water in leather pouches and fruit in one of the long baskets. Arbela remained with the infant Jesus, some time holding Him and at other times speaking to Him while He lay in the cradle. Her joy was great when near the Child; she could feel her heart pounding.

When all was ready they departed, traveling east toward the Nile. Mary rode upon the ass; the infant Jesus was in the sling upon her bosom. Joseph, Seraphia, Arbela and Themeni walked just ahead of the animal. The sky was clear except for a few small clouds north of the village. The road was dry and well worn from the frequent travelers to Ramases. About one half hour later the road turned northward but Seraphia led them eastward along a very narrow road with ruts carved by the farmers' cart wheels. At the intersection of the two roads was a village where no Jews lived; the inhabitants had shops and inns that catered to travelers. Many of the houses had small gardens in which were placed large statues of their god with the body of a lion and the head of a dog. As the Holy Family passed by the village all the statues split from head to tail and the halves crashed to the ground. The villagers rushed from their houses confused and afraid. Some thought an earthquake was beginning while others declared that someone had angered their god. Seraphia, Arbela and Themeni were amazed at what occurred; little did they know the real cause of the destruction. Several of the villagers spied the Holy Family, rushed toward them and picked up large stones. Joseph saw them coming and turned to face them while Mary moved on with the others. When the mob was close enough to hurl the stones they stopped.

One of the men shouted, "You are to blame for the destruction of our god. You are strangers here and you are Jews. You will die for this!"

As they raised their arms to hurl the stones, one of the men ran forward and faced them.

"Wait!" he shouted, "do not harm these people or we will suffer for it. Do you not recall the many plagues inflicted upon Egypt when they wished to leave for their homeland many years ago? And one night all the first born children and first born animals died. There God is very powerful, do not anger Him. Let them pass or we will all feel His wrath."

His words were convincing; they lowered their arms and dropped the stones.

The man who calmed them turned to Joseph and said, "Leave here quickly before their anger is aroused beyond control. Your God protects you still. Go quickly!"

Joseph thanked him and left. Seraphia guided them to a nearby field of high weeds and grass; much of it was as high as Joseph's shoulder. In a few minutes they were out of sight. The villagers returned to their homes still grumbling and making threats against any other Jews who might come near their village. Seraphia quietly guided them through the field for a quarter hour more before returning to the road.

"How much further must we go," Asked Arbela.

"Not far," replied Seraphia, "we should come to a marsh soon. The river is just beyond it."

"Can we travel through the marsh," Joseph asked, "or are we to go around it."

"Yes, we can go through it," she answered. "There is a narrow strip of firm ground that even loaded carts may travel on. All who take their goods to the cities by way of the Nile come to this place. A small pier has been constructed so that the goods can be easily loaded."

As they entered the marsh, Seraphia remarked that it was much drier than usual for there had been little rain. Not long afterward Joseph spied the tops of palm trees that appeared to be in rows. Seraphia indicated they lined the river and they were surrounded by lush grass. Near the trees they saw many white birds with long beaks and long thin legs; the entire flock flew off to the opposite side of the river as the travelers approached. A short distance from the river's edge was a long barge made of timbers and reeds. It was curved at the bow, straight along the sides and had a square stern. A large white sail was supported by a cross beam that was raised or lowered on its mast. The mast was located closer to the bow than the stern. Seraphia called to the men who were busy lowering the sail. Their greeting in return was friendly; they transported her goods often and she paid them well. Using long poles they maneuvered the barge until it was broadside against the pier. The four men, who were dark skinned and bare from the waist up, spoke a language that was unfamiliar to Joseph but Seraphia knew it well. She boarded the vessel and spoke to them for several minutes. They seemed reluctant to take passengers but finally agreed when Seraphia placed some coins in their hands.

She returned to the shore and declared, "They have agreed to take us to Matarea but first they must make some repairs on the side of the vessel. It was damaged when they struck a floating object and caused a leak. It is minor and nothing to be concerned about."

"I am happy," declared Arbela, "now we have more time to be with you before it leaves."

"Yes," Themeni added, "we have time to eat and rest. Let us move under the trees where it is cooler."

Mary welcomed the opportunity to walk about and to attend to Jesus. Joseph, Themeni and Arbela carried the pouches of food and water bottles to the trees and cleared a place for them to recline. Seraphia returned to talk with the men on the barge and to assist them. After attending to the infant Jesus, Mary took the prepared food from the pouches and began to serve Joseph, Themeni and Arbela.

Arbela objected, "I should be serving you, Mary. Please allow me to do so."

Mary replied, " Allow me to serve you Arbela for when we serve we show our love and we receive love in return."

Arbela could say nothing in response; Mary continued to distribute the food and when Seraphia joined them she served her as well. After the repast Joseph carried water to the men on the barge. They received it gratefully and thanked him with a slight bow.

When the repair was complete the men signaled to Seraphia; she in turn informed the others and they gathered at the foot of the pier to say farewell. Arbela wept openly. Themeni embraced

Joseph then kissed Mary and the infant Jesus. Seraphia led Mary to a tent-like covering at the rear of the vessel while Joseph brought their animal to the bow, as directed by the crew, then tied her to a large camel hair rope coiled on the deck. Arbela and Themeni came aboard, embraced Seraphia then returned reluctantly to the shore. As the crew poled the barge into deeper water the two youngsters continually waved farewell. When the men could no longer use the poles two of them went forward and raised the sail. The wind was stronger away from the shore; the white sail was filled by it and moved steadily southward through the calm, silvery water. Mary, Joseph and Seraphia remained standing until they could no longer see Arbela and Themeni then reclined on sacks filled with cotton.

Joseph sat close to Mary. Together they took in all the beauty of the Nile, the terrain on both sides and the many birds and animals. Joseph pointed out a group of crocodiles lying on a small island. Upon their backs were white birds busily pecking at insect parasites that plagued the crocodiles. They made no attempt to snare the birds for the service they rendered. Along the shore on the east bank were herds of animals with short curved horns feeding upon the rich grass. In the trees they saw a large bird, pink in color, building a nest while its mate flew overhead as a sentry.

The beauty of it all caused Joseph to exclaim, "Lord, you have made so many things! How wisely you made them all!"

Seraphia, who was used to these sights, was lifted in spirit by Joseph's words and declared, "All of them depend on You Lord to give them food when they are in need. You give it to them, and they eat it; You provide food, and they are satisfied."

Mary looked skyward, bowed her head toward the infant Jesus and said aloud, "May the glory of the Lord last forever! May the Lord always be happy with what He created. I will sing to the Lord all my life; I will sing praises to my God as long as I live. Praise the Lord, my soul!"

Within an hour and a half the barge was nearing Heliopolis. Joseph pointed out the place where they first saw the Nile after leaving the balsam oasis in the desert. Soon after they passed the sunken idol and the tree that had fallen. No one was at the site; it appeared now to be abandoned. This branch of the great river passed Heliopolis on the west side; several canals left the city and connected to it. Along one of the canals was the shop in which Joseph had worked, and as they passed the city every statue of their false gods, that had not been destroyed, now shattered or split in half. Because the barge was some distance away the Holy Family was not seen; the inhabitants could find no one to blame for the destruction.

"How much further is Matarea?" Joseph inquired of Seraphia. "Not far," she replied, "we should be there in less than an hour. As we approach the city you will see a large white building that will appear to be on the river. It is a storehouse for their cotton and other goods. Matarea is situated on a piece of land that juts out into the Nile but is much higher than the banks of the river. Therefore the city is never flooded when the river rises. We will pass the storehouse then come to a row of cattle pens. Just beyond the pens we will leave the barge. My sister's house is but a short walk from there, and the house you will use is not much further; Before nightfall you will be settled in."

Mary and Joseph were very pleased by Seraphia's promise; they longed to live in a house once again.

As the barge approached the storehouse the river traffic increased. Several small boats and barges passed it going in the opposite direction; they had come from the piers adjacent to the storehouse. Joseph pointed to the many men carrying goods from the barges. He had not seen this much activity since the time he worked in Tyre on the shore of the great sea. Beyond the storehouse was the center of the city; they could see many houses of different sizes and designs. The river curved eastward around the peninsula upon which Matarea was built, then turned sharply to the west. Behind the storehouse were a dozen cattle pens filled with sheep, goats and some of the animals they saw in herds along the river. The crew now steered the boat toward a dock made of stone and timbers with steps rising to a road lined with palm and cedar trees. The Holy Family disembarked while Seraphia thanked the crew. One of the men assisted Joseph with the ass when he saw Joseph was having some difficulty getting the animal to climb the steps for fear of being injured. Finally they got her to the top, helped Mary to the cross-seat then proceeded along the road in a southwesterly direction. In the distance were a line of low rolling hills barren of any trees. Near the hills was a flat arid terrain. Before they reached this dry area they turned toward the south. The terrain became rocky and drier as they traveled. There were no houses, only a few small sheds surrounded by piled stone walls. At the crest of a low hill Seraphia stopped and pointed to a group of houses.

"Below is my sister's home," she said. "The one facing us with four windows close together. Do you see it?"

"Yes," Joseph replied, "it appears to be well built, so do the others."

"They were built by my sister's husband and his brothers six years ago. They know much about building but now they only farm the land and raise a few cattle each year. Come let us go! I long to see them again."

Seraphia hurried down the hill. Joseph and Mary followed but at a slower pace. Seraphia reached the house quickly and entered it. Then as the Holy Family approached she came out with her sister, her sister's husband and their three sons.

"Peace be with you," Joseph called to them.

"Peace be with you," the man answered. "Welcome to our home."

"We are pleased to have you visit us," his wife declared.

Seraphia waited until Mary dismounted then introduced her relatives.

"This is my sister Deborah, her husband Barak and their sons. The oldest, who will be twelve years old soon is called Ehud, his brother, who is eight years old is called Kenaz and the youngest, my favorite, will be seven next month; he is called Joash which was my father's name."

Joseph touched the right shoulder of each boy, bestowed a blessing upon them while they entered the house. Barak performed the ritual of washing the feet of Joseph but Deborah washed Mary's. The three sons crowded around the infant Jesus who was placed in His cradle.

"I have never seen my sons so attentive to an infant," declared Deborah, "What can be the cause I wonder?"

Mary made no reply, nor did Joseph.

Seraphia exclaimed, "Arbela felt much love for the Child! She was almost overcome with joy when she held Him."

Deborah and Seraphia went to the cradle; both felt a warmth flow through them as they gazed upon the Babe. The three boys knelt beside the cradle and stared at the Him in silence.

"Come! Let us take Joseph and Mary, and the Child, to our other house," Barak declared, "so that they may be settled in before dark."

"How far is it to the house?" Joseph asked.

"It is not far," Barak answered, "we will be there in a short time."

He called to his sons, "Come boys! We are leaving."

They went to him without delay. On the way Barak described the house to Joseph and the repairs it would require; the women discussed the furnishings and the facilities it had. The oldest son, Ehud, guided the ass while his brothers rode upon the cross-seat. Joseph saw that the area was barren of trees except for some very large oaks near the road and he noted the poor construction of the houses they passed. He hoped he might do repair work for the inhabitants. Barak led them to a property with low stone walls running alongside a small mud and stone house. Near the house was a shed used as a stable. Between the stable and the house there was a narrow, stony brook which ran parallel to one of the walls. Two large oak trees stood together at the rear of the property which was nearly two acres in size. Mary entered the house with Joseph; he saw that it was well made. The roof was sound and in the center was a stone fireplace with a hearth open on two sides. There were two windows in the front and rear walls and in one of the side walls. The fourth wall was made of stone held in place by a brownish mortar. Window shutters made of thick wood were lying on the stone floor. Near the rear wall stood a wooden table with three stools stacked beside it. A heavy layer of dust covered everything, and a thin layer of brownish sand covered the floor. With his three sons, Barak unloaded all that was on the ass, including the cross-seat, and left everything outside near the entrance. Deborah and Serpahia fabricated two sweepers from the high grass near the brook and proceeded to clean the house, while Mary attended to the infant Jesus. Mary afterward saw to the cleansing of their utensils and a few dishes they brought with them and placed them in a cabinet built into the wall near the table. Using his tools and skills Joseph repaired and rehung the wooden shutters and installed a wood latch on the entrance door. Next he climbed to the roof, gave it a close inspection and laid on new grass wherever needed. By late afternoon the house was secure against the weather. When the cleaning was finished Seraphia prepared a cold meal.

After prayers of thanksgiving and a blessing upon the house everyone sat upon mats on the floor and ate. Joseph asked many questions of Barak about the people living nearby and the availability of food and work. Barak stated that the people nearby were mostly poor Egyptians but there were a few Jewish families. He complained of the poor soil and the meager crops.

"Many of the men work in Matarea proper," he said, "and obtain food at the city markets. The Egyptians in the city have little respect for the Jews and hire them only when they are in desperate need of labor. But the poor families nearby have much less arrogance. They will hire you but pay little for they have not much to spare."

"I must find work as soon as possible, "Joseph declared. "Do you know where a carpenter might be needed?"

Barak thought about this for a few moments then replied, "You may find work in the city proper. There are many buildings under construction."

"I am reluctant to go into the city," Joseph said in return, "we must not come to the attention of the pagan priests as occurred in Heliopolis. Where else may work be found?"

"Well," Barak answered, "you will find that much work is needed on the houses in this area but you will not be paid much for your services."

"I will accept whatever they can give," Joseph replied, "even if it is little."

Mary interjected, "And I can help by sewing or weaving garments. I am sure we will manage."

Seraphia added, "And I will send you vegetables and fruit from our harvest whenever it is shipped to Matarea. The men who own the barge will see that they are delivered."

"I must warn you about the water coming from the brook," Barak declared. "It has a bitter taste and becomes very clouded when the heavy rains come during early spring. There are no wells nearby or in Matarea. The city dwellers and the people in this area cart water from the river."

"Are there balsam plants near here?" Joseph asked.

"None that I know of," Barak replied.

Deborah interrupted them, "Husband, I think we should leave now so that we may arrive home before the light fails, and our guests are tired."

"You are right," Barak said, "and I am sure they wish to be alone for a while. We shall return tomorrow to help with the remainder of the chores."

When Deborah called their sons they came to her reluctantly; they wished to remain beside the infant Jesus. She and Seraphia left with the boys while Joseph and Barak discussed further the repairs needed on the exterior of the house and a section of the stone wall, then he too left. While it was still daylight Joseph walked through the property at the rear of the house. Within Mary attended to the infant Jesus, singing as she moved about. Joseph could hear her from any part of the property; he was delighted to hear her singing again and thought: "Perhaps things will be better for us but as You will Lord our God, as You will."

He returned to the house, cleaned the hearth then built a fire with branches that had fallen from the oak trees. As he stood before the fireplace Mary came to him with the infant Jesus in her arms.

He turned, embraced Mary and said, "The Lord, our God, has brought us to this place far from our home but far from Herod' s power. He has provided this house for us through our friends. Here we will remain until we are told to return to Judea. Let us give thanks for all that the Eternal God has done for us and will do for us in the future. As we are in His hands and the Promised One is with us, of what shall we fear."

"Let us now kneel and give thanks and praise," Mary added. "We shall sing to Him, be glad that we belong to Him, and be glad that we are in His care. He, the Lord, is our God; His commands are for all the world."

Mary gave the infant Jesus to Joseph, placed two oil lamps on the table she had covered with the veils given to her at Heliopolis, then knelt with Joseph before the table.

Joseph began the prayer, "O Lord, I am not bothered by great matters, or with things to difficult for me to understand. But I am content and at peace as the One You sent lies quietly in my arms, so my heart is quiet within me. I thank You, Lord, with all my heart; I sing praise to You before all men. You answered me when I called to You; You strengthened me with Your strength. Even when we are surrounded by troubles, you keep us from harm. You have opposed all our angry enemies, and saved us by Your power. I know You will do everything You have promised; Lord Your love is always constant. Complete the work you have begun."

Mary moved closer to Joseph so that their shoulders were touching; with her head bowed and one hand upon Jesus she began to sing a psalm of thanksgiving. When she was finished Joseph placed the infant Jesus in the cradle before them. Silently they adored Him and meditated upon all that had occurred from the time they departed from Nazareth before Jesus' birth to that day. Although they knelt upon the stone floor for nearly an hour any discomfort they endured was hardly noticed; they were so deep in thought. Joseph stood first, placed a few branches on the fire then walked about the house. Mary began to prepare the food for the evening meal.

Later while they were eating Joseph said, "Tomorrow I will spend time making this house more livable. I will make dividers for our sleeping places and platforms for our bedding. We should not sleep upon this floor. It is damp and there are insects. Our friends will return to assist us, much can be done. On the next day I will seek work at our neighbors' homes."

"Remember, dear husband," Mary added, "to inform our neighbors of the weaving or sewing I will do and I will accept whatever they are willing to pay. In this way we will come to know them and it will add to whatever you may earn."

Joseph nodded in agreement and promised to build a loom for Mary's weaving. After the meal he left the house carrying an oil lamp; he gathered two armfuls of grass for their animal and allowed her to drink from the brook. The night air was cool and the sky was clear. Joseph looked up and marveled at the number of stars. He thought of Abraham and God's covenant with him. He returned to the house all the while praising God for His magnificent creations.

CHAPTER TWELVE
Slaughter of the Innocents

It was the month of Sivan; summer was just beginning. Jerusalem was astir about the reports of debauchery, drunkenness and the lavishness of Herod's birthday celebration within the palace gardens, filled with many guests. Included were the officers commanding the soldiers garrisoned at Hebron, Gilgal and Bethlehem. No expense was spared in their entertainment and each was given a bag of silver coins and semi-precious stones. On the morning following the spectacle Herod's servants found him sprawled across some silken pillows in his private chamber. He was in such a sound sleep they had difficulty waking him. After several attempts he stirred, opened his eyes, looked to his left and right then suddenly sat erect.

"Where is he?" he shouted. "Where is he?"

"Whom do you seek, sire?" asked his body servant.

"The new king of the Jews," he replied. "He was in the courtyard! I saw him sitting in my chair. Call the guards! Find him!"

"Sire, you must have been dreaming," said the servant, "there is no one within the palace that should not be here. But if you wish I will summon the guards."

Herod stared at the servant for few moments then said, "You are right. It was nothing but a dream."

Two other servants helped him to stand; perspiration stained the front and rear of his garments and his hair was in disarray. His servants prepared a bath for him and a change of clothing. They knew well his moods following a tormenting dream.

"Summon Nabat!" he commanded. "I will speak with him in the ante-chamber. Let no one be present or enter until summoned."

Nearly an hour passed when Herod entered the ante-chamber. Nabat greeted him with a low bow then watched as Herod made certain that no servant was near the doors before closing them. He motioned to Nabat to join him at the center of the room.

Nabat thought: "His behavior is very strange. I wonder what this fox is up to now."

"I have had the same dream!" Herod said excitedly. "It occurs more often now. As always the figure of a man, whose features I cannot discern clearly, is moving about the palace, watching and waiting. This man moves into the courtyard where he sits upon the Judgment chair. Before him are the three kings who recently came to Jerusalem and many people. They bow low to him and salute him as their king."

Herod paused for a moment, wiped his brow then continued. "I must find this child and his family. Why have the three foreign kings not returned as I asked? Where can they be?"

Nabat answered, "Sire, a report has come to me that they have left Judea by a southern route. I am certain they will not return to Jerusalem."

Herod's face flushed from anger. He hurled his drinking cup across the room where it smashed against the door to his chambers. The noise startled his servants within but no one dared to inquire about the cause.

"Well, now we must find the child by other means. The scriptures declare that of Bethlehem-Ephrata the ruler will arise. Issue a proclamation in Bethlehem and the surrounding villages that all women who have given birth to a male child within the passed year, no, the passed two years are to receive a special gift from my hands. Instruct them to bring the children with them and they are to assemble in the courtyard of the soldiers' billet in Bethlehem."

"Yes, sire," Nabat responded, "but on what day shall they assemble?"

"Set the time for the day before the third Sabbath of this month. That will be ample time for the proclamation to be made known and for the women to arrive. You may leave now, but return to me in three days. I will have further instructions at that time."

Nabat bowed, backed away from Herod until he was at the door, then turned and exited the ante-chamber. Herod paced back and forth for quite some time before returning to his private chambers with his fiendish plan fully formed in his mind. He was confident of its success. Until the day before that terrible day Herod occupied himself in many matters and attended the nightly festivities within the palace. All who were in his presence were amazed at his jovial mood, and his servants were pleased that his sleep was no longer disturbed by tormenting dreams.

One of his aides remarked, "He appears to have a great burden lifted from him."

Herod left Jerusalem that night accompanied by Nabat and one hundred of his personal guard. His wife and her followers were ordered to remain within the palace until his return. A great commotion was created when Herod arrived at Bethlehem. Many of the women had arrived with their children and were accompanied by their husbands, especially those that came from the most distant villages. At the billet Herod called together the officers in a room used for their dining. Nabat was not present; he was sent on an errand to the elders and the Roman officer quartered in the former residence of Joseph's family. Herod first presented a bag of gold coins to each of the four officers, and proceeded to explained to them his plan. At first they were concerned about the act and the reaction of the people in the area. But Herod assured them that if they did not do as he asked they would lose their lives before the children. He also assured them that the Romans would squelch any uprising by the people. He ordered them to select four teams of six men to act as the executioners. One of the officers suggested the women and children be placed in the soldiers dining hall where there would be enough room. Another suggested the women be brought into the courtyard in groups of twenty which would be easier to control, then led to another section of the billet where additional soldiers would prevent them from leaving before the slaughter was completed. Herod approved their suggestions and declared that all the minor details would be their concern. That night, while Herod slept in a nearby villa, the officers selected six men from each of their companies that would be capable of performing any act without question or hesitation. These men were granted extra rations of food and wine. Others were assigned to the control of the women and were ordered to maintain order no matter what occurred.

The morning sky was overcast and a light rain began to fall as the women gathered at the main entrance to the billet. Some were pushing their way to the front in order to enter first. A small detachment of soldiers left the billet to restore order. More and more women arrived at the building as the morning wore on. At precisely ten o'clock trumpeters standing at the edge of the roof announced Herod's arrival with a series of long blasts on their instruments. Excitement ran through the crowd of women.

The billet was a formidable building with exterior walls made of large stones and mortar about one story high. Above the wall one could see the second floor of the soldiers' quarters. The entire structure was rectangular in shape. The courtyard was completely enclosed so that once inside no one could be seen or heard from without. Herod positioned himself in a second floor room, opposite the main entrance, from there he was able to look down upon the women and children as they entered the courtyard. A small cushioned chair was placed near a large opening; around it stood the officers of Herod ' s personal guard. Herod wore a purple mantle trimmed with white fur and a solid gold crown rimmed with small rubies.   At his signal the gates were opened. The women rushed into the courtyard then formed small groups of five or six. Some allowed their children to run about but most held them close to their side. Another signal from an officer brought thirty soldiers armed with spears from the lower rooms. They escorted the women and children into the dining hall, telling them they would receive refreshments while waiting their turn. Nearly a half hour passed before all the women passed through the gate. Their husbands were turned away by the soldiers in a gentle manner so as not to alarm them. One of the officers came to Herod with a count of 630 women and approximately 720 children. Shortly after eleven o'clock the last of the women and children entered the dining hall. As promised there were tables upon which were plates of small cakes, large bowls of fruit and many cups filled with cheap wine and water. The soldiers within the hall had no trouble maintaining order although the women and children were crowded together. While the women ate and drank more soldiers entered the hall moving slowly along the walls. One by one they stationed themselves before the windows. At a signal from an officer the soldiers closed and locked the heavy wooden shutters on each window. Suddenly the women became nervous and frightened. The soldiers calmed them with various reasons for closing the shutters. Yet the women began to look about nervously and speculated among themselves concerning Herod's motive for summoning them.

Precisely at noon a trumpet sounded in the courtyard and the doors to the dining hall were opened. Twenty women and their children were led into the courtyard. What they saw did not alarm them. At the opposite end of the courtyard was a large chair covered by a striped tent. To the right of the chair was a long, high partition made of wood lattice draped with purple cloth. Nothing could be seen beyond it. The women were positioned in a single file before the chair. They were told to look only at the chair. A line of twenty soldiers moved behind them.

An officer came from behind the chair and shouted, "Now!"

Each soldier quickly wrapped a cloth around the women's heads, gagging them. At the same time a second group of soldiers rushed forward, pulled the children from their mother's arms and hurled them over the partition. The women's hands were bound and quickly led through a large opening behind the chair that led to the soldier's sleeping quarters. The children were heard crying behind the screen for a few moments then all was silent. The first slaughter was accomplished in less than three minutes from the moment the women were led from the dining hall. Herod complimented the officers for their efficiency and directed that the killing continue. A second group of women and children were led into the courtyard; they suspected nothing; not a sound was heard within the dining hall. As before the women were gagged and bound while their children were slaughtered behind the partition. Within the soldiers' quarters the women hurled themselves against the stone walls, gashing their heads. Blood flowed freely across their faces, through their hair and onto their garments. They then fell upon the floor and rolled about wildly for their grief was more than they could bear. A company of soldiers assigned to control the women was stationed in the adjacent quarters. As more women were brought in the number of soldiers in the room was increased. Without interruption the slaughter continued; Herod and his officers watched stoically from the second floor room.

At midday Joseph returned from a nearby house where he had repaired and rehung a door. For his labor he received a few copper coins and a brightly colored urn made by the woman's husband shortly before he died. Before entering the house Joseph carried an armful of fresh grass to the stable trough and filled a bucket with water from the brook. The water was not as bitter as it had been and the color improved. He and Mary disliked the brook water but it was their only supply. He thought of the well water at their home in Nazareth that was sweet to the taste and always clear; he thought of the water they drank from the desert oasis on their way to Egypt, resolving to return to the oasis for a supply. On his way to the entrance Joseph had to pass close to the window near Mary's couch. As he did he heard both Mary and the infant Jesus crying. He was greatly perplexed and ran quickly to the entrance and entered. He found Mary kneeling near her couch with the Child in her arms. She turned to Joseph then lowered her head; he could clearly see the tears flowing upon her face. In that brief moment when she looked at him, Joseph saw great sorrow in her eyes and face.

"What is wrong, Mary?" he asked. "Why are you in such sorrow? Is there something wrong with Jesus?"

Mary stood up, turned to Joseph, reached out and grasped his hand.

"Dear husband," she began, "at this moment a terrible event has begun in Bethlehem."

"How do you know this?" asked Joseph.

Mary replied tearfully, "When we were guests in the home of Seraphia, the same angel that announced to me the conception of Jesus appeared to announce a second time Herod's plan to destroy the Promised One by the slaughter of all male children born in and around Bethlehem within the past two years. This brutal and abominable act, shedding the blood of the innocent, has begun; many children are now being murdered. Come join me in prayer for the grieving mothers and the little victims."

Shocked by this news, Joseph fell to his knees and wept bitterly with his hands covering his face. Mary's heart felt as though it would break when she saw Joseph weeping so. She understood now why he was not to be told earlier for he could not have endured the sadness for so long a time. She then knelt beside him. Mary pressed Jesus to her bosom in order to comfort him; He was aware of the suffering of the little martyrs and their mothers.

When Joseph regained his composure he asked, "What of your cousin Elizabeth and her son John? Do you know of their fate?"

Mary replied, "The angel said they would find a place of safety. "

"Let us pray," declared Joseph, "for all those suffering now and those who will grieve for them. I recall the words of the Prophet Jeremias, 'Thus says the Lord; a voice was heard on high of lamentation, of mourning, and weeping, of Rachel weeping for her children, and refusing to be comforted, because they are not.' "

Joseph was bent over while he wept; now he straightened, raised his head and began to pray aloud. "Lord, I look to You, up to heaven, where You reign. As the servant depends on his master, and the maid depends upon her mistress, so we keep looking to You, Lord our God, until You have mercy on us. Be merciful to them, Lord, be merciful; they have been treated with so much contempt!"

For nearly an hour the Holy Couple knelt side by side praying fervently, when Mary placed the infant Jesus in Joseph's arms, sat back on her legs and bowed low until her face was almost touching the floor. She moaned and cried so pitifully causing Joseph to ask.

"Mary, what are you feeling or seeing now?"

Mary did not answer immediately; she was in great sorrow. Several minutes passed when she was able to answer.

"Oh! Dear husband, I can see the terrible treatment of the innocent ones. I can see also their mothers thrashing about in a dark room. Their hands are bound behind them and they are unable to cry out because a cloth is tied tightly across their mouths. Behind a screen Herod's soldiers are piercing the little bodies with spears and swords. But all around them I see many angels; they are visible to the children and are comforting them. The Eternal God, our Lord, has given them a grace to understand why they are being martyred and the ability to pray. Many of them, before death, are praying for their parents and their executioners. Oh! What an evil and wicked act Herod is guilty of; he shall be despised for all generations to come."

Mary and Joseph did not speak again until the last of the children was put to death.

For almost three hours the slaughter continued without interruption. Herod remained in his place through it all; he was unaware of the anger building in the soldiers below. As each group of women and children were led to the courtyard several soldiers turned toward Herod hoping for a signal to end the senseless slaughter, but none was given. The plan was perfect. Not one woman in the dining hall was aware of what had occurred in the courtyard. In the soldiers' .quarters several hundred women in utterly perfect grief were now so crowded together that not one could fall to the floor or move about. Dozens managed to loosen their gags by snagging them on the pegs used to hold the soldiers uniforms. Their screams and curses were horrendous and their cries now carried to the exterior of the billet. Husbands and relatives waiting for them became alarmed and began to shout for their wives and children. They pounded on the heavy wooden gates until a company of soldiers rushed out to disperse them and to tell them their wives would be released before the start of the Sabbath. Reluctantly the men did as ordered and so too their relatives but moved only to the streets nearby. Many men climbed to the roofs of houses where they could see the walls of the billet but could not be seen by the soldiers.

Within the billet Herod bestowed many compliments on the officers for their efficiency. He was informed that 717 children has been killed and he was assured that no male child in that region had escaped death. Herod gave an order to have only Gentile men living in the area dig the large grave following the release of the women. The children were buried in the courtyard. He also ordered the soldiers to escort the women out of the city even though they lived within it, and to hold them out of the city until his departure.

Finally the order was given for the release of the women. All of the soldiers, except those guarding Herod and those overseeing the men digging the grave, were to escort the still shrieking women out of the billet. A great tumult went up when those waiting for them learned of the slaughter. Their husbands tore their garments and covered their heads with dust from the streets. Young men hurled stones at the soldiers, cursed them and cursed Herod.

"May Herod's name be cursed and despised by all generations to come," they shouted repeatedly. "The blood of the innocent be on him, his children and his children's children."

The women were little trouble for the soldiers; exhausted by their grief they moved out of the city without resistance. Concerned for their wives' safety the husbands followed peaceably. Herod left by chariot accompanied by his personal guard; no trumpets were sounded so that he might leave unnoticed. In less than one hour he would be in his palace in Jerusalem. He had little respect for the Sabbath law or any of the Jewish laws but pretended to follow them to avoid criticism from the priests.

News of the slaughter spread quickly throughout Judea; the entire province was lamenting.

Many cried, "How long, O Lord, must we tolerate the acts of Herod. When will you send us the Promised King?"

CHAPTER THIRTEEN
Life in Matarea

On the eve of the first anniversary of Jesus' birth Mary spent the hours before retiring embroidering a small border of yellow flowers on the hem of the soft, woolen garment she had woven for Jesus. Mary sensed He would walk soon; she had been helping Him to take His first steps during the past week. The garment was light brown and made in one seamless piece with a small opening at the center.

"Perhaps Jesus will walk in the morning," she thought. "How pleased Joseph will be."

Jesus was beside her asleep in his cradle. Joseph was behind the house filtering their drinking water through a large ball of cotton cloth. The filter removed much of the brownish sediment but the bitter taste remained.

Upon entering the house with the filtered water he said to Mary, "Day after day the condition of the water worsens and the river water is just as bad. It is not good for us to continue drinking it. When I have finished the repairs on our neighbor's stable, two days hence, I will leave for the well at the oasis we came to in the desert. I will return within two days with as much water as our animal can carryon its back and with a few balsam bushes to plant near the stream."

"If you must go," Mary said, "please take Barak's oldest son Ehud along to help and to have someone for company."

"I will speak to Barak tomorrow," Joseph replied. "And I will ask him for one of their asses. In that way we may return with water for his family as well. But now I must retire for the day has been long and I am tired."

He embraced Mary, bent low to kiss the infant Jesus then retired to his sleeping place. Mary continued sewing. Many poor women brought cloth and fibers to her rather than do the work themselves. The quality of Mary's work far surpassed any of the tradesman in Matarea and the surrounding villages. Her reputation for excellent needlework and weaving was growing. But she refused requests to make items solely for reasons of vanity and extravagance. Rich women of Matarea who personally brought work to her were indignant when Mary refused to grant their requests. Often she was ridiculed and talked about scornfully among them. When servants brought the work Mary sent them away with short messages of admonition for their mistress. What little income she realized she gave to Joseph to add to the meager payment he received for his work. Mary finished the embroidery just after midnight, placed the little garment on a device Joseph devised for stretching cloth then knelt beside the cradle to say her nightly prayers and to meditate. Several times her meditation was interrupted by thoughts of the journey Joseph must make to obtain fresh water. She was concerned also for her neighbors who were forced to drink the stream water for so long. She lifted her concern to the Eternal God through the infant Jesus in a short prayer. The moment her prayer ended she entered an ecstatic state. Suddenly the small house was filled with a brilliant light and the most beautiful sounds of angelic voices, and there appeared before her the angel who came to her in Nazareth.

"Mary be not concerned for Joseph," the angel declared, "he will not journey into the desert for water. Take with you Joseph's staff; scratch the surface of the soil near the two oak trees; fresh spring water will flow from it. Joseph is to build a wall of stone to contain the water which will not fail for as long as you remain in this land."

The angel then knelt on the opposite side of the cradle silently adoring the infant Jesus with Mary. After several minutes in silent prayer the brilliance of the heavenly visitor's light diminished slowly until he vanished. Mary recovered from her ecstasy in great joy giving praise and thanksgiving to the Eternal God. She continued to do so until first light when, following the angel's instruction, she took Joseph's staff, and with the infant Jesus in her arms went directly to the two trees at the rear of the property. Near the trees the vegetation was dark green and very dense. Between the two trunks Mary spied a shallow ditch about the length of a man and no wider than a spade. While straddling the ditch, she scratched a small furrow in the center with the worn end of the staff. Immediately water flowed into the ditch. Mary saw that it was clear; she drew up a palm-full and tasted it. It was cold and sweet. In great joy she rushed back to the house to inform Joseph. Upon hearing Mary's account of the angel's visit and the discovered water, Joseph rushed out to the site. He found the ditch full and about to overflow. He fell to his knees, took in one mouthful, and then swallowed it slowly. The taste was exquisite. Using his hand he dug around the ends of the ditch. After removing a few inches of dark, moist soil he discovered the edge of a large, flat stone. Noticing chisel marks on the side, he returned to the house to obtain a spade and his tools. Mary remained near the trees with the infant Jesus. Joseph removed all the soil from the stone and placed it around the ditch to form a reservoir. Although the water was several inches deep now he could clearly see the soil and vegetation at the bottom. He soon had the stone uncovered; it was approximately four feet on all sides and four inches thick. Joseph placed a large rock about one foot away from the stone's edge. Using it as a fulcrum he slowly raised the slab with his staff. Below he discovered a well, dug many years earlier, lined with fieldstones and mortar. As the angel directed, Joseph began to build a wall of stone around the opening. Field stones were plentiful and the soil made good mortar when mixed with straw and fine gravel from the stream bed. He worked unceasingly without any thought of eating or taking rest. Mary brought out two leather bottles which he filled and a small basket of fruit, but he ate none of it. Mary knew that he would not rest until the wall completely surrounded the opening. After nursing the infant Jesus, Mary removed His swaddling-clothes and bathe Him in a basin of water she had warmed in the sun. She then placed fresh under-garments on His little body and the brown tunic she had woven.

While Jesus lay on her lap Mary spoke to Him in endearing words. "My son, my Lord and love You have endured the discomfort of swaddling-clothes long enough. Now I place this tunic on You so that You may walk. It is my gift to You on the anniversary of Your birth."

Within her she heard Jesus reply, "My Mother because of the love I have for all mankind, whom I have come to redeem, I was not bothered by the wrappings for when I am a grown man

I shall be bound again and delivered into the hands of my enemies, and it will be sweet to me because of my love for all men. I wish to possess only this one garment during my lifetime. I seek only that which is sufficient to cover me. This tunic only will I wear for it is your gift to me, and it shall grow with me. But one day men shall cast lots for this garment; nothing shall be left to me so that all men shall know that I was born in poverty, lived and died in poverty. So that I may be an example to them and teach them to despise all earthly things that darken their hearts. I wish to show the entire world that it must love poverty and not hate it; for I, who am the Lord of all creation, reject and repudiate all earthly possessions."

Mary was filled with abundant gratitude for the love Jesus had for all mankind; she vowed to imitate the same virtue for the remainder of her life.

She then covered Jesus little feet with sandals made of soft hemp and placed Him upon His feet. For a few moments He held on to Mary's dress then stepped forward and walked unsteadily to the front entrance. He placed both hands upon the wooden latch, turned around slowly and returned to Mary all the while smiling and reaching out to her. Mary was overjoyed at this immediate progress; she lifted Jesus, embraced Him and kissed Him. Jesus kissed her in return. It was a moment of unspeakable joy for Mary and she wished to share it with Joseph. She went to the rear window and called to him. Joseph dropped the stone he was about to set and ran to the house.

"What is it, Mary?" he asked. "I sensed excitement in your call."

Mary held Jesus out to Joseph and said, "We have a surprise for you dear husband. Place Jesus on His feet then let go of Him."

Joseph did as she requested. Jesus leaned against Joseph's legs for a moment then after a glance at Mary walked away from him. Joseph was utterly surprised and greatly pleased. Jesus walked to Mary and stopped. Mary lifted Him and began to weep for the joy she saw in Joseph.

"He is beautiful in His new tunic," Joseph declared, "and it fits Him perfectly. It just barely touches His little feet and the sleeves extend to the middle of His hands. It is a marvelous garment Mary!"

"He will wear it for the remainder of His life," Mary said but sadly for she thought of the time when men will cast lots for it.

"Will you lengthen it as He grows?" Joseph inquired. "It will grow with Him and it will not be soiled or damaged until it is taken from Him," Mary replied. "But I know not under what circumstances or when it will occur."

At that moment Mary lowered Jesus to the floor and He walked directly to Joseph without any unsteadiness. Joseph was amazed by this and exclaimed, "He walks so well, Mary! Look at His sure and steady steps!"

Joseph dropped to his knees, embraced Jesus then lifted Him above his head.

"Not long from now you will work beside me," he said joyfully, "and I know You will always be close to your Mother."

The infant Jesus smiled warmly, and when Joseph lowered Him near to his face Jesus wrapped His arms about Joseph's neck. Mary came and knelt beside them. Joseph placed his arm around her shoulders and embraced her. They remained together savoring the moment until Joseph thought of the wall he must build to contain the spring water.

"I must continue with the wall," he declared, "I want to finish it before dark. Will you both come out to me when you are able for I love to talk with you while I am working."

"Yes, Joseph," Mary replied, "but for a little while I must prepare the food for our meals and I have weaving to do. We will come to you when it is time for the midday meal."

Joseph bestowed a kiss upon Jesus and Mary then returned to the well. The water had risen much higher but it had not overflowed. Joseph thought of the joy this fresh water would bring to Barak's family and their neighbors.

Life during the following years continued to be difficult for the Holy Family. Although they now had fresh water, food was not as plentiful as it was in Galilee. They received little in return for their labor but gratefully accepted whatever was given. Their talents were well known in the region but also their docility and humility. Many of the rich took advantage of these qualities by paying very little even though they were greatly pleased by their work. Some continued to ridicule Mary when their requests for sensual or immodest garments were denied. Despite all the hardships tranquility abounded within that most Blessed Family.

Jesus' developed rapidly for a child His age. Visitors frequently congratulated Joseph and Mary for having such a son. His body was perfectly proportioned, His skin was fair, He had fine, dark hair and dark eyes.

In His fifth year Mary allowed Jesus to accompany Joseph when he had work to do not too distant from the house. While they were gone Mary busied herself with weaving or sewing but every moment longed for their return. Those that hired Joseph were immediately drawn to Jesus because of His great beauty and remarked at His wisdom. They realized, too, a change in themselves and their children while He was present. Some were healed of ailments not knowing Jesus had done so. Occasionally Mary was obliged to deliver finished garments to homes in Matarea; a distance of one league from their home. Mary brought Jesus with her often.

Wherever they traveled idols fell and the pagan temples were heavily damaged. But no one attributed these catastrophes to the Holy Mother and Child. Many of the people declared that their gods were weak and resolved not to worship them any longer. Where Mary and Jesus encountered the very poor or crippled beggars Mary shared with them half of her wages. Those that looked upon Jesus with tenderness and admiration were miraculously healed and He bestowed upon them a silent blessing. News of the healings spread rapidly throughout the city and nearby villages. Soon the streets were crowded with the crippled, diseased and possessed brought there by their relatives.

At the age of six Jesus asked permission to visit the sick cared for in terribly maintained buildings set aside for that purpose in Matarea. Many of the patients suffered miserably from improper attention unless cared for by relatives. The poor were forced by their state to enter these buildings; the rich summoned physicians to their homes. Mary allowed Him to go but only if accompanied by one of Barak's sons. Occasionally Joseph joined Him and witnessed Jesus bestowing His blessing upon those suffering most severely in order to comfort and console them. Many gifts were presented to Him which He then gave to the poor in the streets. Children were especially attracted to Jesus. He welcomed them with great love and kindness, and at once taught them, in a childlike manner, about the Eternal God and the way to eternal life. Their parents often went to Him when troubled or confused. The children readily accepted His counsel and admonitions to live good and charitable lives. In later years many of them would become His disciples and saintly men and women.

When at home Jesus spent much of the day in Mary's oratory in prayer and meditation but always ready to assist Mary as she needed. He gladly ran any errand and performed all of His regular duties. He especially liked to care for their animals; the faithful ass now seven years older but still strong; several white fowl given to Joseph as payment and the many birds that came to live in the two large oaks. Jesus daily brought grain for the birds and the fowl, and cut dry grass for the ass. She, too, ate grain but preferred the grass. He saw that their water was replenished and their sleeping area was clean. After spreading grain around Him for the birds he would sit in the center of it while they ate. They had no fear of Him, the Son of the Creator for Whom all things were created, but peacefully hopped about Him and ate from His hands. When Jesus spoke to them they stopped eating, raised their little heads and looked at Him. He spoke to them of the Eternal God, the life and care He gave to them and the glory they gave to Him in return. Mary often saw wild and dangerous creatures enter the acreage, sit beside the creatures they naturally preyed upon and listen to Jesus. Although insects were plentiful in this area and alighted on the Holy Child none bit Him or caused Him any discomfort. Mary and Joseph were granted the same consideration.

Joseph, now in his fifty-third year, was obliged to work long hours because of the demands for his talents. Often he arrived home well after dark using an oil lantern to light his way when the moon was not visible. His hair and beard were much grayer now. His face was deeply tanned and dried from the many hours he worked in the sun and the strong desert winds. Yet when he came into the house and was greeted warmly by Jesus and Mary his fatigue was forgotten. Jesus happily assisted him by pouring fresh water into his cup and filled a basin used for washing his hands and feet. At first Joseph objected gently when Jesus knelt to dry his feet but acquiesced when he saw the disappointment in Jesus' face. Each night Jesus performed this ritual and brought Joseph clean sandals. The Holy Three would then sit at table because Jesus and Mary would refrain from eating until Joseph arrived. Not wanting to tire him with many questions, Mary and Jesus waited for him to share the day's happenings with them. Following the meal Joseph led the prayers of praise and thanksgiving which lasted for almost an hour. Afterward he would continue Jesus ' lessons in reading and writing while studying Holy Scripture.

One night in the tenth month of Jesus' seventh year, while in a deep sleep Joseph dreamed of Bethlehem, Nazareth and the places he longed to see again. An angel surrounded by a most brilliant light appeared before Jesus who was awake and aware that God's messenger was coming. While bowing low to Jesus, the angel gave Him a royal greeting then conveyed the message he had for Joseph. At the same moment Joseph saw the angel in his dream and heard the long awaited news.

"Arise, and take the Child and His mother, and go into the land of Israel. For they are dead that sought the life of the Child."

Upon awakening, two hours later, Joseph found that Jesus was already awake kneeling in prayer at Mary's oratory. Joseph went directly to Mary woke her and related his dream and the angel's message. Mary, though sad in heart at the thought of leaving their home in Egypt was at the same time joyful about returning to Israel. Mary and Joseph said nothing to Jesus about the angel's message; they sensed that He had knowledge of it. They proceeded to make preparations for the long journey home.

First Joseph finished the work he was contracted for, then he announced to their friends and neighbors that they would be leaving the day following the Sabbath. All were deeply saddened and entreated him to remain a while longer. But Joseph declared that the journey must be made as soon as possible. For two days visitors came to say farewell and were given something to keep as a remembrance. Barak, Deborah and their sons remained with the Holy Family through the Sabbath. Just after the Sabbath ended Joseph and Barak assembled the articles to be distributed to the poor families living near-by. Mary and Deborah saw to the packing of the food and clothing to be used on the journey, while Jesus and Barak 's sons filled the water bottles and tended the animals. When all was ready for loading upon the ass both families joined in prayer near the hearth. During the prayers Deborah wept softly; tears filled the eyes of her husband and children and so too Jesus, Mary and Joseph.

CHAPTER FOURTEEN
Return To Nazareth

Along the east bank of the Nile was a well-traveled road that originated in Memphis to the south, went through Matarea, passed close to Heliopolis, and went northward through Goshen on to Ramases near the Nile delta. It was along this route the Holy Family traveled. While in Goshen they visited Seraphia, Arbela and Themeni, remaining one night with them before resuming their trek. That night Seraphia declared that one day she and her family would return to Israel for she longed to live in Jerusalem until the end of her days. Traveling was easy along this route; the terrain was flat and open and there were many places to rest. The Holy Family turned eastward just south of Ramases onto a road not far from the Mediterranean Sea that led to Gaza. From there Joseph planned to take the road east to Hebron and Bethlehem; it was his wish to settle in Bethlehem once more. On the way to Gaza, Joseph recalled his promise to visit Mosoch the leader of the robbers who took them in on a cold night in the desert. He remembered also Derketo his wife and their child Dismas who was miraculously healed of leprosy when immersed in Jesus' bath water. He told Mary of his desire to visit them; she expressed the same desire. Jesus having heard of their visit many times from Joseph and knowing full well what occurred that night wished to see the family, especially the boy Dismas.

"But how can we find their village," Joseph said to Mary. "I know not where to go for it was not near this road or any landmark."

Joseph questioned other travelers and a few merchants about Mosoch and his people but they would volunteer no information for fear of reprisals from the band of robbers. Joseph decided to remain in the village they had come to hoping to find someone with the courage to help them. He found lodgings in a small inn at the east side of the village. Beyond the inn was the vast desert between Egypt and Israel. That night they heard a great commotion, many men shouting and the clash of weapons. It lasted only a short time then all was quiet.

Early the next day Joseph and Jesus left the inn to obtain fresh water and to make more inquiries about Mosoch and how to find him. Jesus assured Joseph of finding someone who would help them. After filling the leather bottles at the town well they walked about a market of several shops and tables with all sorts of food and household items for sale. Joseph purchased some provisions and a large blanket to protect them from the desert cold if they were to spend a night in the open. And he learned of the capture of two pillagers the night before as they attempted to drive off camels belonging to a trader.

Surrounding the market were two and three story buildings; most were made of stone carried there from the sea coast north of Gaza where loose stones were plentiful. One of the buildings used as a jail had four prisoner stocks before the front of it. Two were occupied with men held fast at the ankles and the wrists. Anyone passing by had the right to insult them, spit upon them or strike their bare feet with small, flat boards tied to the upright beam. Pity and compassion toward the prisoners was not evident; each passerby took advantage of their right to punish them.

Jesus and Joseph were unable to see the prisoners but heard one of them asking for mercy; the other endured the punishment without complaint. Jesus' heart was moved with pity but He could do nothing. As they drew abreast of the men the crowd around them began to move away so that the men were in full view. Jesus and Joseph stopped before them; they were less than twenty feet apart. The crowd became unusually quiet and remained motionless as if in a trance. Jesus walked up to the prisoners, took the water bottle He carried from around His neck, went behind the stocks where He could reach their faces and poured water into their mouths and upon their heads. Joseph remained where he was. Jesus returned to Joseph and they started to leave. But the prisoner who had been silent until then shouted after them.

"Joseph, son of Jacob, do you not remember me?"

Joseph turned quickly and stared at him.

He replied, "Forgive me, young man, but I do not. How is it that you know me?"

"I am Heber, son of Japhet, nephew of Mosoch. You came to our village once many years ago. We gave you shelter during your journey to Egypt. I and my father witnessed the miraculous healing of Dismas my cousin, a leper."

Joseph and Jesus went to the young man.

Joseph said to him, "Yes, I do remember Heber a young boy who was present that night. If you are that one, my heart is heavy to see you in these circumstances. I had hoped that you and your people would change their ways."

"Mosoch and Derketo did so," he replied. "They left the village after bitter arguments with the others who would not give up their trade. My father, Japhet, became their leader but he has died since. We are led now by three men who have been robbers all their adult lives. They rule with strength and ruthlessness."

"How may I find Mosoch and Derketo?" Joseph asked. "I and my family wish to visit with them once more."

"You will find them in a village called Raphia which is south of Gaza," he declared. "He is employed by a camel trader."

"What of his son Dismas?" asked Joseph.

"I have not seen him since they left the village," Heber answered.

"And what will happen to you?" Joseph asked. "How long will you be punished like this?"

"Do not worry about me," Heber replied. "We have but a month to stay in these stocks then we shall be released. I have been through this before and no doubt will suffer it again."

"You must reform your life," Joseph declared. "You are offending the Eternal God by your behavior and will be subject to His justice someday."

Heber made no reply except to thank Jesus for the water and to wish them well on their return to their homeland.

"We will pray for you often," said Joseph. "Peace be with you."

The moment Jesus and Joseph walked away from the stocks the crowd resumed their abuse of the prisoners.

At the inn Joseph related to Mary all that occurred then added, "We will leave for Raphia after the morning meal. If all goes well we should arrive in Raphia shortly after noon."

Mary responded with a question, "Will we enter Judea soon, Joseph? I long to be in our homeland once more."

"It is but a four hour journey from Raphia to the border," he answered.

That night the Holy Family spent much time praying for the band of robbers, Mosoch, Derketo, Dismas and
Heber.

The road to Raphia was hard and wide because of the many carts and caravans traveling between Gaza and Ramases. At many places the Mediterranean Sea could be seen. It was at these points they found resting places and inns, but did not stop at them. Joseph sought places where there were shade trees and grass but no travelers. Mary and Jesus rode upon the ass most of the way but occasionally walked alongside Joseph. Jesus asked many questions about the animals and birds He saw and the places they passed. And He would give a friendly greeting to all the travelers they encountered. Many returned His greeting but some ignored it. Joseph and Mary saw the sadness this caused Him and tried to explain their indifference.

About two hours passed noon Raphia came into view when they reached the top of a long incline. The trees and buildings seemed to be shimmering as the heat rose from the ground. Most of the inhabitants were in their houses during the warmest part of the day but Joseph saw men moving near the corrals. He went straight toward them. Three men were repairing the enclosure which was made of thick camel hair ropes about the diameter of a man's fist, and thick wooden posts spaced ten feet apart. Behind the ropes were dromedaries already trained to carry passengers or merchandise. In an adjacent enclosure the young camels bleated for their mothers now separated from them. Joseph approached the men and inquired about Mosoch. He was told he could find him working for a trader at the other end of the village. Joseph received directions from them and left.

Mosoch was standing near the watering trough speaking to his employer when he first saw the Holy Family approaching. At first they appeared to be just three more travelers but then he felt something within him that he felt only once before.

"Could it be them?" he asked himself. "Have they returned as promised?"

His employer continued speaking but realized Mosoch was not listening. He turned to see what had his attention.

As he did Mosoch yelled, "It is!" and ran toward the Holy Family.

Joseph stopped when he saw him running toward them.

"It is Mosoch," he said to Mary. "We have found him."

Jesus was standing beside Joseph when Mosoch came and embraced him. Both He and Mary had broad smiles and tear-filled eyes.

Mosoch stepped back and said, "The Eternal God is great and good, blessed be His name. He has allowed you to return as you promised. I am very happy to see you my friend! You have been gone a long time!"

"It has been more than seven years," Joseph replied. "We settled near Matarea, a city south of Heliopolis. Where we were given a house and land by friends, and I was able to work at my profession."

Mosoch turned to Jesus and said, "Are you the little babe that came to my house one day?"

Jesus smiled at him and answered, "My father has spoken often of that night and his promise to return. I am happy that we have found you."

He now turned to Mary, bowed to her and said, "Peace be with you, Mary. It is good to see you again."

Mary, her face covered by her veil, nodded and returned his greeting, "Peace be with you, Mosoch."

She only glanced at him then bowed her head.

"Tell us! How are Derketo and your son Dismas?" she continued.

Mosoch's face became sullen as he answered, "Derketo left me two years after we left our people in the desert and she took our son with her. She complained always about having too little money and the poor food and lodgings we had. One morning I awoke and found them gone. To this day I know not where they went. She did not return to our desert village nor did she return to her family in Egypt. I searched for them for nearly a year then returned here where many caravans pass by. I hope someday to find someone that has seen them or knows of them. My heart feels as if it will break when I think of them."

"We will pray that you find them," Joseph declared.

Jesus walked along with Mosoch holding his hand.

He said to him, "You will find them Mosoch. And on that day you and Dismas will find perfect joy."

"Your son has a sympathetic heart," he said to Joseph. " And I thank Him for His kindness."

The tone of his speech changed to one of excitement as he asked, "But tell me, how long will you remain in Raphia and where are your lodgings?"

"We have no lodgings yet for we have just arrived," Joseph replied. And we will be on our way in the morning. We are anxious to reach Judea as soon as possible. There are relatives we long to see again."

"Alas, I was hoping that you would stay in Raphia for a while," said Mosoch, "but I understand how anxious you are. There is a good inn not far from here. I have been living there about three years now. Come I will take you there. The owner is my friend; he will give you a good room and the best of his food. Let me first be excused by my employer."

Mosoch ran back to his employer, explained why he must leave then returned to the Holy Family. He guided them to the inn which was at the northwest side of the village. A well used road leading to the sea went by it. Later that evening, Joseph invited Mosoch to their room. It was a large room with curtained areas for sleeping, a partitioned section containing a tub and a sitting area with a small, brick oven. Mosoch, Joseph and Jesus sat near the oven, which was used only during very cold nights. Jesus listened to Joseph as he told Mosoch of their life in Egypt, and as Mosoch described his search for Derketo and Dismas.

"Where do you intend to settle when you reach Judea?" Mosoch inquired.

Joseph replied, "We will return to Bethlehem, the place of my birth and the birthplace of our son Jesus. Now that Herod is dead we can live there without concern for our safety."

"Why did you flee from Herod?" Mosoch asked.

"Did you not hear of Herod's terrible act against the male children of Bethlehem?" Joseph asked in return.

"Yes," Mosoch answered. "The news of the massacre spread rapidly throughout Egypt and the lands to the east."

"He sought to destroy our son Jesus by that act but we were forewarned and escaped to Egypt," Joseph continued. "Now we may return."

"I know not why Herod wished to kill your son but I must warn you that Herod's son, Archelaus, now sits on the throne and it is said that he is as ruthless as his father. He may act to fulfill his father's wishes. I suggest that you settle further away from Jerusalem."

"I thank you for this information. Mosoch." Joseph said. "And I thank you for your concern for us. I will discuss this with Mary. Perhaps we will return to Nazareth, her village. We have relatives there and a house to use."

Mosoch added, "And if you will, please inquire about Derketo and Dismas wherever you go. Send word to me here for this is where I will remain."

At that moment Jesus saw Mary beckon to Him; it was time for prayer before He went to bed. He took leave of Joseph and Mosoch and went to her. Mosoch remained a while longer then after promising to be with them in the morning, he left for his room. Before retiring Joseph informed Mary about Herod' s son and the possible threat from him. Mary agreed that living in Nazareth would be better but suggested they ask in prayer for the Lord's guidance. This they did then retired.

During the night Joseph dreamed. Once again an angel appeared to him and said, "Joseph you are to take the Child and His mother into the quarters of Galilee and reside in Nazareth. This is to fulfill that which was said by the prophets: 'That He shall be called a Nazarene.' "

Joseph awoke the instant the angel vanished. He sat on his bed pondering the message for a few moments then went to Mary; he found her kneeling and praying.

"Mary," he called softly. She immediately turned to him and said, "What is it, dear husband?"

Joseph told her of his dream and the angel's message.

"The Lord's will has again been made known to us," Mary declared. "Now we must follow it."

"Praise the Lord, our God," Joseph exclaimed. "Blessed is His name and holy is He! I am content and at peace. As a child lies quietly in its mother's arms, my heart is quiet within me. All should trust in the Lord, from now on and forever."

Anxious to resume their journey Joseph arose at daybreak, and with Mosoch 's, aid he reloaded their possessions on the ass while Mary and Jesus prepared the morning meal. When done they joined in prayer in the Holy Family's room before eating. Mosoch expressed a deep sadness to see them leave again but he was at the same time glad for Joseph, Mary and Jesus would soon be in their homeland. He and Joseph embraced warmly at the moment of departure, and he asked Joseph to pray for his intention to one day with his wife and son. He then went to Jesus, knelt on one knee, embraced Him, and kissed His forehead. Suddenly Mosoch felt a warm sensation flow through his entire body, He was greatly perplexed and thought to himself:

"Why does this Child cause this feeling within me?"

Jesus smiled at him and said; "The love you have within causes the warmth you feel."

Mosoch was amazed at this statement and as the Holy Family departed he said to himself: "It is as if the Child knew my thoughts."

The road to Gaza was well traveled. By midday the Holy Family had encountered six caravans moving westward toward Egypt. Joseph thought it best not to speak about their origin or their destination but he did inquire about affairs in Israel, especially the city of Jerusalem. He heard reports of misconduct by Archelaus and his followers but nothing about acts of violence. Nevertheless, Joseph resolved to avoid the roads once they entered Judea; he followed almost the same route they took when fleeing Herod.

On the fourth day after leaving Raphia, at mid-afternoon the Holy Family arrived at Nazara where they stayed with Issachar and Emerentia. Joseph remembered their kindness and promise to visit them upon their return. Because the Sabbath would begin at sunset, the Holy Family remained with Issachar and his wife that night, through the Sabbath and the following night. Their hosts now nearing seventy years and cared for by their sons were greatly pleased by the visit. Issachar invited his sons and the thirteen grandchildren they now had for a special Sabbath meal to honor the Holy Family.

Joseph, Mary and Jesus were well rested when they resumed their journey, and were able to maintain a pace that brought them to the southern edge of Nazareth during the morning of the third day after leaving Nazara. At the crest of the hill, where Anne and Mary Heli saw them last, Joseph stopped their good beast. He helped Mary to dismount and together with Jesus between them stood with their hands crossed upon their breast and gave thanks to the Eternal God for their safe return. Almost a quarter hour passed before they moved down the hill and entered the village.

Joseph saw no one he knew along the road but the few people they passed were curious about them. He went directly to their home where they were surprised to find Anne and her servant Athalia waiting within. Joseph entered first; Mary followed holding Jesus by the hand. Anne and Athalia, the past seven years showing on their faces and hands, had been preparing the house for three days. Anne, in a dream, saw the Holy Family traveling toward Nazareth on the very route they took, and in the dream she heard a voice telling her to expect the Child three days hence. She and Athalia brought fresh bedding, food and linens, hung curtains on all the windows and cleaned bowls and utensils left behind. And she invited all their relatives living in Galilee to a feast to be held two days after their return. No one questioned the invitation; they were well aware that Anne often knew of future events.

Anne went first to the child Jesus fell to her knees and embraced Him. Jesus embraced her in return. Tears filled the eyes of all.

Anne said aloud, "All praise and thanksgiving to the Eternal God, holy is His name, for He has answered my prayer and that I may behold you again before I die!"

She also greeted Mary and Joseph with great emotion and love, which she received in return. Athalia in the meantime took from a wall cabinet a large multi-branched candelabrum, lighted the candles and placed it and a paper scroll upon a table covered with a red cloth. Mary then crossed her arms upon her breast and began to pray. Jesus stood to her left.

"I will praise You, Lord, with all my heart. I will tell of the wonderful things you have done. I will sing with joy because of You. I will sing praise to You, Most High! I will always thank You, O Lord; I will never stop praising You. Proclaim with me the Lord's greatness; let us praise His name together."

Joseph led them in the recitation of a psalm of praise.

"Clap your hands for joy, all peoples! Praise God with loud songs! The Lord, the Most High, is to be feared; He is a great King, ruling over the world. He gave us victory over all; he made us rule over the nations. He chose for us the land where we lived. The proud possession of His people, whom He loves. God goes up to His throne! There are shouts of joy and the blast of trumpets, as the Lord goes up! Sing praise to God; sing praise to our King!

God is King over all the world; praise Him in songs. God sits on His sacred throne! He rules over all the nations.

The rulers of the nations gather with the people of the God of Abraham.

The shields of all the soldiers belong to God; He rules over all!"

Joseph bowed his head and all were silent until Anne spoke aloud her prayer.

"The Almighty God, our Savior, speaks; He calls to the entire earth, from east to west. God shines from Zion, the city perfect in its beauty. He is coming but not in silence; a fire rages before him, a great storm around Him. He calls heaven and earth as witnesses to watch Him judge His people. He says, 'Gather my faithful people to me, those who made a covenant with me by offering a sacrifice'. The heavens proclaim God's righteousness, that He alone is judge."

Suddenly the room became very quiet, and no sounds were heard from without; a brilliant light grew from the child Jesus. His dark hair and garment became white as newly fallen snow. At once Mary, Joseph, Anne and Athalia fell to their knees with a thud but felt no pain. Jesus raised His head and eyes toward the ceiling and extended His arms. He said nothing but was in fact communicating with His Heavenly Father for quite some time. A sudden clap of thunder caused the room to vibrate and instantly two angels appeared before the Child, and bowed to Him. The angels wore fine, blue gowns, had golden hair that just touched their shoulders and pinkish wings that extended from the top of their heads to the lower part of their calves. Each had distinct features but were enough alike to be considered twins. Only Athalia could not see them but she saw Jesus illumined. Mary and Joseph recognized the angels as those that brought to them the messages and warnings from God. Anne fell into an ecstatic state; she began to reflect the light emanating from Jesus, and was granted the knowledge of who Jesus was and His mission, and because her earthly life would end before three years passed. But the angels instructed her to share this knowledge with no one except her daughter, Mary, the mother of Jesus. The angels remained less than one-quarter hour then disappeared. Jesus returned to His normal state, and so did Anne. All remained silent pondering the vision for some time before resuming the homecoming.

While Mary and Anne spoke of the journey, Joseph and Athalia unloaded their belongings. Soon all was in its place and a meal was prepared. For the remainder of the day and that evening Mary and Joseph related the many wonderful things done for them on their way to Egypt, their life in Matarea and the good people they came to know and love. Anne voiced praises for the Lord frequently and was filled with wonder and awe. During the next two days Anne, her daughter Mary Heli and her servants prepared for the feast. Eliud, her husband, rode to nearby villages to invite friends and the chief rabbi of the Synagogue in Capharnaum who was a distant relative. The feast which lasted two days was held at Anne's house; many who attended brought household gifts. A great deal of attention was given to Jesus. He in turn showed much affection to the guests, especially the children. As the days and then weeks passed the people in Nazareth came to realize the holiness of Jesus and His devotion to Mary and Joseph .They saw Jesus often with Mary in the streets as she was returning garments she had repaired or made to the owners. In whatever way His child's body allowed, Jesus assisted Joseph when he was performing household tasks or while working in the shed Joseph framed with old beams salvaged from a neighbor's collapsed stable. It was located at the front of the house but more to the side. Passersby could easily see Joseph at work and the things he was making or repairing. Joseph was very pleased to have Jesus with him and to teach Him the craft of carpentry. After Joseph's death Jesus would use these skills to support Mary. He assisted His parents in every possible way and amazed everyone by His wisdom and maturity.

Soon the parents of children in the village were using Jesus as a model for their own children. And often they would say to them, "What will Joseph's son say when I tell Him this? How sad He will be."

Because the children loved Him they were saddened themselves when thinking they displeased Him. At other times Jesus, though only a child, was asked to admonish disobedient or misbehaving children. In a childlike manner Jesus would speak to them about leading good lives, making sacrifices that benefit others and honoring their parents. He would lead them in prayer to the Eternal God asking for the strength to act as they should. Many times the children were older than Jesus but did as He asked. Following the prayers they would confess their faults to their parents or the person they acted against and earnestly begged their pardon.

Early in the month of Nisan in which the Passover was to be celebrated Joseph and Mary decided against making the pilgrimage to Jerusalem to avoid drawing attention to Jesus while Archelaus was king. Instead they and Anne made preparations to conduct the Seder (the Paschal Meal) at Anne's house with Joseph presiding. Since Jesus was the youngest child in the family Joseph instructed Him in the part played by a child during the recitation of the Exodus events.

On the morning of the 14th of the month, the eve of the holy day, Mary began baking small discs of unleavened bread used exclusively during this solemn meal to commemorate the Jews' hasty departure from Egypt. She and Jesus were alone in the house; Joseph having gone to assist in the examination of the lambs to be slaughtered. As she removed the last of the bread from the hearth she noticed Jesus kneeling with His arms extended and His eyes closed. He was in deep meditation. She placed the bread upon the table then knelt beside it. Mary sensed that something of great significance was about to take place; she prayed fervently for the strength she and Jesus would need to endure it.

Again a clap of thunder preceded the appearance of the two angels who came to them the first day of their return. With solemn faces and their arms crossed upon their breast they bowed before Jesus. Mary saw them move apart, one to Jesus' left the other to His right. Jesus eyes remained closed all the while. In unison the angels reached out and touched the palms of Jesus' hands then disappeared. Jesus' body stiffened the instant they touched Him and emitted a cry of pain. Mary at once felt the same pain but did not make any sound; she began to weep and shudder. The words of Simeon the priest flashed through her mind, "And thy own soul a sword shall pierce, that the thoughts of many hearts may be revealed."

Suddenly the angels reappeared. Jesus opened His eyes and looked at them. He saw in their hands instruments of torture; Mary saw them also. Jesus and Mary were greatly perplexed by this vision, and as Jesus gazed upon them He was shown how the instruments would be used to inflict many wounds upon His body just prior to His death. He became extremely disturbed and frightened. Mary saw His fright but could not move to comfort Him. When the child Jesus could endure the visions no longer He ran to Mary whose arms were reaching out to Him. In His haste a strap upon one of His sandals snapped causing Him to stumble into Mary's arms. She embraced Him and pressed His head against her breast. Jesus little body was shaking and drops of blood began to ooze from the pores of His forehead and temples. Mary held Him against her for several minutes; all the while the angels remained in sight but said nothing.

Jesus turned to the angels and said, "I will drink of the cup the Father has given me."

The angels bowed low again and vanished.

Jesus remained in Mary's embrace for some time in order to render to her in return the comfort she gave to Him. Mary could not speak because of her deep sorrow.

Jesus, deeply saddened by Mary's suffering turned to her and said, "Mother when the time is at hand to drink of this cup of suffering you will suffer in kind. But our greatest comfort will be the fulfillment of the Promise."

'la fine'

Look for the next book of this series entitled "The Stone Rejected" coming in 2019.

Printed in Poland
by Amazon Fulfillment
Poland Sp. z o.o., Wrocław